# THE END OF HER

Also by Shari Lapena
Available from Random House Large Print

**Someone We Know**
**An Unwanted Guest**
**A Stranger in the House**

# THE END OF HER

## SHARI LAPENA

RANDOM HOUSE
LARGE PRINT

Copyright © 2020 by 1742145 Ontario Ltd.

Published in the United States of America by Random House Large Print in association with Viking, an imprint of Penguin Random House LLC.

Cover design: Ervin Serrano

Cover images: (main) Abigail Miles / Arcangel Images; (Trees and Grass) Shutterstock

The Library of Congress has established a Cataloging-in-Publication record for this title.

ISBN: 978-0-593-29540-3

www.penguinrandomhouse.com/
large-print-format-books

FIRST LARGE PRINT EDITION

Printed in the United States of America

10  9  8  7  6  5  4  3  2  1

This Large Print edition published in accord with the standards of the N.A.V.H.

To Pilar

# ACKNOWLEDGMENTS

I will always be eternally grateful to my British, American, and Canadian publishers, who took a chance on me five books ago and have never looked back. Once again, and from the bottom of my heart, thank you to Larry Finlay, Bill Scott-Kerr, Frankie Gray, Tom Hill, and the rest of the outstanding team at Transworld in the UK; to Brian Tart, Pamela Dorman, Jeramie Orton, Ben Petrone, and the rest of the brilliant team at Viking Penguin in the US; and to Kristin Cochrane, Amy Black, Bhavna Chauhan, Emma Ingram, and the entire dedicated team at Doubleday in Canada. I must also thank the many other publishers around the world who do such an excellent job bringing my books to readers in so many different languages.

Huge thanks again to Helen Heller—the best agent a thriller-a-year writer could ever have. I can't tell you how much I appreciate you. Thank you once again to Camilla and Jemma and everyone at

the Marsh Agency for continuing to do a superb job representing me worldwide.

I continue to be amazed that I'm where I am today, and it really is all down to all of you.

Special thanks, again, to Jane Cavolina for being an exceptional copyeditor.

Thanks once again to my adviser on all forensic matters, Mike Illes, M.Sc., of the Forensic Science program at Trent University. I'm very grateful for your help, Mike!

Thank you to Aurora Lydia Dominguez, who won the right to have her name used as a character in this book, in support of the Broward Public Library Foundation.

As always, any mistakes in the manuscript are entirely mine. I have taken some small liberties with the procedural aspects of inquests for the sake of the story.

I'd also like to thank all the readers, booksellers, bloggers, librarians, and the enthusiastic people who tirelessly put on festivals—thanks to all of you for supporting writers and books and reading. Crime writers are the most supportive and the most fun writers of all, and I'm so happy to be part of this community.

And lastly, thanks to my husband, my kids, and the cat—I couldn't do this without you. Special thanks to Julia for being an insightful early reader. Manuel—thank you for the flowers on my desk in that last writing stretch—you are the best.

# THE END
# OF HER

# PROLOGUE

## JANUARY 10, 2009
## CREEMORE, COLORADO

The snow has fallen heavily, relentlessly, for two days now, and shows no sign of letting up. It's madness to go. But the plows are out, Lindsey reminds herself. She stares moodily out the window, feeling trapped and restless. Trapped by the mountains surrounding her in this small Colorado town thirty miles from downtown Denver. Trapped by the endless snow. Snow brings such silence. Sometimes the silence makes her want to scream.

Her husband enters the tiny, crowded living room behind her; the space is cheaply furnished, the teetering bookshelves held together with screws.

"All set?" Patrick asks as she turns and looks up at him, her hands resting on her huge, pregnant

belly. They're still being careful with each other, after last night's argument.

She's glad to be getting out of here, where her sense of isolation is so complete. Snow or not, they're going to visit her mother and sister in Grand Junction for a few days, where the weather is more moderate. Their bags are packed, and standing by the door. She longs to be back in the bosom of her family—she's hungry for the much-needed company and attention. She didn't know this would be so hard. She'll stop in familiar coffee shops, and meet up with the friends she'd left behind. They'll smile and exclaim over how big she is, and want to touch her stomach; they'll be excited about the impending baby. And Lindsey will feel better. Better about everything. And then she'll be able to face coming back.

Or maybe she will stay in Grand Junction.

"I'd better start shoveling the car out," Patrick says, and puts on his boots and coat. He adds a hat and gloves, and says, "I'll warm up the car for you."

She nods and turns back to the window.

# 1

Hanna Bright puts little Teddy in his baby swing on the front porch and sits down to read her novel. It's going to get hot later, but in the morning it's nice here on the porch, out of the sun. She notices two cars parked at the house across the street and a couple of doors down. The house is for sale; someone must be looking to buy.

She soon becomes engrossed in her novel, but looks up a little while later when she senses movement across the street. A heavy-set man in a suit whom Hanna recognizes as the real estate agent is in the driveway talking to a woman. Hanna watches them, idly wondering if she is a serious buyer. The house hasn't been on the market for long, and this is a desirable neighborhood; she imagines it will sell fairly quickly. She hopes it goes to a young

family—she wants lots of friends for Teddy, who's six months old. There's a pair of four-month-old twins with a really nice mom—Stephanie—directly across the street whom Hanna's become friends with. This woman looks to be alone—no husband or kids in tow.

With a final handshake, the woman turns away from the agent and heads for her parked car. As she reaches the street, she looks over at Hanna on her porch and stops. Then, to Hanna's surprise, she crosses the street and walks toward her house. What does she want? Hanna wonders.

"Hi there," the woman calls out in a friendly voice.

Hanna can see that she's probably in her early thirties and is certainly attractive. She has shoulder-length blond hair, a good figure, and enviable posture. After a quick glance to check that Teddy is content, Hanna stands up and walks down her porch steps. "Hi, can I help you?" she asks politely.

"I was just looking at the house across the street," the other woman says, making her way up the drive. Hanna walks over to meet her, shielding her eyes from the sun with her hand. "Do you mind if I ask you a bit about the neighborhood?" the woman asks.

So, she's a serious buyer then, Hanna thinks, a bit disappointed. "Sure," she says.

"My husband and I are interested in this area—is it a good place to raise children, do you think?"

She nods toward the baby swing on the porch and smiles. "I see you've got a baby."

Hanna warms to her then and describes the neighborhood with enthusiasm. Maybe the woman is already pregnant, but not showing yet.

At the end of their chat, the woman thanks her and walks back to her car. Hanna realizes she didn't get her name. Oh well. Plenty of time for that if she does buy the house. Something niggles at the back of her mind, but she doesn't know what. Teddy starts to cry then, and as she lifts the baby out of the swing, she realizes what it is. The woman hadn't been wearing a wedding ring. No matter—lots of people have families without getting married these days, although she'd mentioned a husband. But who looks at a house without her spouse?

STEPHANIE KILGOUR HAS put the twins down in their cribs upstairs for their morning nap. Now she sits down on the living-room sofa for a moment and leans back and closes her eyes. She's so tired that she doesn't know how she actually manages to get up when the babies start crying for her at 6:00 a.m. Nothing—and no one—could have prepared her for this.

She relaxes for a moment, letting her exhausted body sink into the cushions, her head heavy against the pillows. She lets herself go slack. If she's not

careful, she might fall asleep just sitting here. And that wouldn't be good—the twins only go down for about half an hour in the morning, and the difficulty of rousing herself after such a short time won't be worth it. She'll get her own rest when the twins have their longer nap in the afternoon.

Her baby girls, Emma and Jackie, are the best thing that ever happened to her. But she had no idea it would be this hard. Had no sense of the toll it would take on her body, and on her mind too. The effects of protracted sleeplessness are catching up with her. People who knew she was expecting twins—she hadn't made a secret of it—had joked with her about how much more difficult twins would be. She'd merely smiled, delighted with her pregnancy, and was even secretly smug at how good she felt, how easily her body was handling the changes.

Stephanie had always been a little bit of a control freak, and she'd spent a lot of time on her birth plan, wanting everything to go just right. She wasn't so complacent that she thought she could do it without drugs, but she wanted to have a normal birth, even with twins.

Once they were in the labor suite, though, the plan soon went out the window. She'd ended up with two babies in distress and an emergency C-section. Instead of soothing music, low lighting, and controlled breathing, it was all beeping machines, dropping heart rates, swarming medical

staff, and being wheeled hurriedly into the operating room. She remembers her husband, Patrick, holding her hand, his face white with fear. What she remembers most, besides her panic as the babies were whisked away to intensive care before she could even hold them, was the convulsive shivering and nausea after the birth. Fortunately, both babies had been fine—healthy and a good weight.

It was hard not to feel like a failure in those early days, struggling with sleeplessness, the pain of the C-section recovery, and the frustration of breastfeeding two babies, seemingly all the time. . . . Those first couple of weeks after the twins were born were the most difficult of Stephanie's life. The babies soon began nursing well, but she often thinks about how stressful the C-section had been—for everyone. **We don't always get to choose**, she reminds herself. The important thing is that she and the girls were healthy. Now, Stephanie is astonished at how naive she was before the birth. Control is an illusion.

And then, the colic . . . the babies didn't sleep well from the outset, and then around the age of six weeks, it got worse. They cried and fussed and wouldn't go down to sleep. Her pediatrician, Dr. Prashad, told her that it would probably ease at about twelve weeks. That was more than a month ago, and it hasn't gotten any better. These days Stephanie—and Patrick—seem to be operating on pure willpower. They haven't had a good night's

sleep since the twins were born. The fussing starts in the early evening and lasts until about one or two in the morning. Then they're up again at six. **Brutal** is the only way to describe it.

Now, Stephanie's breathing slows and in mere moments, she's out cold.

Suddenly a piercing sound—a loud, insistent **beep, beep, beep**—wakes Stephanie with a start. She's disoriented, her thoughts muddled. It's the smoke alarm—there's smoke in the house—she can smell it. She lurches to her feet, eyes wide with fear. It's coming from the kitchen. Momentarily paralyzed, she thinks of the twins upstairs, then she runs to the kitchen. There's a frying pan on the stove, and it has erupted into flames. For a moment she stands in the doorway, stupefied, because she can't remember putting anything on the stove. Quickly, she enters the kitchen and reaches frantically for the fire extinguisher in an upper cupboard near the stove. In her panic, she can't remember how to work it. She turns to face the fire and the flames are higher now, licking toward the ceiling, but the ceiling hasn't yet caught fire. She can hear the whooshing sound of the flames, and the heat is almost unbearable. Her heart is pounding frantically as she has a moment of indecision. Should she stay here, wasting precious seconds trying to work the extinguisher, or run upstairs to get the babies? Would she even have enough time to get them out? Should she call 911 first? Then all at once

she knows what to do—she wrenches open a bottom cupboard and grabs a metal lid, then slides it onto the frying pan. Deprived of oxygen, the fire is smothered and quickly goes out. She grabs an oven mitt and reaches over and turns off the burner.

Stephanie sags with relief. The room smells of smoke. Her eyes are stinging and tearing up, and she leans back against the counter, shaking now that the danger is past. The alarm is still shrieking, but it's not the one in the kitchen that's going off, she realizes—it's the alarm upstairs. She turns on the fan over the stove, opens the window above the kitchen sink, and runs upstairs. She has to grab the footstool out of the bedroom to reach the screeching smoke detector in the hall. She finally disables it with shaking hands. In the sudden silence, she can hear the babies wailing, startled awake by the alarm.

She hurries into the nursery, whispering shhh, shhhh. . . . She picks each baby up, one at a time, soothing them, kissing their soft cheeks. They won't go back to sleep now; they're too riled up. She carries Jackie and then Emma downstairs and places them both in the playpen in the living room with some of their favorite toys, and returns to the kitchen.

The air is clear but it still reeks of smoke. She stares at the frying pan sitting on the burner as if she's still frightened of it. She grabs the oven mitt and lifts the lid. It looks like there was just oil in

the pan. Was she going to fry something? She can't remember. How could she have put a pan on the stove and forgotten about it and let herself fall asleep? She thinks with horror about how quickly the fire might have spread.

Still shaken, she returns to the living room and sits on the rug with her back against the sofa, cuddling both babies to her chest. She kisses the tops of their soft heads and strokes their cheeks, holding back tears. "I'm so sorry, I'm so sorry . . ." she whispers.

She must remember to get Patrick to look at the smoke detector in the kitchen when he gets home tonight.

# 2

On Monday, just after lunch, Stephanie stares blankly at the wall in the pediatrician's office, fatigue glazing her eyes. The previous night had been particularly difficult. The twins are still buckled, squirming, into their double stroller; it's the easiest way to contain them. She hopes the doctor won't be too much longer. One thing Stephanie's learned as a first-time mother is that timing is everything. She hopes to keep the girls awake long enough to make it through the appointment, and then they can fall asleep in the car on the short drive home. She'll carry them inside for their afternoon nap, still asleep, one after the other, leaving one alone in the locked car while she carries the other in. . . .

The door opens abruptly and Dr. Prashad smiles at her. Stephanie knows that she's a mother, too, that she understands what it's like, although she doesn't have twins.

"How are we doing?" the doctor asks sympathetically.

She might well ask. This is an unscheduled appointment, but it's not Stephanie's first unannounced visit like this.

"Not great," Stephanie admits, giving a wobbly smile. She can feel her eyes immediately welling up. Shit. Why is it that the slightest bit of sympathy can bring her to tears these days? It's sleep deprivation, that's what it is, pure and simple. If she doesn't start getting more sleep soon, she's going to lose it.

She glances away from the doctor to her babies.

Dr. Prashad looks at her with concern. "Colic is really tough," she says. "I can't imagine what it must be like with two at once."

"It's hell," Stephanie admits with a weak smile. "They're both awake crying from about seven p.m. until one or two in the morning. Every. Single. Day. Patrick and I have to put them in the swings and listen to them crying just to bolt down some supper. And then we carry them in circles around the living room for hours." She rubs her eyes with her hands. "I've read all the parenting books, we've tried everything, but nothing works." She hesitates. "Are you sure there's nothing wrong with them? I mean . . . could we have missed something?" She doesn't want to accuse the doctor, but . . .

The doctor sighs and says, "They're healthy babies. They've been fully checked. I know it

doesn't make it any easier that we don't know much about colic, but I promise it will pass."

Stephanie steels herself and asks, "But when? How much longer is this going to go on?" She can hear the exhaustion—even despair—in her voice and hates herself for it. She sounds so whiny, like she can't cope. She can't stand women like that. She has always been someone who copes, and copes well.

The doctor shakes her head. "There's no way to know, I'm afraid. It usually stops pretty suddenly. They'll outgrow it. Like I told you before, most babies get over it at around three months, but it can last up to around nine months. I've never heard of a two-year-old with colic."

Stephanie can't bring herself to tell the doctor what prompted this sudden visit. She'd almost burned the house down while her husband was at work. Patrick had been beside himself when she told him. She can't even remember putting the pan on the stove. What if Dr. Prashad thinks she's an unfit mother?

She doesn't know why she bothered coming. Of course the doctor wouldn't be able to help—Dr. Prashad gave her the same spiel the last time she visited. "Am I doing something wrong?" Stephanie asks, rather hopelessly.

"No. Not by the sound of it. You've told me what your routines are. You're doing everything right. You're just unlucky, that's all." Dr. Prashad's voice

softens. "This will pass." Stephanie nods wearily. "The important thing is that you take care of yourself during this time. Is there anyone who can help out? Can you get a sitter or a family member to watch the babies for a night—or even for a few hours—so you can get some sleep?"

"We tried that. But I couldn't sleep through the noise." The sound of her babies wailing in distress creates a visceral reaction in her that she simply can't ignore. She glances at them now. The twins are fidgeting less in their stroller, starting to look drowsy. She has to leave soon so she can get them home and have a nap herself. The two or three hours she gets in the afternoon and the four hours between 2:00 a.m. and 6:00 a.m. are all she can count on. Most nights she sends her protesting, sheepish husband to bed by midnight and tries to handle the girls on her own so that he is able to go to work and function the next day.

After the appointment, she pushes the stroller out the door of the clinic to where she's parked on the street. She settles the twins into their infant car seats, wondering if it's safe for her to be driving— her reflexes have been dangerously slow these days. She's so tired that after she fastens the babies into their seats and closes the two back doors, she almost drives away without collapsing the double stroller and stowing it in the trunk. Jesus, she thinks, noticing the stroller at the last minute, sitting alone on the sidewalk. That would be a thousand bucks

wasted. It's not like it would still be here by the time she realized her mistake and came back for it. Get a grip, she tells herself.

With extra care, she drives the ten minutes from downtown Aylesford to the comfortable suburb where they live. She turns onto their street, then pulls into the driveway and stops the car. She glances in the rearview mirror and sees that both babies are asleep. Thank God.

She brings them inside and settles them in their cribs. Both are down soundly. Why can't they do this at night? If she bundles them into the car late at night crying, and drives around town until they're asleep, they wake up when they're brought back inside. It's the most frustrating thing. She's never felt as powerless as she does in the face of a crying baby—or rather, two—who won't be soothed.

Relieved, she grabs the baby monitor and makes her way to her own bedroom, ignoring the pile of unwashed clothes in the basket just inside the laundry room, and the rank smell of the diaper pail that fills up too quickly. She only wants sleep. She's heard that people can lose their minds if they go long enough without it—they can start imagining things.

As her head hits the pillow, she wonders again why the smoke alarm in the kitchen didn't go off the other day—Patrick had found nothing wrong with it—and then she is asleep.

# 3

Patrick Kilgour returns to his office after an unsatisfactory meeting with a new client. He'd expected it to go better. But he seems to have lost some of his polish, his shine. Patrick had felt his business partner's eyes on him during the presentation. Niall had given him a hard look afterward. "Get it together," he said and walked away.

Patrick slumps in his desk chair and swivels around to stare out the window, blearily taking in the view: the two arched bridges spanning the Hudson River, and beyond them the Catskills, smudged in the distance. His eyes are burning with tiredness and his body feels stiff. Too many weeks of not getting enough sleep, and it's taking its toll. Maybe he can call the client back when he's got more energy, more focus.

It's four in the afternoon and his lids already feel heavy. He swivels back to face his desk, looks

longingly at the leather sofa along the opposite wall
of his office for a moment, but then turns his atten-
tion to his computer, loosening his tie and opening
the top button of his shirt. He's got work to do be-
fore he goes home, where work is impossible.

He needs caffeine. He gets up and goes out
to the reception area to make himself a cof-
fee from the machine. There's a woman waiting
there, her head down, reading a magazine. He
catches her out of the corner of his eye—her pro-
file, that blond hair—and does a double take. For-
tunately, Kerri, the receptionist with the keen eyes,
is not at her desk, and not there to notice. He's
reached the coffee machine, and now his back is to
the woman. She doesn't seem to be aware of him.

Erica Voss. He would recognize her anywhere.
The sight of her has sent a spasm of disbelief
through him. What is she doing here? It's been
more than nine years since he last saw her. The
past suddenly crowds in on him.

He's not sleepy now; he's shot through with
adrenaline. He wonders what will happen when she
looks up from her magazine and recognizes him.

He hears Niall coming into the waiting area.
Patrick will have to face her to make his way
back to his office. He turns around slowly. She
lifts her head, glances at him—not a flicker of
recognition—and stands up, turning toward Niall.
Niall is reaching his hand out to greet her.

"I'm sorry—have you been waiting long? Kerri

seems to be away from her desk," Niall says. He notices Patrick then, standing near the coffee machine. "I'm Niall Foote, and this is my partner, Patrick Kilgour," he says, gesturing toward Patrick.

Patrick's throat is so dry that he can't speak. He remains where he is, not stepping forward to shake her hand. He gives a brief, frozen smile. She still shows no signs of recognizing him, but he's not fooled. She's better at hiding her surprise than he is. He'd always admired her poise.

"Ms. Voss is interviewing for the temporary administrative assistant position," Niall says, and escorts her down the hall to his own office, oblivious to Patrick's hidden distress.

Patrick hears the office door close and Niall's voice become muffled. He turns back to the coffee machine, goes through the motions of adding milk and sugar to his cup, and notices that his hands are trembling.

What is Erica Voss doing in Aylesford? Last he knew, she was living in Denver.

He decides to go home early. He leaves the coffee on the table, grabs his briefcase from his office, and leaves.

STEPHANIE WAKES FROM a profound sleep to the sound of the front door opening. For a moment she's disoriented. She looks at the clock on the bedside table: it's not even 4:30 p.m. She sits up

quickly, listening. The room is dark, the curtains pulled across the window. She can hear someone moving around downstairs. She glances at the baby monitor; the lights aren't flashing, and the babies are still asleep.

She gets out of bed, a bit dizzy at rising so quickly, a combination of fatigue and low blood pressure. She walks quietly down the hall to the top of the stairs. She sees Patrick at the bottom of the stairs, looking up at her. She can't tell what it is exactly, but something about him seems different. Maybe it's just that he's home uncharacteristically early.

"Did I wake you? I was hoping I wouldn't," he says softly.

"What happened?" she asks as she walks down the stairs.

"Nothing happened," he answers. "I just left early today, that's all. I'm beat."

"Tell me about it," she says, reaching him and giving him a warm hug and a kiss. "How did the meeting go?" He frowns, shrugs, and she feels a twinge of sympathy.

"Not great," he admits.

She knows that he's been struggling lately. He hasn't kept that from her. He's always told her what's going on at work. She doesn't like to be kept in the dark; she wants to know everything.

She's concerned for him—for an architect, mistakes can be costly. He has so many details to stay on top of, and with so little sleep. . . . She tells

herself that they just have to ride this out. The babies will start to sleep, and they will both sleep, too, and be able to cope better.

She looks at him more closely. Now she can see what's different about him; he's clenching his jaw as if he's worried about something. He looks exhausted, like her, but there's a nervous energy running along underneath that isn't usually there. "What is it? You seem a bit tense," she says lightly.

"Do I?" he says. "No, I'm not tense. Just—I was a bit off in the meeting today. Didn't bring my usual energy to it. I don't think they were too impressed." He shrugs. "Maybe I should have told them I've got colicky twins at home." Now there's an edge to his voice and she feels her back go up a bit. It sounds almost like he's blaming her. She tries not to react. Takes a deep breath.

"Look," she says after a moment, "neither of us is functioning at our best right now. We're exhausted. That's just the way it is. But we'll get through it." She puts her hands up and rests them on his shoulders, looks right into his tired eyes. "Things will get better." She remembers how, a couple of nights ago, he'd had to say much the same thing to her. They have to help each other, prop each other up. That's what they've been doing through these long, difficult weeks of colic. He nods back at her, gives her that smile she loves.

Then he kisses her and says, "I know."

"Why don't you lie down on the sofa and close

your eyes for a bit? I'm going to get started on sup-per before they wake up."

She goes into the kitchen, working quickly, be-cause the babies will be up soon. When she glances into the living room a few minutes later, expecting to find her husband fast asleep, she sees that he's wide awake, staring at the ceiling. Then she hears a cry, and steels herself for the long, grueling night ahead.

# 4

The next morning when he gets to the office, Patrick opens his email, runs his eyes down his messages, and stops cold. There's one from Erica Voss. His finger hovers over the mouse. He considers deleting the email unread, but that might be unwise. He clicks it open.

Hi Patrick,

I imagine it was a surprise, seeing me again. I was wondering if we could get together and talk, for old times' sake? Maybe for a drink?

Best, Erica

It seems harmless, but he feels uneasy. He would rather let sleeping dogs lie, doesn't want to nudge

this one awake. But he can't simply ignore her. He hesitates and then types a reply.

Hi Erica,

I could meet for a quick drink. Small world.

Patrick

He stares at what he's written for a long moment, wondering if he's making a mistake. Then he hits send. He watches his computer anxiously for a few minutes, waiting for her to respond. It doesn't take long.

Great! I'm actually living nearby, in Newburgh. I could meet you for a drink after work today in Aylesford, if that works for you?

Erica

His stomach drops. She's supposed to be in Denver. What is she up to? Why was she in his office? Why does she want to see him? His feelings of uneasiness intensify.

· · ·

ERICA SITS IN the living room of her apartment in Newburgh and stares at her laptop screen, waiting for a response. She imagines Patrick at his computer in his office on Bleeker Street, his handsome face taken aback. Wondering this very minute how to respond.

It was fun, seeing him in his office yesterday, his reaction. He's a partner in his own small architectural firm, with offices on the fourth floor of a shiny new building downtown. It looks like he's doing well for himself. She isn't surprised. He always was ambitious. He'd obviously been shocked to see her.

It's been more than nine years since she's spoken to Patrick. She turns away from the computer for a minute and glances around her sparsely furnished apartment. She's only just moved in, and it shows. She hears a ping and looks back at her computer. She smiles.

> How about the Pilot, at 5 o'clock? It's on Bristow Street.
>
> Patrick
>
> Sounds perfect. See you there.
>
> Erica

She didn't think he'd refuse to see her. They have too much history. She wonders what he's like

now, whether he's changed. Somehow she doesn't think so.

SHORTLY BEFORE 5:00 P.M., Patrick leaves his office and walks to the bar on a small side street in the downtown center. He doesn't expect to run into anyone who knows him; the Pilot is just this side of a dive—not one of his usual upscale haunts. He straightens his tie nervously as he walks into the bar. He's five minutes late on purpose. His gaze darts around in the semidark, looking for her.

He spots her in a corner, sitting alone, drinking a beer out of the bottle. She looks much the same, although not quite as whip slender as she used to be. In her early twenties she was a knockout, a natural blond with fine features and beautiful skin. For a moment he stares at her, and then she turns and sees him and seems to go still.

He swallows and walks toward her. "Erica," he says, as he reaches her table. He catches the faint scent of her perfume—exotic and seductive—the same perfume she wore all those years ago. It's disconcerting. For a moment, he's back in Colorado, and they're all sitting in their favorite bar, laughing and drinking beer, so young, all their lives ahead of them. Lindsey beside him with her hand resting placidly on her pregnant belly, Erica watching him from across the table.

"Patrick," she says now, as he sits across from her, "you're looking well."

He wishes he'd thought to grab a beer at the bar on his way over, rather than waiting for someone to come by so he can order. He smiles tentatively at Erica through his discomfort. He's normally so good with people, but he can't seem to read the situation. There's an awkward silence. A server sees him and approaches. Patrick changes his mind about the beer and says, "Scotch, please." His tastes have changed; he wonders if hers have as well, and she simply doesn't trust the cleanliness of the glasses in this place. Can she tell he's nervous? "So . . . you live in Newburgh now?"

"Yes, I moved recently, from Denver. I felt it was time for a change."

He nods, tries to seem nonchalant about it.

"A short drive from here," she says, "only half an hour."

He waits, but she doesn't volunteer anything else. "What a coincidence," he says, "you showing up at my firm."

There's another awkward pause. His drink arrives and he gulps it greedily. Patrick can't think of anything else to say. He's thinking, **Of all the places she could have relocated to, why here?**

She leans in a bit closer, elegant hands around her beer, peeling at the label. He remembers this from before. "I knew you were here somewhere,

so I looked you up. When I realized you were so close, I thought, why not?"

He stares back at her. "You're not interested in the job at my firm, are you?"

She smiles. "No. I already have a job."

He takes another big swallow of his drink, his unease growing. What is she playing at? "So why did you apply?"

"I wanted to see if it was really you."

"You could have tried to get in touch with me in the ordinary way."

"I'm not sure you would have responded," she says. He doesn't answer that. "When you left Colorado, all I knew was that you had talked to Greg about returning to New York."

And there it is. He'd left Colorado rather quickly, after Lindsey's funeral, with no forwarding address. He'd wanted to run away from everything. And he'd thought no one there—Erica included—wanted to stay in touch with him. It was all just too hard. Better for everyone if he left. Erica had been his first wife's closest friend. Perhaps she's here to apologize for the way she treated him afterward, at the funeral. She's had time to get her head on straight. They were all a bit out of their minds. It was a terrible time.

"Yes, well," he says at last, "probably better for everyone." She looks back at him thoughtfully. He goes on. "With Lindsey gone, I just wanted to come

home." He'd left a few months into his architecture internship; he'd had to start all over again in New York State. He didn't care. He takes another deep drink of his Scotch and realizes that somehow he's finished it. He leans forward a little and lowers his voice. He pauses for a moment and then says, "I was absolutely devastated by what happened."

"I know. So was I."

WHEN PATRICK ARRIVES HOME a little later than usual, he can tell Stephanie's been waiting impatiently for him to help her with the twins. He pitches in, but his mind is elsewhere, thinking about his meeting with Erica. The conversation had remained fairly superficial. She hadn't volunteered much about herself, but he'd noted the absence of a wedding ring. She'd flirted with him a little, but she was subtle about it. He hadn't flirted back. He'd told her he was happily married, with twin baby girls.

After half an hour, he'd made a show of looking at his watch, and said he had to go. He thought that might be the end of it, but she'd insisted on exchanging cell phone numbers before he left. Now it feels . . . unfinished. And that worries him.

# 5

Cheryl Manning waves at her son, Devin, from the side of the soccer field. He's almost nine years old, going into fourth grade in September. For the month of August, though, he's spending his days in soccer camp. He loves the sport, he's good at it, and she's proud of him. She and her husband both. Devin, it turns out, is a talented athlete.

She watches him run out onto the field. They spend a lot of money on him. This specialty camp is expensive, and the gear is pricey, but they can easily afford it, and there's nothing they won't do to help their son realize his potential. They **enjoy** spending money on him; she finds it strange when the other moms she knows—who can also afford it—complain about how much their kids' activities cost.

There's nothing quite as satisfying, Cheryl thinks, as seeing your kid excel and feeling in some

measure responsible. She stands on the edge of the field watching him for a moment. He's a good-looking boy. His brown hair tosses in the wind as he runs. He grins as he maneuvers the soccer ball skillfully with his feet. He waves at her, and she waves back. She's pleased that he's confident. He calls out to the other boys on the field, a natural leader. He makes friends easily. She knows she should go, not hover like this, but she stands a minute longer to enjoy the morning sun on her face, and to enjoy her son, appreciate his abilities.

The coach walks over to her. "Devin's doing really well," he tells her. "He's a natural."

She smiles at him. One doesn't like to brag. "So we've been told," she says modestly.

The coach smiles at her and heads onto the field, blowing his whistle. He takes attendance and starts lining the kids up for drills. It's time for her to leave. All the other parents have already gone—often having to take a second child, or even a third, to a different camp somewhere else. But Devin's an only child, and she's a stay-at-home mom, so she doesn't have anywhere else she has to be. She always seems to hang around longer, as if she can't let go. As if she still can't quite believe that Devin is hers.

It would have been perfect if they could have had a daughter too. She might have been one of the mothers racing to drop off at soccer so that she can get to ballet camp on time. But they only have

one, and she and her husband, Gary, are desperately grateful for that.

She can't have children.

It had been such a shock to discover she was sterile.

It was more than that—it was traumatic, profoundly disorienting. The years of trying, the heroic efforts—none of it had paid off. The chronic disappointment had led to depression. She felt like a failure. All around her women were having babies, seemingly effortlessly. She was secretly afraid Gary might leave her. It was a dark time.

They'd come to adoption only after exhausting all other options, including IVF. Even then, things hadn't gone smoothly. They had arranged an adoption to get an infant girl, but the birth mother had changed her mind right after the baby was born. They were heartsick—left with empty arms, and out of pocket for all her expenses. It had been devastating. There was nothing they could do but suck it up and try again.

But then, working again with the same private adoption agency, another birth mother chose them. It was an open adoption, so they were able to meet her. They were cautiously optimistic. She seemed smart and they liked her right away. She didn't seem flaky; she seemed to have her head on straight. No drug or alcohol problems. She told them she wasn't ready to have a baby on her own—she wanted to finish school. She didn't want her baby to be raised

by a single mother without any money, and she had no extended family to help her. She wanted what was best for him, not what was best for her.

She was also physically attractive; more importantly, she looked a lot like Cheryl herself—blond and blue-eyed, fairly tall and slim, with fine bone structure. Cheryl had wanted a child who might resemble her in some way. They didn't know anything about the father, except that he was white, university educated, and wasn't interested in becoming a father.

Devin must have taken after his biological father, because as he grew, he didn't look anything like Cheryl.

Cheryl takes one last look at Devin on the soccer field and waves goodbye, but he's not watching and doesn't notice. She turns back to her car and drives home, thinking about how lucky she turned out to be in the end. Devin's such a great kid—he's even good in school. So many of the moms she's gotten to know are discovering that their kids have learning disabilities, allergies, all kinds of problems. Finally, she's one of the lucky ones.

Nobody around here knows that Devin is adopted; they haven't even told him yet. They've decided they'll tell him when he's twelve or thirteen. Everybody except close family thinks he's their biological child. She doesn't really want anyone to know—it's none of their business. Devin can tell people once he finds out, if he wants to. She hopes

he keeps it to himself, though. She hopes he never wants to know about his birth mother. So many adopted kids do nowadays. Nothing good comes of it, Cheryl thinks. Why rock the boat? He has all the love and everything else he'll ever need, right here, with them.

She arrives home and lets herself in. She's grateful for the blast of air-conditioning—it's so humid today. They live in a lovely house; her husband makes a very good living in commercial property development. Maybe she'll make herself an iced coffee and go out and sit by their pool.

But for some reason, she finds herself thinking about the past. She makes her way upstairs to Devin's bedroom and opens his door. She's seen some of the bedrooms of Devin's friends. They make her shudder. The other moms complain about how messy and lazy their kids are, but Cheryl thinks maybe they aren't bringing their kids up properly. Kids need boundaries, expectations. Good parenting is so important. She and Gary make Devin tidy his room every weekend.

She looks at his bed, with the quilt with the airplanes on it. Devin has always loved airplanes. He wants to be a pilot someday. She thinks maybe there's nothing he can't do. How ambitious she is for him—she hardly likes to admit it to herself, how invested she is in him—perhaps because he's an only child. She often daydreams about his future—what it will be like for him, and what it

will be like for them as his parents. He'll have every advantage. Her eyes fall on his dresser, which has several trophies on it: for track, soccer, hockey. His closet is full of sports equipment, his walls plastered with posters of favorite sports figures.

She searches his bookshelf for the photo album. She pulls it out and sits down on his bed. Why is she looking at this today? She thinks she knows why. There's a reason her mind has turned to the past.

She opens the small album, which has a few baby pictures, carefully selected, printed, and glued into it. Photos are all digital these days, but she wanted a proper album of Devin growing up. She studies the very first photograph—a picture of him in the hospital, right after he was born. He's all red and scrunched up and wearing a blue knitted bonnet. Cheryl and Gary hadn't been there, at the hospital. They'd waited at home, eager for news, terrified that the birth mother would hold her newborn in her arms for the first time and change her mind like the last one had.

Because this woman, Erica, who they'd been so taken with in the beginning, had begun to make them feel uneasy. At first it was little things. She'd had an extra cost when her car had broken down— could they cover it so she could get to her medical appointments? Of course they expected to pay her regular expenses—her rent and groceries and

maternity clothes and so on. Erica had given up her job, after all, for the health of the baby. She told them she'd been working part time at a dry cleaner and she'd read that the chemicals might cause birth defects, so she'd quit as soon as she found out she was pregnant.

And then, one day late in her pregnancy, she'd dropped by to see them, at their home. This was unexpected and not really done. She hinted that she really needed money, or "she didn't know what she would do." Cheryl and Gary had been deeply unsettled. They asked delicately what she needed the money for. She explained that it was for her education, or she might have to give up her dream of going to medical school and instead raise her child herself. She asked for a hundred thousand dollars.

Stunned, they left Erica sitting in their living room while they retreated to the kitchen to make her some herbal tea and discuss the problem in hushed tones.

"What are we going to do?" Cheryl whispered to her husband, in distress. She was starting to cry. Meanwhile, Erica sat in their living room, huge with their child, waiting serenely for her herbal tea while shaking them down for a huge amount of money.

"We have the money," Gary said. "Let's just pay her."

Cheryl felt the blood drain from her face. "But

it's illegal—you know that! We can't pay her more than the allowed expenses." She added, "We have to tell the agency."

Her husband looked grim and said, "No, we don't. She's not going to tell anybody, or she could go to jail. Nobody has to know."

"But—what if we pay her and then she doesn't let us have the baby?" Cheryl cried.

"That's a chance we have to take," Gary said. "Do you want this baby or not?"

"Yes, of course I do."

"So do I."

They returned with the tea tray and Cheryl's husband offered to write her a check.

Erica said it might be better if he got it for her in cash.

Miraculously, Erica hadn't changed her mind. She'd taken the cash, and later, after the baby was born, willingly signed the papers terminating all parental rights to her child. She told them that she'd decided she didn't want to maintain contact with them and the baby after all; she thought it would be easier if she didn't. They'd been relieved to hear it, though of course they hadn't said so. The period allowed for her to change her mind passed, Devin was theirs, and she disappeared from their lives. But before she left, she'd given them a copy of the birth photo, and Cheryl had treasured it.

She looks at it now, thinking back to that time, almost nine years ago. She's remembering it now,

because after all this time, she's afraid that Erica might be back. Cheryl thought she saw her a couple of weeks ago, in the park, watching Devin kick a ball around, and she had a camera around her neck. But she was gone before Cheryl could be sure.

# 6

Erica showers, dresses in a short black skirt and silky sky-blue blouse, and applies her makeup carefully. She studies herself in the mirror, pleased, thinking about the meeting with Patrick the day before.

She hadn't really known what to expect. It's been a long time. He was looking good, she has to admit. Older, of course, but he's the kind of man who looked better with a bit more maturity. His tall frame had filled out a bit. His dark hair was shorter, nicely cut, and he'd been wearing an expensive-looking suit.

He hadn't been happy about her showing up at his firm, that was obvious. He was nervous; that was obvious too. He's probably afraid of her coming back into his life, afraid of the old attraction firing up again, getting between him and his new wife. Maybe he should be afraid. He never could keep it in his pants.

Her attractiveness has always been one of her best weapons.

PATRICK STRUGGLES ALL MORNING at the office, unable to concentrate. He notices that Niall is humming quietly to himself, which only irritates Patrick. Around lunchtime he hears Niall leave his office and talk to Kerri at the front desk on his way out.

From his window, Patrick stares out at the river, his mind dull. He has so much work to do, but instead he thinks about how Erica had come to his office, pretending she didn't know him, when she'd known he was here all along. She'd deliberately put him in an awkward position.

Yesterday, he'd casually asked Niall how the interview went and Niall had said, "She's not the best candidate," and Patrick had felt relief. She wouldn't be back in the office. He will never have to explain that they actually know each other, although they hadn't let on. And she's not interested in the job anyway.

He rises from his chair and walks tiredly over to his drafting table. He's working on a high-end new build of a house for a prominent doctor, and he needs to focus.

.   .   .

NIALL LOOKS ACROSS the seat to the woman driving the car. The windows are down and the wind is blowing her hair around her face. He notices she's wearing designer sunglasses. Again he wonders why she was interviewing for a temporary admin position. Perhaps her husband has left her recently. Perhaps he will find out.

He'd been surprised when Erica Voss called him at the office that morning, inviting him to lunch. Not typical behavior for someone hoping to get a job—a bit forward. He'd hesitated briefly, until she said she could pick him up in front of the fountain downtown.

He feels a familiar stirring in his blood—he suspects he knows why she asked him. She's looking very sexy today, he notices. When she came to the office on Monday for her interview she'd been conservatively dressed in a trouser suit, but today she's wearing a tight-fitting skirt and a silky blouse, and showing some leg and cleavage. He studies her appreciatively.

"What?" she says, glancing at him playfully.

"I'm wondering why you've asked me to lunch." He hadn't called her back about the job. In fact, he's not going to make her an offer. She's too gorgeous—too sexy—to have around the office. His wife, Nancy, would go ballistic. He hopes she doesn't think this is how she's going to get the position. If so, he'll have to let her down. He doesn't mix business and pleasure.

"It's a celebration lunch," she says.

"What are we celebrating?"

"I've just got a job at the hospital in Newburgh."

He feels his smile broadening. This isn't going to be a problem then. The mutual attraction he'd suspected during their interview hadn't been his imagination after all.

She brings the car to a stop in the parking lot of the Connaught Hotel, at the end of Water Street.

"I've made a reservation," she says and gets out of the car. Together they step up the front stairs of the hotel, past the doormen, and proceed into the fine dining room on the first floor. As they're escorted to their table, he follows her, his eyes watching her as she weaves among tables. They're seated by the window. He glances around quickly to see if he recognizes anyone—Aylesford is not a big town. There's no one here he knows, and he begins to relax. If someone should recognize him—perhaps one of his wife's friends—he will introduce her as a potential client, a custom home build. She certainly looks the type.

She smiles at him and he orders wine.

"So, Niall," she says, "tell me about yourself."

The lunch goes as he expected. She's interested in him, he's interested in her. The only question is how to go from the dining room to the hotel room with a minimum of fuss and notice. And how to pay for it. He can't let her pay, and he can't have a hotel room in Aylesford showing up on his credit

card bill. Nancy will check. She checks everything since she caught him in his first—and only—indiscretion. He'd made it through eight years of marriage—past the seven-year itch—but last fall he'd had a brief, thrilling affair with a woman he'd met at the golf club. His wife had found out. There had been tears and recriminations; it had been awful and the fallout had gone on for weeks. She'd insisted they do marriage counseling. He'd gone because he didn't want his marriage to end; he loved Nancy and their young son, Henry, and he couldn't imagine life without them—and divorce would be both inconvenient and financially ruinous, it always was. So he'd broken off the affair and done everything Nancy had asked. He'd promised her he would never stray again. He'd been as good as his word, but now, there is a gorgeous woman flirting with him right across the table, and he is sorely tempted.

In the end, he doesn't really struggle with the decision. He's only concerned about not getting caught. He tells himself that what Nancy doesn't know won't hurt her. What possible harm can there be—as long as his wife doesn't find out?

He glances toward the lobby and wonders if there's an ATM out there. He needs to get some cash. Erica meets his eyes and they both know what's going to happen next.

They smile at each other and he pays the lunch bill with his business credit card and then they

leave the restaurant. He withdraws cash from the ATM and takes a room under an assumed name while she goes to the ladies' room. He texts her the room number when he gets into the elevator. On the ninth floor, he lets himself into the room with the key card and takes off his jacket and loosens his tie. He sends a quick text to Kerri that his lunch is running late and to reschedule his 3:00 p.m. meeting, then he hears a soft knock on the door.

He's doing it again. Nancy must not find out. And then he opens the door and forgets all about his wife.

IT'S A LOVELY SUMMER DAY, perfect for an outing to the wading pool in the park beside the public library. Stephanie and Hanna had arranged to get together, and Stephanie had invited some of the women from her moms' group to join them. Amy and Jen are there with their baby boys, and Barb with her little girl.

Stephanie wiggles her bare toes in the warm, shallow water, sitting on the concrete edge of the pool. Hanna is nearby, splashing with Teddy beside her. Jackie and Emma happily gurgle at each other in front of her. All the babies are in swim diapers and brimmed hats, and Stephanie has her girls in bath rings to help support them because she can't really hold them both up at once. The women chat

about the babies companionably. They've already been in the library and picked up some baby board books to take home—a caravan of baby strollers. They all had lunch in the park, Stephanie and Hanna sharing tuna sandwiches. By the time she gets the twins home, Stephanie thinks, she will be able to put them down for their afternoon nap and she can get some sleep.

"Isn't this great?" Hanna says grinning, watching Teddy laugh.

Stephanie has to agree with her. She feels a little more rested than usual today and it's done wonders for her mood. She felt able to reach out to these other women, whom she doesn't really know well. It's hard to be social when you're exhausted. She looks at her two baby girls, their big, round blue eyes, so cute splashing in the baby rings, chortling with glee. She's lucky, and she knows it. She's so lucky to have Patrick, and Emma and Jackie—two perfect, healthy babies. She has everything she ever wanted. The colic will pass.

"Oh, looks like somebody's getting sleepy," Hanna says, smiling at Jackie, who is yawning.

They all start to pack up for the walk home.

# 7

Toward the end of the workday, Patrick gets a call on his cell from Erica. He's been expecting it, but his heart still begins to pump uncomfortably when he sees her number.

"Meet me for a drink?" Erica asks. "Same place? In half an hour?"

He briefly considers refusing. But he knows he must meet her. "Okay."

For him, at least, the attraction is gone; if anything, she frightens him a little. He will be absolutely clear that he's faithful to his wife, and then he will leave. He's not going to make the same mistake twice. And she needs to know it.

On his way from the office to the bar, he tells himself that things have changed. He's with Stephanie now. He has a family.

He spies her in the same corner as the day before. He tells himself to relax. He's got nothing to worry

about. He'll set her straight and he can be on his way. He sits down across from her—he can smell her perfume again, and it bothers him.

She gives him a conspiratorial, seductive look over her beer. For a long moment neither of them speaks. Finally she says, "So . . . you're probably wondering what I'm doing here."

He smiles uncomfortably. "I am, actually."

She tilts her head at him. "You know, Patrick, we could pick up where we left off . . ."

He smiles—as if with regret—and shakes his head firmly. "No. It was a long time ago." He exhales heavily. "I'm not going to cheat on Stephanie." He leans back, putting distance between them.

"Really?" She raises her eyebrows at him as if she doesn't believe him.

"Yes, really."

"Why not? It didn't bother you to cheat on Lindsey."

It hits him like a blow. "That was different."

"How was it different?" Her voice has surprise in it, and a bit of an edge.

He hesitates. "I was younger then—I was only twenty-three, for Christ's sake. I was a kid. I only thought about myself."

"Aren't you going to order a drink?" she asks.

He hadn't been planning on it, but now he changes his mind and beckons the waiter over. He orders a Scotch and they both wait until the server is out of earshot.

She considers him for a moment. "Do you love her, your new wife?"

"Yes, I do. With my whole heart."

"So that's what's different," she says. "You didn't love Lindsey."

"That's not true," he says quickly. "Of course I loved her."

She watches him closely and says, "That's not how I remember it."

He looks back at her, feeling a chill.

He'd slept with his wife's best friend. He had behaved badly, but so had Erica. He had betrayed his wife, she had betrayed a friend. He studies Erica sitting across from him in the dimly lit bar. He has to put this to rest once and for all.

"Look, Erica . . ." He tries to read her expression as she looks back at him. She'd avoided him after the accident. He thought it was remorse for what they'd done. He remembers how she'd caught his eye across the room, the casket between them, and pushes the memory away. "I'm married, with newborn twins. I'm not looking to have an affair. I should have made that perfectly clear yesterday. I came here today to make sure you understand that."

She answers him. "I see." Her mood seems to have changed on a dime.

For a moment he simply stares at her. She can't seriously be hoping to rekindle what they had. What **is** she doing here? His uneasiness grows.

"It's been almost ten years," she says. "A long time to think."

"About what?"

"The accident." She looks at him intently. "Do you still think about it?"

"I try not to. But sometimes."

"I do, a lot." A silence descends between them.

"You miss Lindsey. Of course you do," he says finally. "I do too."

She looks up at him. "That's not what I mean. I think about **how she died**."

He stares back at her, unnerved. "You blame me."

"Of course I blame you. Everyone does."

It's like a punch to the stomach. "I blame myself too," he says. His voice is bitter. "Every day. But it was an accident."

Into the fraught silence Erica says, "Just because they said it was an accident doesn't mean it was."

He recoils in surprise, his heart pounding. "What?" When she doesn't respond, he says, his voice low, "Are you saying—are you accusing me of killing my wife **on purpose**?"

"It's crossed my mind."

"Why—why the hell would you think that?" he asks. His heart is racing now. It had been ruled an accident. There was no question. No suspicion at all. It was a sad, tragic event. At the time, everyone had shaken their heads, looked at him with terrible pity, but no one had suggested that he'd done it on purpose. That he'd deliberately murdered his wife.

She spells it out for him now, and there's cold calculation in her voice. "You remember. You told me you felt trapped, you were unhappy. I thought you were in love with me. Imagine what it was like for me when she died. I thought—I was afraid— that you'd done it on purpose." She adds, "And I've had to live with that ever since."

Patrick's mind reels. Where was this coming from? He'd told her no such thing, and they both know it. He remembers again how she'd spurned him at the funeral, turned her back on him. "You're out of your mind," he says shortly.

"Am I?"

He looks back at her in growing horror. So this is why she's here. Then he takes a deep breath and speaks, trying to keep his voice steady. "You're wrong. I was a bad husband, and you were a bad friend, but that's it," he assures her. "I didn't **kill** her so that I could be with you, and you damn well know it."

"And I'm supposed to just take your word for it?" Her voice is sly.

His uneasiness spikes; he can feel his heart pounding hard in his chest. He says, trying to keep his voice even, "I don't know what else to tell you, Erica. It was an accident. The police thought it was an accident. The press thought it was an accident. You're the only one who seems to think otherwise— and we both know you're **pretending**." He tells himself that he has nothing to be worried about.

But he still hasn't told Stephanie the truth about what happened to his first wife. He wants to tell her at some point, he always meant to. And he will. He'd told Stephanie that his first wife had been killed in a car accident. But Erica knows what really happened. What if she tells Stephanie? Now, when she's so worn out and frazzled with the twins? It wouldn't be the best time—it would be the absolutely worst possible fucking time. Stephanie wouldn't be able to deal with it rationally. She wouldn't understand.

Why the fuck had he come here today? He should have known better.

As if reading his mind, Erica says, "Does your wife know about what happened?"

He feels himself coloring. He must not give himself away, but he's afraid he already has.

"Ah, she doesn't," Erica says, confirming his fears. "You never told her." She's goading him now. "I mean, who would marry a man who cheated on his first wife? A man who **killed** her—even if it was by accident?" He stares back at her stonily, saying nothing. "I wonder if I should tell her?"

"Why the hell would you do that?" he asks.

"Maybe she should know who she married. What if you have something like that in mind for her?"

He's struck with a sudden fury. "You miserable bitch," he says. "You have a twisted, fucked-up mind." They eye each other in silence. He feels

sick. "What's going on here, Erica?" he asks coldly. "Why are you here? What do you want?"

"Money." Her blue eyes stare back at him, cool and unwavering.

It hits him like a blow. That's what this is. She's blackmailing him. She wants him to pay her so that she won't say anything to his wife. Why didn't he see this coming? How could he have been so naive? He snorts. "Well, that's too bad, because I don't have any."

"A successful man like you?"

So that's what she's been doing, snooping around the edges of his life. Coming to his office, trying to get an idea of what he's worth. He can feel himself sweating with nerves. "Look," he says, trying to sound reasonable, "business has been bad lately. I haven't got any spare cash to give you, even if I wanted to."

She leans in closer to him. "Who do you think you're dealing with? I've done my research. I know your business is doing just fine. And I happen to know that your wife is **loaded**." She pulls back and looks at him, very matter-of-fact. "Money is not one of your problems."

He feels his stomach drop. How does she know about that? Now he's truly frightened. He sees it all, how his future might unfold—so very differently from what he'd planned. He must shut this down. He musters every ounce of resolve he has

and says clearly, "I'm not going to pay you any-thing. You need to understand that."

"Is that so?"

"Yes. I'll tell Stephanie everything." He'll tell her as soon as he gets home today, and then Erica will have nothing to hold over him. He has to hope—to believe—that Stephanie will stand by him, even after he admits to cheating on his first wife, even after he tells her exactly how she died.

"Everything?" She looks at him, disbelieving.

"I'll tell her the **truth**," Patrick says. "And I'll tell her about you and what a liar you are and what you're trying to do. Because I don't lie to my wife." He leans forward so that he's right in her lovely face and says, "I'm not afraid of you, and I'm not paying you a fucking cent."

She says, "Maybe it's not your wife you have to worry about."

"What?"

"Maybe I'll finally go to the authorities and get them to take another look at the death of your first wife."

"Why the fuck would you do that?"

"Because I can."

He stares at her in shock, finishes his drink in one go, gets up, throws some bills on the table, and walks out. He doesn't look back.

# 8

The twins are in their high chairs and Stephanie is in the middle of giving them their little bit of baby cereal mixed with breast milk. Patrick hasn't come home from work yet and she tries not to resent it. She'd smelled the Scotch on his breath the day before—he'd obviously been out for a drink after work, but she didn't mention it, tries not to begrudge it. She expects him any minute. She could use a hand. She's got a high chair on either side of her and she's spooning the milky cereal into one little mouth after the other. **My little birds**, she thinks fondly.

There's a sound at the front door but she's focused on the babies. She hears Patrick come in, but he lingers in the front hall for a moment. Another spoonful for Emma—most of it ending up on her chin—then Stephanie scoops it from the baby's face with the spoon. She wonders what Patrick is

doing. Why doesn't he come through to the kitchen and help her? "Patrick?" she calls.

"Yeah, I'm coming," he says.

"What's wrong?" she says, the moment he appears in the kitchen, looking as if he's had terrible news. Her stomach clenches. It must be worse than she thought at work. Maybe he has been shielding things from her after all, because she's got her hands full with the twins. Her anger flares, along with anxiety.

He pulls out a kitchen chair and slumps into it. "There's something I have to tell you."

She imagines the worst. A serious problem—a lawsuit of some kind, a mistake. Architecture is a fraught, difficult field. And she's never completely trusted Niall, even though Patrick does. "Is it work?"

He looks at her, surprised. "No."

Now she's the one who's surprised. What else could it be?

"Christ, I don't know where to start," he says.

She's forgotten about the cereal and now Jackie and Emma start to whimper. She goes back to feeding them, trying to remain calm, fake smiling at the babies. "There you go, yum-yum," she says, in a singsong voice. Then, to Patrick, "Just tell me. I can handle it."

"You know I love you, Stephanie," he says earnestly.

She turns her head away from the twins and

stares at him. Now she's really worried. He has the tortured look of someone about to confess. What has he done? They haven't had sex since the twins were born. Is that what this is about? She waits.

"You know I told you that my previous wife, Lindsey"—now tears are coming into his eyes—"died in a car accident."

"Yes." Her voice is uncertain. She can't imagine what he's about to say next.

"I didn't tell you everything."

She goes absolutely still, staring at him.

His face has gone pale. "I never told you because . . . it was my fault."

Oh, dear God. Her entire body tightens, as if for a blow. This is coming at her out of the blue; she's not prepared for it.

He sags further into the kitchen chair. "I have to tell you what happened."

"Okay," she says.

"It was winter," he begins. "There was a storm. We were going to visit her mother. There was so much snow. I didn't want to go, but she insisted. . . ." His face is anguished and he stops, as if he can't go on.

It's difficult for her to look at him in such obvious, raw pain. "You were driving?" she whispers. Even the babies are quiet now, as if they can sense the tension in the room.

He shakes his head. "No. We never got off the street."

She doesn't understand. He's not making sense.

"She got in the car to get warm. Lindsey was always so impatient. I told her to wait inside the house, but she came out before I was done. I didn't know it was dangerous." He swallows.

"What was dangerous?" she asks, confused.

He takes a deep breath. "I had to shovel out the car. It was taking a long time because the snow was almost up to the roof. She was so desperate to visit her mother and her sister." He hesitates. "She was finding it hard, being away from her family—she was eight months pregnant—and I was working such long hours."

Stephanie feels her stomach turn. She hadn't known his wife had been pregnant when she died. She steels herself for the rest.

"She wouldn't stay inside. It was very cold. I told her to go back in the house, but she got in the car. And I just kept shoveling—I had no idea that the exhaust pipe was plugged with snow, that carbon monoxide was getting into the car—killing her." He chokes back a sob.

Stephanie gapes at him in horror, but he doesn't meet her eyes.

"When—when I finished, I put the shovel away and went up and got the bags from the apartment and locked everything up. I put the bags in the trunk. And then I opened the driver's-side door." He pauses, and it looks to Stephanie like he can't catch his breath. "At first I thought Lindsey was just

asleep." He glances at her, and quickly looks away. "But then suddenly it struck me that she didn't look right somehow, that she didn't look normal. I grabbed her by the shoulder and shook her, but her head just fell forward. And—I knew she was dead. I started to scream. I lost my mind for a minute. I backed out of the car, screaming for help, fumbling for my cell phone. I called 911. Some of the neighbors came running out. I was hysterical—I don't remember much more than that, other than people dragging Lindsey out of the car and lying her down on the snow. Someone did CPR on her. The paramedics got there really fast, but it was too late. She was declared dead. The baby too."

He puts his head in his hands and says, "If I'd only known what was happening. If I'd checked on her first, before putting the shovel away, going upstairs to get the luggage—" He collapses into ragged sobs.

Stephanie stirs herself out of her shock and goes to Patrick, putting her arms around him. She doesn't know what to say. She watches him break down, his face in his hands. The babies start to cry too. She's numb. She had no idea. No idea that he'd been carrying this awful burden the whole time that she's known him. She clasps him in her arms as he sobs, his body heaving. "Shhhhh," she whispers, holding him tight. It's the saddest thing she's ever heard. She can't even imagine—

"It was an accident," she whispers, holding him

tight until his body stops trembling. She has never seen him like this, in such inconsolable grief. As if he's been torn apart.

He looks up at her finally, his eyes wet and red. "I'm sorry. I'm sorry I didn't tell you."

The babies are bawling now and together Stephanie and Patrick wipe the girls' faces and hands and unbuckle them from their high chairs. Then they carry them through to the living room and put them in the swings so that Stephanie and Patrick can talk. The twins like the swings, and they're distracted, at least for a few minutes.

Patrick collapses onto the sofa as if all the strength has gone out of him. Stephanie sits down close beside her husband and turns to face him. "Why didn't you tell me?" she asks softly.

He looks back at her, completely spent. "I was too ashamed. I can't tell you the guilt I carry around. I didn't think. I didn't know it was even possible to get carbon monoxide poisoning that way."

She nods. It wouldn't occur to her either. It was a simple but tragic mistake.

"I was only twenty-three. I was almost destroyed by grief, by guilt. I left Colorado after the funeral, came back to New York. It took a long time to just begin to feel normal. I still think about it, about what happened, every day." He looks at her, his face overwrought. "And then I met you three years ago, and started to feel like living again." He turns

away. "I'm sorry. It isn't fair to you. To dump it on you like this."

"You don't have to apologize to me," she says. "I wish you'd told me before, but I'm glad you've told me now." She wonders why he chose today to do it.

"I didn't want it to be part of our life together. I didn't want to burden you with it too. It should be mine to bear, alone."

She reaches out, takes his face in her hands, and says, "Patrick, I love you, and I always will. We have two beautiful little girls together. What happened is horrible and I'm so, so sorry." She pauses and then goes on. "I don't mean to minimize it in any way, but it's in the past. You have to let it go, forgive yourself. We're building a future together."

He looks back at her, but his face is still bleak, and he turns away and stares at the floor. "I want to put it behind me. God knows I've suffered enough for it."

"You **can** put it behind you. Have you ever seen anyone, a grief counselor, to help you with this?"

He shakes his head, sniffs. "No."

"Maybe you should," she says gently.

He's still looking down; he takes a deep breath. "There's a bit of a problem that you need to know about."

She waits, worried.

"Lindsey had a friend, Erica. She's recently moved near here, to Newburgh. She got in touch

with me a couple of days ago and wanted to meet for drinks."

"Okay," Stephanie says, remembering the smell of alcohol on her husband's breath, wondering where this is going, feeling uneasy.

"She's threatening me."

# 9

Erica leans back in her bathtub, the hot water up to her neck, breathing in the smell of lavender. Her mind drifts to Niall. He's an attractive man, surprisingly good in bed. She'd enjoyed herself.

She'd applied for the job at Foote and Kilgour only to freak Patrick out; she wanted to catch him off guard. But there was an undeniable attraction between her and Niall in the interview. Plus she couldn't help noticing that Niall was married, with a child—she'd seen his ring, the photos on his desk—and most married men, especially those with children, don't want their wives finding out if they're getting a bit on the side.

Her mind shifts to Patrick. Of course he said he wouldn't pay her. But he doesn't mean that.

. . .

STEPHANIE STARES BACK at her husband, alarmed. "Threatening you, how?"

He sighs deeply, miserably. "She threatened to tell you what happened, and I said I'd tell you myself. I have nothing to hide."

Stephanie is silent, her anxiety spiking.

Finally he says, "She wants money, or else she says she'll go to the authorities in Colorado and try to get them to look at the accident again, maybe reopen the case."

"What?" Stephanie says in disbelief. "She's trying to **blackmail** you?"

He nods. "Yes."

"What is she talking about, reopening the case? What case?" Stephanie cries, feeling a terrible anxiety creep over her.

He's not looking at her. He's staring at the floor again. "It was an accident, and it was officially ruled an accident, obviously. There was never any suggestion that it was anything else! But now she says she can go to them and get them to reopen it. She says she might tell them that—that I did it on purpose."

Stephanie is stunned. She can hardly process what she's hearing. "Why would she do that?"

"For money! She's just trying to frighten me into paying her."

"But she can't do that, surely? She can't just ask them to reopen a case. That's absurd."

"Of course it's absurd. She's out of her fucking

mind." He looks at her then. "And that's what I told her."

"But"—Stephanie doesn't know how to put it— "but . . . can she do that? Do we have anything to worry about?"

"I don't know." He looks more worried than she would like. "She's just doing this because she knows we have money. She found out about your inheritance somehow. She would never have shown up here otherwise."

Stephanie has kept her inheritance very quiet. How would this woman know? "Wouldn't she have to have some grounds?" Stephanie protests. He's silent for a long time. He's not looking at her. "She doesn't have any grounds, does she?"

"Of course not, but . . . she says she does."

"What?" She feels like she can hardly breathe.

"It's too ridiculous."

"Tell me."

He shakes his head, as if at the absurdity of it all. "She says she'll tell them that I wanted to get Lindsey out of the way." Now he looks terribly uncomfortable. He glances at her uneasily.

"Why would she tell them that, Patrick?" Stephanie is feeling sick to her stomach.

He swallows. "She says she'll tell them I was in love with her, which is absolute bullshit. I know it and she knows it. But she'll tell any kind of lie if she gets something out of it." He looks at her desperately. "I really think she might be a sociopath,

Stephanie. She has no scruples, no conscience at all. Who knows what she'll say, what she'll make up? It's obvious she just wants money, but when she talks, it's like she believes her own lies. She's a hell of an actress."

Stephanie's mouth is dry. She tries to swallow. "How did you know her?"

"She was Lindsey's best friend," Patrick says.

"And how well did you know her?"

He looks her in the eyes and says, "I was young, just a kid, really, and very stupid. I don't want you to think . . ." He hesitates.

"Think what?" She's nervous now, afraid of what he's going to tell her. She thinks she knows. He doesn't answer her. She says sharply, "Did you sleep with this woman?" His silence is all the answer she needs. "Oh my God." She gets up off the sofa and stands in front of him, looking down at him, aghast. "You slept with your wife's best friend and now she says you were in love with her. Were you? Were you in love with her?" Her voice is accusing.

In the swing, Jackie begins to cry. Almost instantly, Emma joins in. They don't like hearing their mother speak this way.

"I slept with her a couple of times," Patrick admits. "That's all it was. We were drunk. We were kids. It meant nothing. Nothing! And now she thinks she can use that against me, because she needs money." He stands up, too, running a hand wildly through his hair. "She never said

anything before. Because she **knew** it meant nothing. She **knew** it was an accident! She **knew** I was devastated by what happened." He reaches out to her, pleading. "You have to believe me, Stephanie. I would **never** cheat on you, if that's what you're worried about. I'm a different person now."

But her thoughts are reeling. He cheated on his first wife. She can hardly believe it. It was almost ten years ago, she thinks, but do people ever really change? She says, with absolute conviction, her voice cold, "If you ever cheat on me, I'll leave you and take the twins with me."

He looks at her in surprise, as if taken aback at her tone. "Okay. I know that. I will never be unfaithful to you, I swear. I never have been and I never will. Let's not even go there, because that's not going to happen. What we have to deal with now is—this situation."

She takes a deep breath. It's hard to think straight because both babies are crying. They've had to raise their voices to be heard over the din. She walks over to the swings and turns on the timers again to set the babies back in motion. That calms them for a bit. Then she paces around the living room, suddenly filled with a nervous, restless energy, her exhaustion gone. She turns to him. "What are we going to do? If she goes to the police with her lies, that would be—" She can't even imagine what it would be like. "She's accusing you of—**murder!**" Stephanie says, her voice strained. "Think of what

that would do to us, what it would do to us personally, to your reputation—"

"It would be in Colorado, not here," Patrick says, his voice tense. "Worst case is I'd have to go back to Colorado and give my side of the story, which I've already done. They believed me then. They won't believe her and they won't reopen it. I don't think anyone here would find out."

"I think that's naive, Patrick," Stephanie says.

His face darkens. "Fuck." He begins to pace as well. "She can't be allowed to get away with this! It's all lies!"

"Should we talk to an attorney about this?"

Patrick shakes his head. "Not yet. Maybe she'll give up when we don't pay her."

Stephanie thinks for a minute, her breathing fast and shallow. "You said you think she might be a sociopath. Do you really think so?"

"I don't know."

"If she's crazy, no one's going to listen to her."

He exhales deeply. "But she doesn't **seem** crazy. She comes across as completely normal, but **I** know she's lying," he says. He adds tentatively, "I don't know—maybe we should pay her something, just to make her go away."

"No way," Stephanie counters. "If we pay her once, she'll ask again. She'll be after us for money for the rest of our lives. She'll drain us dry." They have to stand up to her, come what may. She feels ill at the prospect of what's ahead. "We're not going

to use my parents' hard-earned money to pay off some woman who's trying to blackmail you over something that you didn't do. Think about it, Patrick! This is insane. I can't believe you'd even **consider** paying her anything."

"No, you're right," Patrick says, nodding.

"Maybe I should talk to her," Stephanie says suddenly.

Patrick looks taken aback. "Why?"

"To show her that I believe you, that I'm standing by you. That might take the wind out of her sails. Maybe I can reason with her," Stephanie says.

He shakes his head. "No! There's no reasoning with her. I don't want her anywhere near you, or the twins. She's toxic—and possibly dangerous." He adds, "I mean, who in their right mind would make up something like this?"

# 10

Nancy Foote has put her son to bed and is now gathering up the day's laundry to pop in the machine overnight. She picks up the shirt her husband wore that day—he's thrown it on the bed, he never bothers to put anything in the laundry hamper—and a faint smell of perfume wafts from it. She freezes.

No. He wouldn't. Not after last time.

In disbelief, she brings the shirt to her nose and sniffs. A woman's perfume—floral and exotic, very faint. She tells herself that it doesn't necessarily mean what she thinks it means. Maybe someone at the office was doused in scent today. . . .

But Nancy can't stand being lied to, and she won't lie to herself either. She hasn't smelled anything like this on her husband or his clothes since she forced him to break off his affair with Anne O'Dowd.

She sinks down onto their bed, her heart racing

with the fear of betrayal. She hasn't trusted him since she caught him cheating. She's been keeping an eye on him, slipping her hands into his trousers and jacket pockets at night, looking for signs— a receipt, a cocktail napkin, a note . . . but there's been nothing. She doesn't know the password to his phone, unfortunately.

She sits on the bed feeling like the wind has been knocked out of her. She doesn't want to go through this again. Should she confront him? She knows from experience that he'll deny it. He'll deny it until there's incontrovertible proof, like last time.

She'd told him she'd forgiven him for Anne, but it isn't really true. She hasn't forgiven him. But she wants to stay in her marriage. She still loves him, and they have a young child to think about. Henry is only four years old. She doesn't want to be a single mother, making arrangements week in, week out, reminding Niall to make his support payments, because she knows—she has divorced friends, and she knows what it's like.

He'll be smarter this time, more cautious. Because he wants the marriage to survive too. He'd been completely undone, before, when he realized that his little fling might cost him his marriage, his family. He'd been shattered. He wasn't lying about **that**.

So why does he do it? Why does he cheat on her?

· · ·

PATRICK CLIMBS INTO BED just after midnight. Stephanie shooed him away as she sat on the sofa with the twins, one propped up on each breast. He knows they'll be quiet while they're feeding, but soon after, the crying will begin again, and she will have her hands full for a while yet before they finally cry themselves to sleep. This is their routine—he gets a couple of extra hours at night and she gets the afternoon nap. They're both functioning on about six hours of sleep a night and have been for months. Even so, when he gets into bed now, he can't sleep.

They'd walked in circles while holding the crying babies all through the long evening and night. He'd longed for his bed, but now that he's here, he can't shut off his mind. To pay Erica would be a stupid thing to do. They must stand up to her, call her bluff. But what if she doesn't give up? What if she goes to the authorities and they take her seriously? Would they, after all this time? Surely it will make them doubt her, the fact that it took her so long to come forward. He'll tell them that she's tried to blackmail him. Surely that would put an end to it right there. He really shouldn't have anything to worry about.

Even if nothing comes of this, though, Erica has already done enough damage. He could see the doubt in his wife's face—not about the accident, but about him. He'd been unfaithful to

his first wife; he could see the calculation behind Stephanie's eyes—**Would he be unfaithful to her?**

He'd had a fright when Stephanie suggested she meet Erica. No, they mustn't meet. He must make sure of that. He'd always sensed something dangerous coiled inside Erica. Maybe that had been part of the attraction all those years ago. But now he has so much more to lose. What if Erica comes around to the house, spouting her lies? She can be very convincing. He has to trust Stephanie. Trust that she loves him enough to tell the truth from the lies.

Finally, he drifts into a troubled sleep.

THE NEXT MORNING, Nancy pours herself a cup of coffee and decides she is not going to be made a fool of. If her husband is starting to see someone else, she has to know what's going on. This morning when Niall left for work, he was whistling—a bad sign; he used to whistle when he was seeing Anne.

Now, she sits down at the kitchen table with her cell phone. She's never been very good with technology; she learns only as much as she needs, and beyond that she tries to ignore it as much as possible. She doesn't use apps. She can work her computer, and she's adept enough at social media, but she's not one to adopt new technologies with enthusiasm. Unlike her husband, who has an app

for everything and who's in love with his flashy new Tesla Model X with its gull wings and futuristic features. She's afraid to drive it—she finds it intimidating. She has her own car, anyway. Still, when he bought it, in his first flush of enthusiasm, he'd given her one of the black key cards to keep in her wallet, installed the app on her phone, and tried to explain to her how it all worked, but she'd glazed over and hadn't looked at it since.

Now she opens up her phone and clicks on the Tesla app. She studies it and decides there's some valuable information on here. She can see right now that her husband's car is parked at 111 Bleeker Street—he's at the office. She realizes that she can open the app at any time and see exactly where his car is. That might come in handy.

ERICA LEAVES HER spartan apartment and climbs into her car. Despite what he said, she doubts Patrick has told his new wife anything at all. He's always been the secretive type. No, his wife probably doesn't have a clue. She won't know what's hit her, if and when it all comes out. She should be grateful, Erica thinks—maybe he was going to try to kill her and her babies one day. A man like that. Erica tells herself that really, she's doing the woman a favor.

She turns onto the highway to Aylesford,

consumed with curiosity about Patrick and his new little family. She already knows where they live, what they look like. She's been there. She's even viewed a house for sale a couple of doors down from the Kilgours' on Danbury Drive. It's one of the nicest suburbs in Aylesford, according to the real estate sites. She knows they've got money. She'll drop by again today, to Danbury Drive. Take another look at his new wife.

STEPHANIE WAKES WITH A START. She has no idea how long she's been asleep—it could be minutes, or hours. She looks at the digital clock to orient herself. It's 2:37 p.m. Someone is calling her name. Who is it? She sits up, thinking she's imagined it.

"Stephanie?"

She recognizes Hanna's voice, calling her from downstairs. What is Hanna doing in the house? Is something wrong? Stephanie remembers the fire in the kitchen and gets out of bed and rushes to the stairs—no smell of smoke; she's halfway down when she sees Hanna in the front hall, the door wide open behind her. "What are you doing here?" Stephanie asks, confused.

Hanna looks up at her, her face showing concern. "I saw your front door was open. I came by to check on you."

Stephanie reaches the front hall. She thought

she'd locked the door on her way in from the gro-
cery store—but maybe she hadn't. She can't re-
member.

"Maybe I forgot to lock it," she says, worried,
one hand to her forehead. "I must be losing my
mind." She shakes her head and frowns. "Honestly,
if these babies don't start sleeping soon, I'm going
to completely lose it." She hasn't told Hanna about
the incident with the stove. She hasn't told anyone
but her husband. Hanna only has one baby, and
his sleeping habits are excellent; she might judge,
even if she doesn't mean to.

"Sorry to wake you," Hanna says, "but I was
worried." She closes the door now.

"No, it's fine," Stephanie says, giving her a wan
smile and looking dully at the area near the door.
She'd dropped her purse there on the floor, by
the narrow table in the entryway. She's sure of it.
"Where's my purse?" she says, looking around for
her large black bag.

Hanna's eyes sweep the vestibule, following her
anxious gaze.

"I left it right there," Stephanie says. It's obvi-
ously not there now. She goes into the kitchen and
checks the counter and the table. The floor. She
doesn't see her bag anywhere. Hanna has gone into
the living room to look, and now comes back to
join her.

"Could it be upstairs?" Hanna suggests.

Stephanie shakes her head, but charges up the

stairs anyway, looks in her bedroom, then goes swiftly down the hall and checks on the still-sleeping twins. But the purse isn't there either. She's getting upset now. It's dawning on her: someone was in the house and took her purse. They could have taken the babies, too, and she wouldn't have known. And it's her own damn fault for not locking the front door properly. And she left her purse right there on the floor, by the front door. "How could I be so stupid?" she fumes at Hanna, back downstairs once again. "My wallet was in there, all my ID. Everything! I'll have to get it all replaced." Just the thought of the effort that will require is enough to flatten her.

"Don't blame yourself," Hanna tells her. "You should be able to leave your door unlocked and not expect someone to come in and steal your purse."

"You said it was wide open."

"It was when I saw it," Hanna admits.

"Patrick will be upset. He worries about me," Stephanie says. "I'm so absentminded these days, so forgetful."

"I'll help you get your ID replaced," Hanna offers. "I've done it before. I had my purse snatched once in New York City."

Stephanie manages to swallow her dismay. "Thanks, Hanna. I don't know what I'd do without you." Then she realizes something else. "I had a spare house key in there too. I'll have to get the locks replaced."

She wants to invite Hanna to have a cup of coffee and tell her everything—about Patrick's past and the woman who is threatening them. But she can't. She must keep it to herself. Even if it feels almost too heavy to bear.

# 11

Stephanie struggles to get the double stroller out of the trunk. It had rained overnight, but now it's cleared and it's going to be a nice day. It's not even 11:00 a.m. but she's already been up for hours. She's had two coffees to clear the fog in her head. But today it's more than sleep deprivation that's bothering her, making her forgetful and distracted as she packs for an outing with the twins. She and Patrick are both on edge, waiting to hear again from Erica Voss. And Patrick had been upset last night when she'd told him about the theft of her purse. He'd insisted she be more careful and called a locksmith immediately.

Her exhaustion makes everything seem even more unmanageable, more overwhelming. How can life throw such curveballs at you? She's just a normal wife and mother, but now she and her husband are the subject of attempted blackmail. That Patrick had cheated on his first wife was bad

enough—she can hardly believe it. And the rest of it . . .

Last night, they'd discussed going to the Aylesford police. Patrick wasn't in favor of it. But to her it seems the most sensible plan. Maybe they could charge this woman, or at least frighten her off. For now, they've agreed that when Erica gets in touch again, Patrick will tell her that Stephanie knows everything and they're not going to pay her a cent. Maybe then she'll go away.

She's keeping her phone close, waiting to hear from him.

The babies are dressed in their adorable complementary outfits. She has to get out of the house. The best thing is to go for a walk in the fresh air, showing Jackie and Emma the butterflies and the flowers, and then stopping at the park nearby. There, they'll sit on a blanket by the sandbox with the toys she's brought and she'll do her best to keep them entertained. Most days she runs into someone she knows at the park, something she usually looks forward to. She's not sure she wants to see anyone today, though. She can't tell anyone what she's dealing with—not even Hanna, her closest friend.

She lifts the babies into the stroller, buckles them in, and locks up the house. Then she gives her girls a smile and a little chuck under each chin, talking to them as she pushes them along the sidewalk. Then she pulls out her cell phone, takes a cute

picture of the twins in the stroller, and texts it to her husband.

He doesn't respond. Maybe he's in a meeting. She imagines how difficult it must be to focus on work with all this going on.

When she finally gets to the park, there are a couple of other mothers sitting with their babies on blankets beneath the trees while their older children play in the nearby sandbox. No one she really knows except by sight. She lifts the babies out of the stroller onto their blanket. She has to keep her eye on them, but she quickly glances at her phone. She hasn't heard from Patrick, and she's getting more and more nervous. Has he heard from Erica? She threatened him on Wednesday, and now it's Friday. Is she trying to make them sweat?

She hears her phone ping and takes a quick look.

**Haven't heard from her.
Will keep you posted.**

She puts her phone away, unhappy. She thinks they should go to the cops. They're law-abiding citizens, victims of an attempted crime. Patrick hasn't done anything wrong. The police here won't be interested in reopening a case in Colorado. She thinks they are their best option.

"So adorable," a woman says, sitting down near her on the ledge of the sandbox.

Stephanie glances at her, pulled out of her

thoughts. "Oh, thanks," she says, smiling absently. She gets this a lot, especially with twins, but no woman ever tires of hearing some stranger tell her how adorable her kids are. The woman looks familiar.

"Do I know you?" Stephanie asks.

"No, I don't think so. No—wait—I think I saw you yesterday in the drugstore. In the line for the cashier."

"Oh, that's right. I remember now," Stephanie says.

"You were buying diapers and dark chocolate," the other woman says.

Stephanie is a little taken aback that this woman noticed what she bought.

"How old are they?" the other woman asks.

"Four and a half months, just about," Stephanie answers, wondering absently where the woman's own kids are. She doesn't appear to have any with her. Why is she here at the sandbox, then? Stephanie looks at her more closely. She's very pretty, with blond hair in a loose ponytail, snug jeans, and a smart blouse. Stephanie is suddenly aware of her own untidy hair, the spit-up on her T-shirt, and the fact that she's still wearing maternity jeans. It's going to be a while before she gets her body back, and she has a momentary twinge of jealousy, even regret, looking at the trim, attractive woman in front of her. But then she glances at her babies, and she doesn't care what she looks like. It's totally

worth it to have Emma and Jackie. They're every-thing to her. So what if she's put on a few pounds?

"Twins are so cute," the woman says.

Stephanie nods. "Yes, twice as cute and twice as exhausting," she says ruefully.

"My sister has twins," the woman says. "Her hus-band is a lawyer, and he says it's like serving your sentence concurrently rather than consecutively."

They laugh. "Do you live around here?" Stephanie asks, curious.

"Not yet. My husband and I are looking. I thought I'd walk around and check out the neigh-borhood and shops and hang out in the parks and coffee shops a bit before we buy. I don't think you should just fall in love with a house without know-ing what you're getting into, the bigger picture."

"No," Stephanie agrees, although that's what they had done—looked at the house, fallen in love with it, and taken everything the real estate agent had told them about the neighborhood as gospel. Fortunately, they have been happy here.

"How long have you lived here?" the woman asks.

"About two years," Stephanie tells her. "We moved in right after we got married." She notices that the other woman isn't wearing a wedding ring.

"And you like it here?"

"Oh yes, we love it. It's been great."

At that moment, the other woman takes out her phone and the pleasant expression seems to

disappear momentarily from her face as she types a brief message.

"A problem?" Stephanie asks lightly.

"No, not really," the woman says, and looks up at her again, smiling, as her phone rings. "Nothing I can't handle."

PATRICK CAN'T STOP THINKING about Erica and his situation. It creeps into his mind every minute, even when he's talking to a client. He checks his messages obsessively, but there's been no word from Erica. He needs to deal with this. Get it over with.

Finally, a text comes in from Erica.

## Call me

He stares at his phone. He realizes he's clenching his jaw tight; his entire body is tense. Is this the right thing to do? Does he dare call her bluff? He has a terrible moment of doubt. It's her word against his. And she's such a brilliant liar.

He calls her cell. "Erica?"

"Yes."

He says, "I've told Stephanie everything. And she's agreed—we're not going to pay you a dime."

He waits for her response. When it comes, it's not what he was expecting.

# 12

She disconnects. Then he gets the ping of a text message.

**I'm at the park, talking to your wife. The twins look like you.**

Patrick feels dizzy, as if all the blood has left his head. For a moment he can't think at all. Then his mind clears and the thoughts come quickly. Would Erica harm Stephanie and the babies? She's not violent—as far as he knows. But she **is** manipulative. She knows this is going to get to him— that's why she's done it. She must have followed Stephanie when she left the house. He realizes that his breathing is irregular and tells himself he must calm down. He takes a deep breath, in and out,

and again, staring at the message, trying to figure
out what to do.

His phone pings again.

**I really think your wife
and I could be friends.**

And attached to the text is a photo. Of Stephanie
and the twins, sitting on a blanket. Stephanie is
turned away, lifting one of the smiling babies,
probably unaware of the photo being taken. Does
Stephanie know who she's talking to? He texts his
wife urgently.

**It's her. You're talking
to Erica. She just sent
me a picture of you.
Take the babies and get
away from her!**

But he gets no answer. The lack of a response
is maddening. He'd told Stephanie to keep her
phone close. Has she got her hands full with the
twins, or has something happened? He tells him-
self that the park must be full of people this time
of day. Nothing can happen to his family in broad
daylight.

But the silence from both of them is making
him crazy. Finally he hits speed dial to Stephanie's

cell. He hears the phone ring and ring. He's start-
ing to panic when his wife answers. She sounds out
of breath.

"What's going on?" he demands frantically.

"What? What's the matter?" she answers, sound-
ing normal but defensive. "I was just getting the
twins into the stroller."

He lowers his voice. "That woman with you, is
she still there?"

"No, she left a minute ago. How do you know
about her?"    •

Patrick closes his eyes. "That was Erica."

STEPHANIE TURNS AND LOOKS in the direction that
the blond woman had gone, just moments before.
Stephanie can no longer see her.

As Patrick explains everything, she feels a chill.

"She didn't say who she was?" Patrick asks.

"No," Stephanie says, her voice hollow. "She just
chatted with me, then she got a call on her cell."
It unnerves her that she was here with Jackie and
Emma while her husband was talking to his black-
mailer and she didn't even know. "She seemed so
nice," Stephanie says, faltering.

"She's not **nice**, Stephanie," Patrick says ada-
mantly. "She's trying to mess with us."

"I've seen her before," Stephanie says. "Yester-
day . . . I was in the drugstore, and she was behind

me in line." She adds, "She even remembers what
I bought."

"Jesus," Patrick says under his breath.

"I've got to get the twins home and fed. I've got
to go," Stephanie says shakily.

"Okay, I'll let you know if I hear anything else
from her."

Stephanie adjusts the twins in the stroller, now
casting nervous looks over her shoulder. The
woman who Patrick is convinced was Erica seemed
perfectly harmless. But people can seem harm-
less and be anything but. You can't judge people
by appearances—they can fool you. She pushes
the stroller rapidly along the sidewalk, eager to
get home and inside, where she will carefully lock
the door. She thinks anxiously about how things
stand. Patrick told Erica they wouldn't pay her—
while she was sitting six feet away from his wife
and babies. Stephanie feels more certain than ever
that they should go to the police.

When she gets home and gets the twins fed and
changed and down for their nap, she's too wired
to crawl into bed herself. Instead, she goes into
the living room and opens her laptop and does
something she hasn't been able to bring herself to
do until now. She opens a Google search, and it
doesn't take her long to find what she's looking for.
There's an article in a Denver newspaper.

## TRAGIC ACCIDENT CLAIMS LIFE
## OF PREGNANT WOMAN

January 10, 2009

A tragic accident this morning has claimed the life of Lindsey Kilgour, aged twenty-one, in the Colorado mountain town of Creemore. The Grant County Coroner has determined that the woman, who was eight months pregnant, died of carbon monoxide poisoning. She was in the running car while her husband, Patrick Kilgour, dug out the vehicle from the recent snowstorm. The couple had been intending to visit family in Grand Junction.

The husband found his wife unresponsive and called emergency services. Emergency personnel tried to revive the victim at the scene but were unsuccessful.

The death has been ruled accidental. Carbon monoxide is a colorless, odorless gas that can kill within a matter of minutes. The authorities are again reminding everyone of the dangers of being

inside a running car surrounded by snow. Especially in times of heavy snowfall, care must be taken to ensure that the exhaust pipe is not blocked, as the deadly gas can seep up beneath the floorboards of the vehicle.

Stephanie feels numb. Worst of all, there are photographs. One is of a small car in the snow, a thick layer of it on the roof. She stares at it. Her husband's first wife died in that car. She feels a shiver along her back. But it's the second, larger photo that she studies the longest. It's a picture of her husband. It's blurry, but it's a close-up, and his face is a grimace of pain. He looks so much younger, thinner, with longer hair, but it's unmistakably him. She feels overwhelmed by it for a moment, absorbing his obvious pain.

Stephanie sits back in her chair. She hadn't known. She wasn't much into social media, but she had googled her husband's name once, when they were first dating, of course. But there were so many Patrick Kilgours that she'd immediately given up. She googles his name again now. She has to go through several pages before she finds this news report again.

She looks once more at the photo of her husband. That expression, that grainy black-and-white image will haunt her now, for the rest of her life.

She can't help herself, she looks for more. She finds other stories, with the same pictures of the car, of her husband. But in some articles there's a picture of his first wife, too, smiling into the camera. And what strikes Stephanie about this photo is that she looks so **happy**.

# 13

Niall knows there's something going on. Something is bothering his partner, Patrick, and he thinks it's more than just colicky twins. He remembers their recent conversation.

Patrick had slumped in the chair in front of Niall's desk, looking both nervous and deeply exhausted at the same time. He'd apologized for his recent poor performance, particularly the lackluster client meeting earlier in the week. He'd blamed it on lack of sleep, said he felt like he was walking in a fog half the time from sheer tiredness.

"Can't Stephanie take care of the babies?" Niall asked. "I mean, she gave up her job and she's home with them, right?"

Patrick had given him a sharp look, which Niall didn't care to interpret. Okay, maybe he was being harsh, and his own wife would have kicked him in the shins for that one, but they couldn't afford mistakes. Patrick's performance was making Niall

worried these days. They'd built up quite a good business in the last four years, and he doesn't want to lose it all now.

"You don't know what twins are like," Patrick said. "Your kid never had colic either."

This was true. Niall had a four-year-old and they weren't planning to have another. Henry had not been a difficult baby. Nancy had stayed home and dealt with it all so that he could focus on the business. Obviously things were a bit different in Patrick's household. But it was frustrating that there was nothing Niall could do about it.

Niall decided to take a gentler approach. "You know how important you are to this enterprise, Patrick," he said. "We both need you at the top of your game."

"I know," Patrick admitted. "I'll—I'll try to figure something out."

And they'd left it at that, with no concrete plan to deal with the problem.

Now Niall stands perfectly still over his drafting table. He'd just heard Patrick on the phone, talking loudly, as if he were arguing with someone. He'd distinctly heard him say, "What's going on?" Niall froze, listening. But then Patrick lowered his voice and he wasn't able to hear anymore.

Now, he pops his head into Patrick's office and asks, "Is everything all right?"

"Yeah, fine," Patrick says. But he looks distraught, and as if he's trying not to show it.

"I thought I heard you arguing with someone on the phone," Niall says.

"Oh, that," Patrick answers, giving a little laugh. "Just talking to Stephanie. The twins were both crying and she couldn't hear me. It can be a little frustrating sometimes."

"Okay," Niall says, and returns to his own office. He wonders again if there's something else going on, something that Patrick is keeping from him.

Patrick isn't the only one around here keeping secrets, he thinks, his mind turning to Erica, and how she looks lying on her back, naked against the sheets. He wants to see her again. She knows he's married, and she's fine with it. He just has to make sure Nancy doesn't find out.

She'd only found out about Anne because he'd been careless. He won't make that mistake again.

PATRICK GRABS HIS SUIT JACKET and leaves the office. He feels like Niall is breathing down his neck—the last thing he needs right now.

Patrick is anxious and unfocused, unable to concentrate on anything but his immediate problem. He needs to check on his family. Suddenly the urge to see them, to know that they're all right, is overwhelming. He walks quickly to the lot where he parks his Audi.

**I really think your wife and I could be friends.**

The idea makes his blood run cold. She was sitting within feet of Stephanie and the twins when she texted him to call her. She'd guessed that he might refuse to pay her, and she was applying pressure. She could lie to Stephanie, tell her that they'd been having sex in a hotel room somewhere. Erica is toying with him. Showing him that she could blow his world apart if she chose to.

He reminds himself that Erica just wants money. She's not going to harm his family.

He drives out of the parking lot and toward home as fast as he dares. Suddenly his phone pings. He glances at it and sees it's another text from Erica. His hands immediately begin to get clammy on the wheel. He pulls over at the first opportunity, into a gas station, and parks the car. He sits for a moment, breathing deeply, before he opens the message. Now, he's a little more afraid of her. Of what she might say or do. He'll tell her to go to hell. He'll tell her he's going to go to the police.

He reads the message.

**Let's meet. Now.**

He hates her peremptory tone. He wants to tell her to go fuck herself. He responds,

**I can't. I'm busy.**

She immediately answers.

**I'll be at the park at
the foot of the Skyway
Bridge in twenty
minutes.**

This is fucked up. Completely fucked up. He smashes his hands against the steering wheel, feels the pain radiate up his forearms. What does he do now? He's never been blackmailed before. What are his options? He could go to the police and tell them Erica is threatening him and stalking him and his wife. He could call them right now. The police could meet her at the park. But what happens then?

His phone pings again.

**There's something you
need to know.**

As soon as he reads the message, he knows he's going to meet her.

# 14

Erica puts her phone down and looks at herself in the rearview mirror. She's pretty sure Patrick will show up, and she wants to look her best. She takes her hair out of the ponytail and brushes it. She puts on fresh lipstick. She looks a lot better than his current wife does. It's not Stephanie's fault—she's postpartum and it takes a while to get back to looking good after you've had a baby. She's sure Stephanie is an attractive woman, just not right now.

She thinks about going to see her son before she left Denver to move to Newburgh. She hadn't seen him in years—not since he was born. But she needed to get a current photo. So she'd watched the house and then followed the family from a distance one evening when they went to the park. Fortunately he looks a lot like his dad. She got a nice shot of him, had it printed, and put it in her wallet.

She drives closer to the Skyway Bridge, parks her car, and walks toward the river and sits down on a bench where she can easily be seen. She knows exactly what she's going to say.

PATRICK DRIVES AROUND for a few minutes, killing time. He doesn't want to go back to the office and park the car and leave again on foot. Niall might wonder what he's up to. He'll drive to the bridge and leave the car somewhere nearby.

Patrick parks on a side street and walks down to the river. His body is tight with tension. There's a small park at the foot of the Skyway pedestrian bridge that spans the Hudson to the Catskills on the other side. Sometimes he and Stephanie sit on the benches here and enjoy the view, with an ice cream. This will spoil it for him.

When he enters the park, he sees her immediately. She's sitting on a bench, looking out at the river. She's not watching for him; it's like she knows he'll sit down right beside her, like a good dog. It makes his blood boil. He's told her he won't pay her. What happens now?

Like an automaton, he walks over to her and sits down next to her on the bench. He can't bear to face her. Instead, he looks out at the river too. It's like they're two spies, pretending they don't know each other, he thinks, about to conduct business. It's all too surreal.

"I'm glad you could make it," she says.

Finally he turns to her. She looks so innocent—with her fine skin, blond hair, and blue eyes, her serene smile. Almost angelic. He knows better. A flash of something carnal arises from his memory, flits through his head. He musters up his courage and says, "I don't know how to get this through your thick head. I'm not afraid of you. We're not going to pay you anything. This is the last time I'm going to meet you." She just smiles at him. "If you don't drop this, I'm going to the police. They'll arrest you for attempted blackmail."

"I don't think so. Not when you hear what I have to say."

He turns on her then. He hisses, "What is it you think you have? What makes you think you can get them to take another look at a perfectly open-and-shut case? It was an accident! Everybody knows that. You can't change that, no matter how much you may want to. There was never any question that it was anything else."

"But they don't know everything," she says. "They don't know that you had a motive to kill your wife."

"Motive! What motive? You can't be serious!"

"Oh, I am deadly serious," she says, in a lowered voice.

His heart is pounding furiously. She means to go on with this—he can't believe it. "You can't honestly think that because I had meaningless sex with

**you**, that I deliberately murdered my wife! No one will believe you." His voice is low but he can hear the desperation in it; he knows he needs to calm down. He shouldn't let her see how riled up he is.

"Perhaps it wasn't as meaningless as you say," she says slyly.

He feels a chill down his spine. She's going to make it out to be more than it was. "You lying bitch," he says venomously. "It's your word against mine."

She reaches into her purse, takes out her wallet, and withdraws a small photograph. "What you don't know is that I had a baby. It's yours." She holds out the photo of a newborn in a blue crocheted hat. He looks down at it in horror, then back at her, stunned. "What?" He can't process it. This must be another lie. "That's impossible."

"Why is it impossible? We had sex." She leans in closer to him now and says, "And if you remember, it was very, very good."

He recoils from her. "You're lying. There was no baby."

"How would you know? You got the hell out of Colorado as fast as you could. But yes, about eight months after the funeral, I gave birth to a bouncing baby boy."

"It's not mine."

"I **know** he is."

"You can't prove it," he says, and then immediately

realizes, stupidly, that he's wrong. Of course she can prove it—she can force him to do a paternity test. His fear grows, threatening to overwhelm him.

"He's almost nine years old now." She takes the photo of the infant and returns it to her wallet, and pulls another one out. She hands it to him.

Patrick takes it from her reluctantly. It's a picture of a boy with dark eyes and hair and a crooked grin. A cute kid. His anxiety spikes. The boy looks remarkably like he did at that age.

He draws away from her, shaken. This is terrible news, the worst news. He might have a son. A nine-year-old son. With her—a lying, manipulative bitch. **If** it's his. But he knows it's quite possible that it is. The timing is right. The photo is convincing, but what if there is no baby, and this is just another lie? "Why didn't you tell me back then?"

She looks out at the river. "I was afraid to. After Lindsey died, I thought—I still think—that you killed her on purpose. So that we could be together. We talked about it, remember?"

"No," he says, shaking his head in disbelief. They had never talked about that. It was just sex between them. "What utter horseshit."

"We talked about being together," she amends, "not about you killing her. I thought you meant divorce."

There's a funny buzzing in his head. He feels like

he's having trouble breathing. "No. We didn't," he says, appalled. "You're making it all up!"

She looks at him through narrowed eyes. "Of course, you say that **now**."

His heart is pounding furiously; he's afraid.

"I thought you'd killed her to be with me," she says again. "It did something to me. It really messed me up. And I'd just lost a close friend. I couldn't bear to look at myself and I couldn't bear to look at you. I was sick with guilt at what you'd done."

**She looks so convincing**, he thinks, staring back at her in horror. Anyone would believe her. A jury would believe her. He's absolutely terrified now. He swallows, his throat dry, and says, "I didn't kill her at all—it was an accident and you know it! You're making all this up; you've never felt guilty about anything."

She turns wide eyes on him, smiles, and says coyly, "But I don't believe you, you see. And it's been bothering me all this time."

"Bullshit! Then why wait all this time? You only came to me now because you want money. Everyone will see that."

She shakes her head. "I was young, and stupid, and afraid after what happened. Afraid they might think I was a part of it. You know what we'd been doing. I'd just learned I was carrying your child. I was even afraid of what you might do to **me**, because I knew what you'd done. And I

knew you were clever—I mean, you got away with
**murder**."

She seems to almost believe her own lies. He
finds himself clenching his hands and forces them
open. He'd love to wring her neck.

She continues. "So I moved away and had the
baby. But now I'm older, and not so stupid. I've
had time to think. I have leverage, and I mean to
use it. And I'm not afraid of you anymore."

"No?" he says. "Maybe you should be." He didn't
mean to threaten her, it just slipped out.

She looks at him as if taking his measure. "Yes,
maybe I should be," she agrees.

"So is that what this is all about? You want
child support? Why didn't you just fucking say so?
We could have worked something out. You don't
need to make all this up about what happened to
Lindsey."

"I'm not making anything up," she says. "I'm
just telling the truth."

"You are so full of shit," he says acidly.

"I think the authorities would appreciate having
all the facts, don't you?"

They stare at each other for a moment. He has to
set her straight. "I told you—we're not going to pay
you anything. Stephanie knows everything. She
knows I would never hurt anyone, and she's very
tight with her money." He takes a deep breath, ex-
hales. "Look," he says, trying to sound reasonable,

which is difficult, because he is completely enraged. "A child is different. If it's mine, and you can prove it, I'll pay the appropriate support. Out of my own earnings."

She glances at him. "Are you going to tell your wife about our son?"

He cringes at the words **our son**. He bites back his immediate response. "I tell Stephanie everything."

She snorts derisively; he lets it go.

"I don't understand why you're doing this," he says desperately. "I didn't kill Lindsey on purpose. And even if I wanted to pay you, I couldn't get you any money—not without Stephanie knowing, and she'd never agree."

"You have to find a way. I want two hundred thousand dollars. In cash."

He gapes at her in disbelief. "That's not going to happen." He shakes his head. "For the last time—I didn't **murder** her—it was an accident!" He's hissing at her now, spit flying.

She waits for him to calm down and then says coolly, "If your wife was dead, you'd have lots of money."

He stares at her, aghast, as the silence lengthens. He lowers his voice and says, "Surely you're not suggesting I murder my wife?"

"You did it before," she says coldly. "Don't pretend you haven't thought about it."

"You're out of your mind," he says. He clenches

his hands tightly again. "You're a fucking psychopath!"

"Takes one to know one," she says, rendering him speechless. He stares at her in horror. After a moment she says, in a reasonable voice, "If she were to meet with a fatal accident, it would make things easier—for both of us."

Patrick continues to stare at her, his eyes unblinking. Finally he says, his voice trembling with rage and fear, "You stay away from her or I'll go to the police."

"No, you won't."

Silence stretches out between them as the awfulness of his situation sinks in.

"You got the insurance money," she says eventually. "What, you didn't think I knew about that? Two hundred thousand dollars," she says. "That was quite a bit of money, nine years ago, for someone in his early twenties. Enough for a fresh start, back in New York. Enough to get started in business, maybe."

"You absolute bitch," he whispers, his face contorting with emotion.

"The authorities will be interested in that, I think, don't you? And they'll be interested in us."

"How do you know about the insurance?" he spits at her angrily.

Instead of answering, she says, "Tell me, who insures a young wife for that amount of money?"

He protests, furiously. "We were expecting a

baby. My dad was in insurance. He always said a young family should have life insurance."

"Right."

He tries to calm himself, regain control. "Look, if you're telling the truth about this kid, I'll figure something out." He gives her a hard look and says, "But stay away from my wife."

She doesn't answer. She gets up off the bench, turns her back on him, and walks away.

He watches her go, a sick feeling in the pit of his stomach. He realizes that he's between a rock and a hard place, and Erica has put him there.

# 15

The twins are still down for their nap, and Stephanie lies in bed in the darkened room. Even though she's bone tired, she doesn't fall asleep. Her mind is racing. She sees the photographs in her mind's eye—the car almost buried in snow; the smiling, dark-haired young woman; her husband's younger, anguished self. All of this happened a long time ago, but it's all new to her. It's been there, on the internet, all this time. It's been in her husband's mind—**I still think about it, about what happened, every day**—and she hadn't known. It makes her wonder what else she hasn't known about him.

She'd never pressed him on the subject of the death of his first wife. She knew there had been an accident—he'd told her that she'd died in a car accident—but nothing more. She sensed that he didn't want to talk about it and she let it be. He would tell her when he was ready.

He'd never told her he'd cheated on his first wife. Why would he? She knows so little about his life before. What had that marriage been like? Should she ask him? She has become very curious now about this earlier marriage. Does it presage anything? Will he be unfaithful to her?

She thinks about Erica in the park that morning—how attractive she was, how lovely she must have been when Patrick slept with her. Suddenly she wishes she'd known that the woman talking to her near the sandbox was Erica, her husband's one-time lover. She might have asked her questions. This woman knows things about her husband that she doesn't know.

She's angry at Patrick for bringing this on them. He never should have cheated on his first wife. Then they wouldn't be in this awful position. Who knows what lies Erica will tell? In today's climate, people seem willing to believe just about anything—the more outrageous the lie the more gullible people seem to be.

She turns over in bed, feeling ill. The media would love a story like this. An extramarital affair, a possible murder disguised as an accident, blackmail . . . they'd never be left alone. Even after it was proven, again, to be an accident, the taint would remain. Everyone would know that her husband had cheated on his first wife, and how his first wife had died. Their daughters would grow

up being the daughters of **that man**, the one made infamous in the news.

She's going to have a hard time forgiving her husband for sleeping with another woman while he was married to his first wife. She has never felt resentment toward her husband before—she's never had reason. She knows that resentment can poison, even destroy, a marriage. She doesn't want that to happen to her. She tells herself that it was a long time ago. He's not going to cheat on **her**; he wouldn't dare. After all, she's the one with the money.

NIALL CLOSES THE DOOR to his office and pulls out his cell phone to call Erica. It's been two days since their tryst at the hotel together, and he can't get her out of his mind. He's eager to see her again.

"Hello, Niall," Erica says.

Just hearing her sexy voice gives him a jolt of pleasure. He smiles into the phone. "I need to see you," he says, his voice low. "But—somewhere more private."

"You could come to my place, if you don't mind the drive," she suggests.

"I don't mind at all," he says, and takes down her address. They arrange a time for after work that day and then he disconnects, takes a deep breath, and calls his wife. "Hi, honey," he says.

"Hi, what's up?"

"I'm really sorry, but I've got to visit a job site after work—problems to deal with."

"Oh." He can hear the disappointment in her voice. It's Friday, the one night she can usually count on him coming home from work at a reasonable hour. "How late will you be?" Nancy asks.

"I'm not sure—a couple of hours probably. Depends on how it goes."

WHEN PATRICK ARRIVES HOME from work that evening, distressed and exhausted, his wife meets him with anxious eyes, one baby in the playpen, one in her arms.

"Hey," she says, worry etched on her tired face, Jackie grabbing at her hair.

Should he tell Stephanie about this possible child of Erica's? She might be bluffing; it might not be true at all. He takes the baby from Stephanie, gives them each a kiss. He knows Stephanie wants to go to the police, especially after what happened this morning in the park. But if Erica has a child by him, it will look bad, no matter what he says. He won't be able to deny he slept with her. He doesn't want to go to the police, not now.

He needs time to look into things himself— maybe it isn't even possible for her to have the accident investigation reopened. Maybe they're all empty threats, and this frantic worry is for

nothing. Maybe there is no child. But how is he to find out? He would be an utter fool to submit to a paternity test if Erica asks for one—because what if she's right?

Stephanie takes Emma out of the playpen and they slump together onto the sofa, a baby on each lap.

"Any news?" Stephanie asks anxiously.

Patrick shakes his head, avoiding her eyes by playing peekaboo with Jackie. He doesn't want to tell her what Erica said to him in the park.

"I think we should go to the police," Stephanie says tentatively.

"No," Patrick says, not looking at her. "Not yet. I think she's bluffing. I don't want to piss her off. Maybe she'll just go away."

"Look at me, Patrick," Stephanie says. He finally turns toward her. Her eyes are worried. "I don't think she's going to just go away. You told her we wouldn't pay her. Do you think she'll really go to the police in Colorado?" Her voice is anxious.

"I don't know, Stephanie." He's exhausted. He lets his head fall back against the sofa and closes his eyes.

"You slept with her," Stephanie persists. "She can exaggerate about that, tell all kinds of lies about the two of you, about your relationship with your first wife. She can make up anything she wants."

He feels a trickle of sweat starting along his back, between his shoulder blades.

"Did anyone else know—that you slept with her?" she asks.

He lifts his head from the back of the sofa and opens his eyes. He shakes his head. "No." He can't bring himself to tell her about the possible child, not until he's sure the kid exists. He tells himself that Erica is lying, and he almost believes it.

"Was—was your first marriage a good one?" she asks.

She's questioning him, as if she might not believe him, as if she doubts.

He leans in closer to her. "Stephanie, yes, I loved her. We argued a little, but only because we were young, and trying to get by on very little money. It was tragic what happened to her." His voice takes on even more urgency. "You must stay away from Erica, Stephanie. She's a liar, she's vindictive, and she's very clever."

"I know. That's what I'm afraid of," Stephanie says anxiously. "If it's her against you, who will people believe?"

NANCY RATTLES AROUND THE HOUSE, keeping an eye on the Tesla app. At five o'clock, she sees that the car is moving. It's a little blue dot on a map on her phone screen. She sits anxiously on the couch in the living room and watches the blue dot as if she's watching her life fall apart. Maybe he really is going to a job site. It occurs to her that she should

find out where they all are. There can't be that many—why hasn't she paid attention?

She watches the dot turn onto the highway, toward Newburgh. She certainly doesn't know of any work Niall is doing out that way. She decides to drop Henry off at her mother's, making the excuse that Niall has asked her to join him for a last-minute dinner with clients.

She gathers up Henry and a few toys and tells him he's going to visit Grandma. Once she's dropped him off, she gets back in her car and looks at the app on her phone. The car has stopped now. The address is 884 Division Street.

She can follow him wherever he goes without being seen, which is rather convenient. She puts the address into her GPS, and after twenty-five minutes arrives at a low-rise apartment building. **Job site, my ass**, she thinks. How will she know which apartment it is?

She parks across the street and gets out of her car. As she walks toward the building, she sees her husband's shiny Tesla in the parking lot. The bastard.

She walks up to his beloved car. The urge to deface it is overwhelming. There's no one around. She could key it; he'd never know it was her. Maybe if she defaced his car every time he came here, he'd stop coming.

She pushes the driver's seat handle and opens the door; the key card in her wallet unlocks the car and lets her in automatically—she doesn't even

have to take it out of her purse. She sits in the driver's seat for a moment; she's so upset her breathing is fast and shallow. The car has automatically turned itself on. She stares at the computer screen for a minute and then hits the Navigate button. That pulls up a screen that shows the addresses he's recently entered into his GPS. Oh, look, he's put in the address—**and the apartment number**—of his new lover. Good to know. Apartment 107. She uses her cell phone to take a photo of the address on his monitor.

She gets out of the car and slams the door. She takes a picture of his car in the parking lot, with the building in the background. Then she enters the apartment building—where her cheating husband is sleeping with another woman while she's down here at the locked doors—and searches the directory. There it is—number 107, E. Voss.

Well, at least now she knows. She uses her phone to take some pictures of the directory too.

What now? Does she stay here and face him when he comes out? Create a scene? Does she wait in his car? Wouldn't it be fun to see his face when he comes out to his car and finds her sitting in the passenger seat? Or should she stay out of sight and wait for him to leave, and then buzz this E. Voss? Get a look at her?

She can't decide. Finally she gets back into her own car, fighting back tears. She'd told her mother she might be late. She decides she doesn't want to

be home when her husband gets back; she needs to calm down. Instead, she drives back to Aylesford and goes to a movie.

She's alone in a movie theater on a Friday night. In the darkness of the theater, she discreetly wipes her tears away with a tissue and keeps an eye on the app. Soon she sees the little blue dot coming back down the highway. She watches it arrive at their home and stop.

**You bastard**, Nancy thinks.

She sends him a text.

> **I'm at the movies with a friend. I'll pick up Henry from my mother's when I'm done.**

# 16

That night, as they try to soothe the babies, Patrick's mind is working overtime; he needs to know what he's up against. He needs to find out the truth.

He walks blearily around the living room, a crying infant in his arms. He and Stephanie have given up trying to be heard above the noise; besides, they are all talked out. Now it's as if they are both existing within their own cones of misery.

Patrick thinks back to those early days in Colorado, when he was newly married. Lindsey was pregnant; they had moved to the little bedroom community of Creemore for him to take an internship in Denver. There he'd met Greg Miller, who was also interning at Wright & Fraser Architects. They worked, socialized, drank together. Erica and Lindsey had become good friends, having met at a photography class, although initially one might think they had little in common.

Lindsey was pregnant, putting most of her energy into preparing for the baby, homesick for Grand Junction. Erica was working part time at a pharmacy and pining for something more.

For Patrick, it was all about keeping his head above water. He was in his first real job, trying to support a wife and expecting a new baby too. Adjusting to life, wondering what the future held. He hadn't planned on marrying and having a family so young. And then one night Erica started looking at him across the table at the bar, and his eyes wandered, and his thoughts, and he'd betrayed Lindsey.

And now he was paying the price.

He's lost touch with Greg. They'd worked together day in and day out, but were not so close that he'd told him about sleeping with Erica. He's glad about that now. Patrick wonders, as he tries to comfort little Jackie, red-faced and squalling, if he should get in touch with Greg. He's already looked him up; he knows Greg now lives in Denver, and has found out where he works, and has located a home number. Should he talk to Greg? Would he know if Erica has a son? Should he tell Greg what Erica is doing? Or should he hire a private investigator? He's already tried to find Erica on Facebook but there was no sign of her.

How would Greg react to what Erica's doing? Surely he would be appalled. He would be on Patrick's side. Greg had been very supportive after

the accident. Greg was the first person he'd called, after 911. . . . Maybe the fewer people who know about this the better. Patrick mulls over the decision for hours. By the time he surrenders the babies to Stephanie and his head hits the pillow, despite his reservations he's decided to call Greg.

STEPHANIE SITS ON the sofa with the twins as she feeds them; they will go down soon, and she will be able to go to bed. She's so tired. It's affecting her ability to think, to cope with even the littlest things. She remembers her visit to the pediatrician. . . . Was it only a few days ago? And now . . . how the hell is she supposed to cope with these revelations about her husband's past, and this woman who's threatening them?

Her thoughts are anxious, confused. She can tell that her husband is afraid of Erica. And he's more afraid of her today than he was yesterday, she can tell that too. But what's changed? Is it because Erica was there, at the sandbox? In the drugstore? Or is there something he isn't telling her?

He'd told her his first marriage was good.

But then why was he sleeping with his wife's best friend?

THE NEXT MORNING is Saturday—usually their favorite day of the week. Patrick makes pancakes and

they laze around together with the twins like they usually do, but this Saturday feels entirely different from the Saturday before. So much has changed since Erica showed up at his office last Monday.

Midmorning, when the twins go down for a short nap, Stephanie tells him she's going out to run a quick errand and Patrick closes himself in the upstairs office. He opens his laptop. The house is quiet. Should he call his old friend Greg? Or send an email?

He decides it would be better to talk to him. Finally, he dials Greg's home number and waits for the call to connect.

"Hello," a voice says, and even over the line, and despite the years, Patrick recognizes it immediately. It gives him a start, just how familiar it sounds. They could be in Colorado again, on the phone; it's as if almost ten years have fallen away. Suddenly he's feeling all sorts of emotions that he'd long buried. He's waited too long to speak, so long that Greg repeats, "Hello?"

"Greg," Patrick says, trying to sound relaxed and comfortable, "it's Patrick Kilgour." He waits for the reaction. The pause on the other end indicates surprise, certainly. But of course he would be surprised, Patrick calling out of the blue like this.

"Patrick! Holy shit! It's been ages!"

Patrick is relieved to hear genuine pleasure in his old friend's voice. . . . What had he been expecting? The truth is, he hadn't been sure. He'd wondered if

Erica had been in touch with him, after everything that had happened. Or perhaps more recently. "I know, it's been a long time. How have you been?"

"I've been all right. How about you—I saw you started your own company a few years back. Business good?"

"Can't complain," Patrick says. "How's the family?" He's done his research—Greg is married now, with a little boy and little girl.

"They're grand, really good. You?"

"Married, four-month-old twins."

"Twins! God. What's that like?"

"Oh, you know. Hell." They both laugh.

"Are you coming to Denver?" Greg asks next.

Patrick feels an immediate alarm. Why would Greg think he's coming to Denver? "No, why?"

"Just—figured that's why you called me up."

"No, I have no plans to come to Denver," Patrick says. "But you never know," he adds.

"So what's up? I mean, it's nice to hear from you, but what can I do for you?"

Patrick's hand is clammy on the phone. His gaze flits automatically to his office door, which is firmly closed. Should he confide in Greg? He'd always trusted him; there was never any subterfuge about him, any hidden agenda. When he takes the plunge, it feels like he's jumping off a cliff into water far below. "You remember Erica?"

A wary pause. "Yes, of course." Greg doesn't say anything else.

Patrick tenses. **What does Greg know?** "Are you in touch with her?"

"No. I lost touch with her after—afterward."

Patrick pauses, closes his eyes. This is difficult. "I'm sorry I just left and never kept in touch—"

"No apology necessary," Greg says in a lower voice. "It was a hellish time. I don't know how you survived it."

"Thanks."

"Why are you asking about Erica?" Greg says.

Patrick hesitates and then says, "She's been here, in New York. In Aylesford."

"Really?" Greg sounds taken aback. "Why?"

Patrick takes a deep breath. He can't seem to find the words, and the silence grows.

Greg says, "She was a bit hard on you at the funeral."

"It was my fault," Patrick says. "It was an accident, but I'm to blame. I—I should have known better." His mouth is dry; he can barely get the words out. "Anyway, she's here now, saying some crazy things."

"What kind of things?"

He exhales heavily. "She's saying that we were having an affair, that I wanted Lindsey out of the way so that I could be with her. She's saying that I killed Lindsey on purpose." He pauses. "Like I said, crazy."

"That's pretty crazy," Greg agrees slowly, sounding shocked.

"Yeah."

"Christ."

"I know. I think she might be losing it. She seems . . . different."

"I don't know, I haven't seen her since then. She moved away and we didn't stay in touch." He pauses and adds, "Shit, Patrick. Of course it was an accident. They found it was an accident and I've always believed it was an accident."

Patrick is relieved to hear him say it.

There's a long pause before Greg speaks again, and when he does, he sounds awkward. "I don't think for a minute that you deliberately did anything to your wife, Patrick. But—"

"But what?"

"Erica, before she left, she said she was pregnant. And she said it was yours."

# 17

Patrick feels his heart start to pound. He wants so much for this not to be true. He can hear the question in Greg's voice—he wants to know if the child was Patrick's. Perhaps he's wanted to know this for years. Patrick asks, "Do you know for sure she was pregnant?"

Greg is quiet for a moment, then sighs and says, "I'm not sure of anything. She said I was the only one she was confiding in. She might have been lying; I have no idea. But I know at the time I believed that she was pregnant. She left soon after that. I have no idea where she went."

"She's trying to blackmail me, Greg. She's been stalking my wife and babies. I think she's unbalanced. I'm—I'm afraid she might be dangerous."

"Jesus. Maybe you should go to the police."

He can tell Greg wants to know if he slept with Erica. He takes a deep breath, exhales, and says, "I did sleep with Erica a couple of times. We were

drunk. You know what she was like. But it didn't mean anything. Certainly not to me."

There's silence at the other end of the line. Then Greg says, "Okay. I wasn't sure."

"But the rest of it—she's delusional. It was just a couple of one-night stands. I loved Lindsey. I would never deliberately hurt her." He swallows noisily.

"I know."

"Somehow she's found out that my wife inherited money. She wants us to pay her or she says she'll go to the police in Creemore and tell them I had a motive to kill Lindsey. It's absurd!" He finds himself running his hand through his hair. "Do you—do you think she can even do that?"

"I don't know. But I think you might need some professional help, my friend," Greg says uneasily.

PATRICK HAS HEARD nothing from Erica since he saw her on Friday at the Skyway park. Her silence makes him nervous. He knows she hasn't gone away; she's biding her time. Waiting for the fear to get to him; waiting to see what he'll do, what kind of influence he might have with his wife.

When the twins go down for their nap on Sunday afternoon, Patrick tucks Stephanie into their bed and tells her that he's going into the office for a bit, to catch up on some work. Then he gets into his car, but instead of turning toward downtown, to his office, he takes the highway to Newburgh.

He's already looked up Erica's address—he found it on her job application.

He doesn't know exactly what he has in mind. He's so overtired and stressed that he can't think clearly. He just feels that he must do something. He has to turn the tables somehow, but how? He must get Erica to stop this—this **madness**.

When he arrives in Newburgh it doesn't take him long to locate the apartment building. It's a five-story building on a residential street. He wants to confront her on her own ground, to see how she likes it. He's been too passive; it's time to shake things up. He needs to frighten **her**.

He realizes that she might not be home. He hopes she is; he's spoiling for a fight. He indulges himself for a moment—imagines knocking on her door, her surprise at seeing him, and then pushing his way in. He imagines himself on her balcony, bending her back over the edge, until she's afraid for her life. Maybe that's all it would take. She seems willing enough to think him capable of murder.

But then he remembers her apartment number, 107—she must be on the ground floor. He enters the building and looks at the buzzers. He wants to catch her off guard at her door if he can. A woman walks toward him from the elevators; she opens the door and he slips in behind her. He locates Erica's apartment and knocks firmly on her door, hoping she'll answer. No such luck—she's not home.

He clenches his jaw in frustration. But she's on the ground floor—he can at least look in her windows, see if there's any sign of a nine-year-old boy. He goes back outside, circling around to the back of the building. It's fairly private. Unit 107 has a patio on the ground floor, with sliding glass doors. He creeps up to the glass and looks inside.

The place doesn't look very lived in. He sees a pale blue sofa, a coffee table with some newspapers on it, and not much else; it's barely furnished. There's a galley kitchen beyond the empty dining room—a pendant light hanging over where a dining table should be—and a hall off to the right. He's guessing it's a one-bedroom. There's no sign of a child. He breathes a sigh of relief. She must have taken a photo of some random kid about the right age who looks like him. Is there any length she won't go to?

But he does see something he recognizes—his wife's missing purse, on the floor beside the sofa.

His heart almost stops. But before he can fully process the fact that **Erica has been inside his house**, he sees the door to the apartment open. Patrick steps back out of sight, but then peers carefully around the edge of the sliding-glass door. Erica has entered the room, and there's someone behind her. For a second the other person is blocked from view by Erica, but she steps away and Patrick gets another shock as he recognizes Niall. Niall closes the door behind him and then

sweeps Erica into an embrace. In disbelief, Patrick watches Erica and Niall kiss hungrily and peel off their clothes on their way to the bedroom.

**What the fuck is Niall doing with Erica?**

STEPHANIE WATCHES HER HUSBAND, her stomach in knots. Patrick's upset. His hair is a mess, as if he's repeatedly run his hands through it, and his movements are rushed and jerky. He's pacing the kitchen while the babies sit in their high chairs babbling and smashing their spoons against their trays. He's just told her that he went to Erica's apartment and saw Stephanie's missing purse on the floor through the window.

She's thinking, **He didn't go to the office at all.** "Why is she doing this?" Stephanie asks, her voice shrill. This horrible woman has been inside her house. She's stolen her purse, her ID. She feels a terrible anxiety coursing through her. People can steal your ID and use it to destroy your life. She's at the mercy of this maniac, and it's her husband's fault.

Patrick looks at her warily. "There's something else you should know."

She regards him with dread.

"She's sleeping with Niall."

She looks back at him, speechless with disbelief.

"I saw them in her apartment. They started kissing and then went off to the bedroom." He says,

"I know how she operates. She seduces people. She seduced me and she's obviously seducing Niall."

"Why, though?" Stephanie exclaims. "Why would she sleep with Niall?"

"For the same reason she came inside our house and took your purse—to intimidate us! To make me worry about what she might tell Niall. To show her power over me. That's why she's been watching you, showing up at the park."

Stephanie shudders. It's only now beginning to dawn on her exactly who they're dealing with. Maybe she's planning on blackmailing Niall, too—maybe she'll threaten to tell his wife that he's cheating on her. Stephanie knows that Niall cheated before; Nancy had told her. It almost broke up their marriage.

Patrick continues pacing. Stephanie stares back at him, her mind racing. They refused to pay her. Maybe they've made a mistake. The thought makes the world go all sideways on her. She needs Patrick to stay still for a minute so she can think. But her mind is numb.

She looks at her husband, still pacing across the kitchen, not even seeing her or the twins. Her anger erupts. "You never should have slept with her."

He stops then. "I know that!" He looks at her desperately. "But it meant nothing, Stephanie. She's revising everything in her head, telling it differently from how it really happened. That's what's so scary—I don't know what she'll make up next!"

Stephanie asks bluntly, "Other than the fact that you slept with her a couple of times, she doesn't have anything else, does she?"

Patrick looks at her and there's something in his face that she doesn't like. A mixture of shame and fear. A pleading look comes over him and she knows he's about to confess to something awful. She wants to turn away, flee from the room. She doesn't want to hear anymore. She's sick of all of this and suddenly almost hates him for bringing it all down on their heads. They have two precious little girls to think of—how will all this affect their future?

"She says . . ." Patrick starts, but his voice falters and he can't seem to finish the thought.

"She says **what**?" Stephanie demands, her voice strident. One of the babies begins to cry, and the other immediately joins in.

"I think she's lying, but—after she saw you at the park, she asked me to meet her, and she said she had a child, and that it's mine."

Her heart sinks like a stone. Oh, God. She slumps in her chair, puts her hands to her face.

"Don't look like that," Patrick says, his voice pleading.

She barely hears him; everything seems to fade away into the background, even the twins' noises, and all she can hear is the pounding of her own heart, thudding in her ears. A child. If this woman had a child by him, it changes everything. Finally

she looks up at her husband. She realizes with a sickening feeling that he's even more frightened than she is.

"Stephanie, it probably isn't true," he says. "That's—that's why I went to her apartment—and there was no sign of a child at all. She must be lying." When she doesn't say anything, he says, "I have to find out for sure. There must be a way."

"Yes, there must be a way," she says coldly. "You must be able to find out if she had a child. Hire someone if you have to."

He hesitates and says, "She also told me how much money she wants to make her go away."

"How much?" Stephanie asks.

"Two hundred thousand dollars," he says, his eyes flicking to hers and away again.

She can tell, reading him, that he thinks that's a reasonable amount, considering what Erica's threatening to do, and considering what they have in the bank. She has it in her power to solve this problem for him, for them. But she knows that if they pay her once, she'll just come back for more.

"Over my dead body," she says.

# 18

On Monday morning, Patrick hears the door at reception open and cocks an ear. Niall has just come in. All last night Patrick hadn't been able to stop thinking about Niall sleeping with Erica in her apartment. What had she said to him when her head was next to his on the pillow?

Patrick tries to tamp down his concern, but it's hard to stop worrying about the two of them together. Fear paralyzes him. Erica had waltzed into this firm on a pretense, had pretended not to know him. And Patrick had pretended not to know her. He doesn't want to admit now that he does. How would he explain it? He can't warn Niall about her—about the kind of woman he's getting involved with. How can he confront Niall about Erica without admitting he was peeking in Erica's window yesterday? He can't. He can't say anything.

But Erica knows things about him, things he'd rather his business partner not know.

He hears Niall coming down the hall, and then Niall's cheerful face appears at his door.

"Good morning," Niall says.

"Good morning."

"Are you okay?" Niall asks, looking at him more closely. "You look like you've seen a ghost."

"I'm fine, just—tired."

STEPHANIE PUTS THE TWINS down for their afternoon nap and starts tidying up the house. She's deeply exhausted—she's been stumbling through her routine tasks, her eyes are burning, and her body aches all over—but her mind is racing, flitting from thought to thought, unable to settle on anything. She knows she should lie down herself, but how can she sleep with all this running through her mind?

Can she really trust Patrick to tell her everything? Should she talk to Erica herself? Patrick has warned her to stay away from Erica, told her that she's dangerous. But the doubts have started to creep in. . . . What if Patrick just wants to keep Stephanie from talking to Erica? From hearing her side of the story? Everything she's heard so far has been mediated through Patrick.

Maybe Erica will turn up again. If she does, Stephanie decides, she won't run away. She will

ask questions. Maybe even try to get Erica to see reason.

She finds herself in their bedroom, but instead of lying down, she glances restlessly around the darkened room.

She turns on the overhead light and starts searching through her husband's dresser. She doesn't even know why she's looking—there's nothing there; she puts away his clothing in these drawers all the time. She looks anyway. When she's done with his dresser, she goes through his side of their closet, feeling disloyal and wondering why she's wasting her time. She searches through shoeboxes on the floor. He keeps his handgun, a Glock 19 9mm, in a safe on the top shelf. She knows the combination. She opens the safe and looks inside. Nothing in there but the gun and a few rounds of ammunition. There's nothing else in the closet but clothes.

Next, she tries his office at the end of the hall. Patrick's old computer is on the desk. She has her own laptop and so does he; he never uses this one anymore. Is there anything about his old life on this computer? It doesn't matter, she has no idea how to get into it. It's a mystery why he even keeps it. She pauses and thinks.

Why **does** he keep it?

Maybe there is something there. She turns it on, tries a few combinations related to her name and the twins' names and birth dates, but nothing works. Sighing, she turns it off again and searches

through his filing cabinets. There's absolutely nothing there pertaining to his earlier life with his first wife.

She's reaching around inside his filing cabinets, about to give up, when she feels something stuck to the underside of a drawer. She touches it tentatively—it seems like a small key, covered by tape. She tears at the tape gently, careful not to rip it.

She pulls it out and looks down at it. She's right: it's a small, silver key, covered with masking tape. It can't be the key for the filing cabinets, because they aren't lockable. She studies it closely. There's nothing on it except a number: 224. She has no idea what it's for. But if it didn't come with the filing cabinets, what is it doing there? The only conclusion is that Patrick must have put it there, where she wouldn't find it.

It doesn't look like any of the other keys they have in the house. She wonders if it's for a lockbox, or a safe. If it is, it isn't in the house or she'd know about it, unless he'd hidden it somewhere. She hurries down the stairs, after looking in on the twins briefly. She probably has about another hour before they wake up. She tears the basement apart looking for anything that looks lockable, but finds nothing, not even in the crawl space.

She finally comes to the uncomfortable conclusion that whatever the key fits, it isn't here. And

then it hits her. Of course. It's a key to a safety deposit box.

And she doesn't know anything about it. He's hidden it from her.

STEPHANIE IS CONFLICTED when Patrick returns from work that evening. She's worried about him—he's pale and tense—but she's angry and suspicious. Why did he hide that key from her? Why has he hidden the fact that he has a safety deposit box from her? Should she broach it with him?

She'd wrestled with it the rest of the afternoon. She thought of holding the key up under his nose and saying, "What's this, Patrick?" and dragging the truth out of him. What else is he keeping from her?

If she'd been able to, she would have gone to the bank and looked in the box herself. But she knew he'd be home soon. Finally, she'd retaped the key to the same spot on the underside of the drawer of the filing cabinet.

So much for honesty.

They put the babies in the swings in the living room so that they can talk.

Patrick looks more worried every time she sees him, and she feels a rush of concern for him. She watches him, waiting.

"I've talked to a lawyer in Colorado," he says.

"Okay."

"If she goes ahead with this, it might be expensive." He looks at her guardedly.

"Of course it will be expensive," she says. "Lawyers always are." She reflects bitterly that she will be using her own money on a high-priced lawyer to get her husband out of this mess, rather than paying off his former lover. It doesn't make her any happier. Her concern for her husband diminishes.

"His name is Robert Lange; he's with a large firm in Denver."

"How did you find him?" she asks.

"He was recommended by a friend."

"What friend?"

"A friend of mine from Colorado, Greg Miller. I used to work with him, in Denver. I've spoken to him."

"And?"

"I told him what's going on. He knows Erica, too—he knew her back then. He's completely on my side. He knows it was an accident."

Stephanie feels relief. It's good to hear that someone else who was there, when it all happened, believes her husband is telling the truth. It makes her realize just how worried, how uncertain, she really is. "What did the lawyer say?" she asks. She sees the concern in Patrick's eyes.

"Well, you know what they're like. He wouldn't say anything definitive without looking into it further. But he remembers the case."

Stephanie hasn't told Patrick about reading those articles on her laptop. The images crowd into her mind again—the snowy car, Patrick as a grief-stricken young man. His young wife, smiling at the camera. She tries to push them away. "Did he say whether it was even possible to reopen a case like that?"

He looks at her, worried. "Yes. It's possible, in theory."

Stephanie looks away from him and down at the floor, frightened. **It could happen. Her husband could, possibly, be investigated for murder.**

# 19

Patrick watches his wife's reaction and thinks back uneasily to the phone call earlier that day. It hadn't exactly been reassuring.

Robert Lange, the criminal attorney, had seemed surprised, initially, to hear that Patrick thought someone might try to have the case reopened. Then Patrick told him about everything—Erica's attempts to blackmail him, the original investigation—the lawyer interjecting with the occasional question, but mostly listening in attentive silence.

"Why don't you go to the police?" the attorney asked.

"I don't want to provoke her," he admitted. "I'm still hoping she's bluffing and that she's not actually going to do anything. We haven't heard from her for a couple of days." He added, "And I don't have any proof of the blackmail."

"I see."

"So," Patrick asked, "do I have anything to worry about? It was ruled an accident. It **was** an accident. But can she get them to reopen it, and try to make it look like something it wasn't?"

The lawyer cleared his throat and spoke. "Well, I do have some concerns, especially from what you say about how the matter was dealt with at the time. I mean, it wasn't much of an investigation, from the sound of it. They seem to have wrapped it up in a matter of hours." There was a hint of a question in his voice.

"Yes, well, it was so obvious that it was an accident."

The lawyer said, "If this woman were to go to the authorities and give them new information, they might decide to take another look. Especially if there is a new coroner, or a new sheriff, as there might well be, after almost ten years. The fact that she was having an affair with you, and that she might have had your child—that would, of course, be . . . relevant."

Patrick's heart sank. "Can you find out if she ever had that child?" he asked.

"That'll be the first thing I do," he said. "Don't worry, I'll find out what's going on and get back to you."

Now, looking at his wife, Patrick is reluctant to tell her what the lawyer said.

"What did he say, exactly?" Stephanie asks. "Tell me everything."

"Well, he had some . . . concerns." Patrick gets up off the sofa and starts pacing the living room. He can't remain still with all this anxiety running through him. And he can't stand looking at Stephanie, so rigid with tension.

"What? Did he think they'll believe her?"

Patrick says carefully, "He said that if she went to them with new information, they might take another look." He doesn't want to tell her the next bit, but feels he must. "He was concerned because the original investigation was—as he put it—'thin.'"

"What do you mean?"

"There wasn't much of an investigation at the time," Patrick admits. "They took her body away for an autopsy. The sheriff asked me to come down to answer a few questions. I went in his car. I was a mess. I don't think I was making much sense."

He rubs his face with both hands. "At the Sheriff's Office, they asked me what happened. They were trying to comfort me, telling me that these kinds of accidents happen, that every year something like this happens somewhere."

"Are you saying there was no investigation at **all**?" Stephanie asks.

He looks at her sharply, a bit taken aback at her tone. "They obviously believed it was an accident. They did the autopsy very quickly—that afternoon, I think—and it showed that she had died from carbon monoxide poisoning. So why would they do anything else?"

He doesn't like the way she's looking at him, as if he's to blame for there not being a more thorough investigation. It seems to him that the fact that they'd ruled it an accident so quickly is in his favor.

"They never talked to anyone else?"

He frowns, shaking his head. "No, I don't think so."

"It isn't good that they weren't thorough," she says now, clearly uneasy.

"Yeah, well, I disagree. Obviously they thought there was nothing to investigate."

"But if Erica—"

"Fucking Erica!" It comes out explosively. The babies startle in their swings. He tries to calm down. "She's a greedy bitch. There was never any question until Erica came along. She should mind her own fucking business." He looks at Stephanie, at her pale, anxious face. He takes a deep breath and tries to keep his anger in check. "The lawyer's going to find out if she had a baby. Apparently the sheriff can investigate, if he wants to. And the coroner can also decide to call an inquest, call witnesses—even after all this time." He clenches his jaw and looks at his wife nervously. "The lawyer warned me that if there's a new sheriff, or a new coroner, that might be more likely. And it has been a long time."

"Oh my God," Stephanie whispers.

"She might get them to take another look,

Stephanie, and I think we need to be prepared for that. But what you have to believe is that there's **nothing** to what she's saying. I slept with her a couple of times. That's it."

She looks back at him, nodding automatically, as if not even aware she's doing it. She seems almost to be in a trance.

"There's one other thing you should know," he says. "It's not important but I'm sure it will come up."

"What?" Stephanie asks.

He sees her clenching her hands on her knees as if she's bracing herself for more bad news. "There was a life insurance policy on Lindsey. We were both insured, because we were going to have a baby. It was the responsible thing to do."

"Okay."

"Erica's trying to make a big deal out of it. Saying I stood to gain financially from the death of my wife."

"When did she say that? You never mentioned this before."

He realizes he has made a misstep, and curses inwardly. "I—I forgot to mention it."

Stephanie looks back at him, saying nothing for a moment. Then she asks, "Did the police—the sheriff or whatever—know about the insurance?"

He shakes his head. "No, I don't think so. It never came up at the time. They never asked and I—I

didn't even think of it. My wife was dead. I was in shock." After a moment he adds, "But I don't think it's something we really need to worry about. It's perfectly legitimate to have life insurance once you have a family. I mean—it's stupid not to."

# 20

The next morning, after a particularly difficult night with the twins, Stephanie is completely drained, moving like a zombie around the kitchen. She finds herself reaching to put the milk into the cupboard instead of the fridge and shakes her head at herself. She has to get more sleep. She can barely function. And emotionally, she's a wreck. Even when she does finally get to bed, she's sleeping badly, a bundle of nerves.

She kisses her husband goodbye when he leaves for work, the same as she always does. But this morning she turns her eyes away—because she's keeping a secret from him. In a little while, she's going to put the babies in the car and drive to the bank and try to find out what's in the safety deposit box.

Whatever he's keeping from her, she must know what it is. She will find out, and she will confront him. Tonight.

She gets the twins ready. She checks that the double stroller is in the trunk, puts the twins in the playpen, dressed and ready to go, and then goes upstairs to the office. She kneels down, pulls open the drawer, and reaches in for the hidden key. Once she has it in hand, it suddenly occurs to her that Patrick might not have the safety deposit box at their bank. If he wanted to keep it from her, he would probably choose a different bank.

She makes her way back downstairs. The babies start to fuss, but she ignores them.

She calls the bank from the kitchen phone, a finger over one ear to muffle the sound of the babies' crying. When she's put through, she asks to speak to the manager.

"Yes, what can I do for you today?" the manager asks.

"I've been trying to reach my husband to ask him, but he's in meetings all day. Can you tell me, has he been in to our safety deposit box yet this morning? He was supposed to get me some documents. His name is Patrick Kilgour."

"Hang on a sec."

Stephanie waits at the end of the line, her heart pounding.

She hears the manager come back on the line, sounding puzzled. "I'm sorry, we don't have a safety deposit box here for a Patrick Kilgour. Maybe it's at another bank?"

"Oh, of course," she says. "My mistake. Sorry to

bother you." She quickly hangs up the phone. She stands in the kitchen, the babies wailing now from the living room, her hand still on the phone, trying to breathe.

WHEN PATRICK ARRIVES at the office, Niall says he needs to speak to him. Patrick's anxiety spikes. What if Niall knows what's going on? What might Erica have told him? He's still hoping that somehow he can make Erica go away. But if Erica's already told Niall—

"Come into my office," Niall says, his quiet voice relaying concern.

Patrick enters the other man's office, slumps, exhausted and uptight, into a chair.

"How are things going at home?" Niall begins.

Patrick feels a slow spreading of relief. Maybe this isn't about Erica, then. Maybe this will just be the same old conversation. At that, he feels a stab of annoyance. Niall already knows how things are at home. They're bloody difficult with the twins, and so little sleep. He takes a deep breath. "No better," he admits. "If the twins don't get over the colic soon, I think we're both going to lose our minds."

Niall purses his lips tightly. "I'm sorry," he says simply. Then he says, "I've been looking at the cost overruns on the Melnyk project."

"I know. I'm doing my best," Patrick says defensively.

Niall studies the top of his desk and says, "Kerri tells me that you cancelled an appointment yesterday."

Now he feels anger wash over him. Is there anything Kerri doesn't tell Niall? Did she have to mention it? Does she have no loyalty to **him**?

"I didn't cancel. I asked her to reschedule."

Niall looks up from his desk and meets his eyes. "Why?"

"Because I didn't feel up to it," he says bluntly. "I didn't feel properly prepared. I thought it was better to appear too busy and have to reschedule than do it unprepared."

"So why weren't you prepared?" Niall asks, raising his voice. "You're always prepared—at least you used to be. What the hell is going on?"

Patrick begins to breathe a little easier. Niall doesn't know—not yet, anyway. Erica's keeping her mouth shut so far. "Nothing's going on. I'm sleep deprived, I told you. Sleep deprivation can really mess you up. They use it as a method of torture—didn't you know?"

Niall looks back at him and narrows his eyes. "That's not it, Patrick, so don't try to bullshit me. Something's going on, and I want to know what it is."

Patrick tilts his head back and decides to bluster his way through. "Why wouldn't you believe me, Niall? When have I ever been less than completely honest with you?"

Now Niall shrugs. "I know. You've been a good business partner and a good friend. I've always trusted you. It's just—I'm worried, Patrick. You seem—off lately, as if something is bothering you. I wondered if maybe you were having marital problems, if that's what's been distracting you." He leans in slightly, and says, "You can tell me, you know."

"Maybe I should ask **you** how things are at home," Patrick says, with an edge to his voice.

"Why would you say that?" Niall responds quickly.

But Patrick doesn't want to push it; he doesn't want to let Niall know he knows about him and Erica. Doesn't want to let him know he has a history with Erica himself. Better let sleeping dogs lie.

"To see how **you** like it," he says. Then he shakes his head, gives a tight smile. "Forget it. I have a short fuse these days. Everything is fine. I just need to get some sleep." He gets up. "I'll take another look at how to offset some of those costs on the Melnyk project."

# 21

Stephanie blinks her eyes. For a moment there, she completely forgot what she was doing. She feels a wave of dizziness and grabs the kitchen counter. She can hear the twins babbling from the living room, content for the moment, at least.

Right, she'd come into the kitchen for another cup of coffee.

She was going to get herself a coffee and try to think for a minute.

She reaches for a clean mug out of the cupboard and pours from the carafe. She feels like shit. She has to eat better. She has to get more sleep. Would it be wrong to fall asleep on the sofa with the twins safely in the playpen? She closes her eyes again for a minute, then blinks a couple of times and reaches into the refrigerator for the milk. It seems like she's doing everything in slow motion. She feels detached, as if she's watching herself go through

the motions of getting her coffee ready. Weird. She shakes her head, quickly takes a couple of gulps of caffeine. Sleep deprivation can really mess with your head. She knows if she stares at the pattern on the wallpaper for a minute it will almost put her into a trance.

Things are still calm in the living room. She pulls out a chair at the kitchen table and sits down. She doesn't want to go back in the living room for a bit because she knows that as soon as she does, the twins will see her and start demanding her attention. For now, she's better off here.

She presses her fingers to her burning, itchy eyes. She needs to think. But her mind is such a crazy mess right now she can't make sense of anything. If only she could talk to someone, lay it all out clearly, get someone else's perspective, someone objective—but there's no one she can possibly talk to about this. Patrick is too close to it, and he's freaked out himself. She wants to tell Hanna, but she can't, even though she and Hanna have become close over the last few months, as first-time moms. Patrick would be furious if she told her.

Although it might be in the newspapers soon enough.

Her mind keeps circling back to Patrick's safety deposit box. Where is it? She's already called half the banks in town and hasn't found it.

She gives her head a shake and forces herself to get up and get ready to take the twins out. She

fumbles through her preparations, almost forgetting her keys at the last moment, then going back into the house to get them. As tired as she is, she needs to get them all some fresh air. She'll call the rest of the banks when she gets back. They can't stay in all day.

STEPHANIE PLAYS WITH THE TWINS on a blanket on the grass at the park, her eyes scanning sporadically for a glimpse of Erica. Patrick had suggested she avoid the park because of the run-in, but she had protested. What the hell else is she going to do with the babies on a nice day? She can't keep them inside—they'll all climb up the walls.

Patrick had then suggested she put them in the car and drive to another park farther away, for a change of scenery. She'd turned away and said **maybe** as he looked on worriedly. But she's not going to do that. She's not going to be afraid to use her own neighborhood. And maybe she wants to talk to Erica. So here she is, sitting with the babies under a tree, a bundle of raw nerves. But there's no sign of the attractive woman that her husband slept with a long time ago.

Finally it's time to go home. She picks the twins up, one at a time, to put them in the stroller, lifting them up and down in the air and smiling at them, making them giggle. God, how she loves them. And every time she looks at them now she

feels a clutch of fear at her heart—what will happen to their once-happy family? What if they're all dragged through an investigation—what will that do to her and Patrick? Thank goodness the babies are too young to understand what's going on.

Her cell phone rings—it's Patrick. "Hi, what's up?" she asks anxiously. She's always anxious these days.

"I just heard from the attorney."

She feels her heart rate shoot up. "What did he say?"

"Erica did have a baby. But she gave it up for adoption, privately, after it was born."

Stephanie tries to digest this news, the implications. "That explains why she never came after you for child support," she says after a moment.

"Yeah, but even better, I don't think it's going to be so easy to prove it's mine."

She hears the relief in his voice and it sickens her.

She pushes the stroller home, feeling unbearably weary. At last they arrive at the house and she sings out to the twins, "Home at last! We'll have some lunch and then—" She stops in her tracks, her voice silenced. She's staring at the front door.

It's wide open.

Surely she locked it. She must have, especially after last time. And then she remembers that she'd forgotten her keys and run back in to get them. Did she forget to lock the door on the way back

out? Did she forget to **close** it? Jesus. She has to be more careful.

She maneuvers the stroller up to the bottom of the porch steps and unbuckles Emma and lifts her out. "Mommy is so tired and getting way too forgetful, Emmie," she whispers. She carries her up the steps and inside the front door, and screams.

# 22

er scream fills the front hallway and startles little Emma into crying.

There's someone inside, sitting in her kitchen. It gives her a terrible shock. Then she recognizes Erica and she can't breathe.

"Get out!" she hisses when she gets enough air in her lungs, clasping the wailing baby to her chest. "Get out or I'll call the police!"

"Honestly, Stephanie. Calm down," Erica says, standing up and walking toward her, sounding perfectly reasonable. "I'm not going to hurt you."

"You broke into my house!"

"No, I didn't, the door was open. You should be more careful."

For a moment, Stephanie is confused. She might have left the door open; she doesn't remember. But she does know this woman has no business being in her house, even if she did leave the door open. "I know who you are," she says.

Erica nods. "Good. I wasn't sure you would. I don't know how much Patrick has told you."

"You were in here before—you stole my purse!"

Erica's eyebrows go up. "I did not. Why would you think that?"

Stephanie doesn't believe her. "Because Patrick saw it in your living room, through the window."

"He was at my apartment?" Erica says, surprised.

Stephanie doesn't answer that. "You shouldn't be here," she insists.

"Shouldn't you bring the other baby in?" Erica asks.

Stephanie steps back a few paces and looks out the door at Jackie, still buckled into the stroller. She stands in the doorway, not sure what to do. Erica is inside her house; she's been waiting for her. Should she take the babies and flee? Should she grab her phone from her pocket and try to dial 911?

"I'm not going to hurt you," Erica says again calmly. "But there are some things you should know. About your husband."

Stephanie hesitates. She remembers her earlier decision—this woman knows things about Patrick that she doesn't. Erica knew him back then, when it happened. She wants to hear what she has to say, even if it might be all lies. She might learn something useful. So far she's heard everything from Patrick's perspective. She looks at the woman now leaning against her kitchen doorway as if she might

be a friend, dropping by for a visit. Surely she isn't actually **dangerous**?

She can't take the chance. She's not going to bring her twins into the house with this woman— who knows what she might do behind closed doors?

"We can talk," Stephanie says finally. "Outside, on the porch." She turns away and buckles Emma back into the stroller at the bottom of the steps. She makes sure each baby has a toy clutched in a little hand and then sits in the chair on the front porch closest to the stroller. Her phone is in her pocket. She's not really frightened here, where they can be seen; people go up and down this street all day long. But she is distraught.

Erica has come out of the house and seated herself in the other chair. "Nice neighborhood," she begins.

Stephanie doesn't say anything for a moment. She's trying to gather her scattered thoughts—and her courage. Finally, she turns to Erica and says, "I know what you're doing, and it's not going to work. We aren't going to pay you. I thought Patrick made that clear."

"Are you absolutely sure about that?"

"You're not going to get a **dime** out of us, much less two hundred thousand dollars."

Erica gives her an annoyed look. She doesn't speak for a moment, but then she bites her lip and

says, "So he's been telling you what's going on? I wasn't sure. He didn't tell his first wife much."

Stephanie feels a sense of revulsion overtake her. She says bitterly, "How would you know what he told his first wife?"

Erica turns and looks at her. There's no hatred on her face, no venom in her voice. "You know we were lovers?"

"He told me, yes."

"He must actually love you, then."

"Of course he loves me," Stephanie says firmly. "And I love him. And all this crap you're threatening us with isn't going to go anywhere. I don't know why you're bothering. He didn't kill his first wife. You must know that." Her voice is shaking.

"You have no idea who you're dealing with," Erica says seriously.

"Don't threaten me," Stephanie says in a hard voice.

"I don't mean **me**," Erica clarifies. "I mean your husband."

Stephanie recoils from her. "Look, I know my husband far better than you ever did. Just because you slept together a couple of times doesn't mean you actually know him at all."

"Is that what he told you? That we slept together **a couple of times**?"

Now Stephanie looks back at her warily, afraid of what she might say next. But she needs to hear it.

She knows that Patrick and this woman are going to have very different versions of events, and she wasn't there. She can never know for sure. "What's your version?" Stephanie asks dryly.

"We were in love," she says simply.

Stephanie goes cold. The woman is delusional. Fully delusional. "That's not what Patrick says."

"That's what he wants you to believe." She looks earnestly at Stephanie. "But I was there. I was with him. We were very secretive, because he was married, and Lindsey was my friend. I feel terrible about it now, that I treated her that way. That I'm at least partially responsible—morally responsible—for her death."

"That's bullshit," Stephanie says, her heart hammering.

Erica shakes her head. "He would come to my apartment at lunchtime almost every day. He told everyone he went home to eat, but Lindsey made his lunch every morning. He'd eat it in my bed, after we made love, before he rushed back to work."

Stephanie feels ill. "I don't believe you."

"Not yet, anyway," Erica says.

"Can you prove it?"

"I don't know. Maybe. We didn't tell anybody, but I had neighbors. Someone might have heard us through the wall. People might have seen him coming and going."

Stephanie shrinks back into her chair, as if trying

to put distance between her and this disturbing news—and the person delivering it.

"I know how upsetting this must be," Erica says. "And believe me, I don't enjoy doing this to you."

"Is that right?" Stephanie says, her voice bitter. "Patrick warned me that if I spoke to you, you would tell me lies and try to drive a wedge between us."

Erica shrugs. "He would." She looks at the babies in the stroller and says, "I was pregnant with his child—did he tell you about that?"

"Yes."

"So ask yourself—If Patrick didn't kill her deliberately, and it was just a horrible accident, and I was carrying his child, why did I stay away from him all this time?"

Stephanie doesn't know how to answer. She can't think straight. Her head is buzzing with tiredness and confusion, and from trying to keep up her guard.

"I'll tell you why," Erica says. "Because I thought he'd killed her on purpose—my friend and her unborn baby daughter." She turns her eyes away from the twins, looks out at the street. "We talked about being together. I wanted him to leave his wife." Erica glances at Stephanie and looks away again. "I was very impatient and very selfish when I was twenty-one. I didn't like myself for stealing Patrick away from Lindsey, but you have to understand

how it was—we were in love. I thought Patrick and I were meant to be together, and somehow, in my immaturity, I thought Lindsey would just get over it, move on. I thought she would move on more easily from a broken marriage as a single mother than I would move on from a broken heart." She adds, "God, I was stupid."

Stephanie stares at her, appalled, wondering if she's telling the truth. She can't know for sure, but she certainly seems believable. Patrick had warned her that Erica could be very convincing.

"He kept telling me how unhappy he was. We argued, and he agreed things had to change. That was the day before she died." Her face takes on a pained expression. "But I thought he meant divorce. I never thought he meant murder."

# 23

Stephanie stares at her, her mouth hanging open. "You think he killed her deliberately, to be with you." She shakes her head vigorously. "You're crazy. I **know** my husband, and he's not capable of what you're accusing him of!"

"I think we're all capable of things we might not want to admit to," Erica replies. She pauses and then carries on. "I remember it so clearly, as if it were yesterday. Even now, I can't stand heavy snowstorms."

Stephanie doesn't get up and tell Erica to leave. No, she listens. She wants to hear it all, no matter how dreadful her account.

Erica says, "Lindsey hated Creemore. She hated the snow. She missed her family in Grand Junction. She was finding it hard, Patrick not being around a lot." Erica shrugs. "Of course, she didn't know he was with me; she thought he was at work. They were leaving to visit her family. Patrick didn't want

to go—at least, that's what he told me, and I believed him, because he didn't care much for her family and the roads were bad. But I wondered afterward if he just said that, to make it look more like an accident, as if he hadn't planned it.

"I saw Lindsey fairly regularly. I'd drop by when I wasn't working, see how she was doing, trapped in that tiny apartment. I liked her, and I felt guilty, but that wasn't all of it. I wanted to hear from her how things were going between her and Patrick. I knew they were fighting a lot, and it made my heart glad, because I thought it was only a matter of time until he left her." She looks up. "Okay, so that **does** make me look heartless, but at least I'm telling you the truth.

"That morning, the day they were supposed to leave—it was a Saturday, and I was at home, asleep. Greg—he was Patrick's best friend—called me and told me there'd been an accident. By the time I arrived the paramedics were already there, and Lindsey was laid out in the snow, dead. They'd tried to revive her but hadn't been able to."

Stephanie listens in dismay; Erica looks so earnest, so troubled. She reminds herself that Patrick had been equally distressed and convincing when **he'd** told her what happened that day. Either Erica is a very good actor, or she really believes what she's saying, even though it may not be true.

Erica continues. "Patrick was so distraught—but I caught his eye, just for a moment—and there was

something in that look, just for a second, between the two of us, something **triumphant**—and I knew then that he'd done it on purpose. There was absolutely no doubt in my mind."

There's a moment of silence. Then Stephanie says, not hiding her astonishment, "A look. Your belief that my husband is a cold-blooded murderer is based on a **look**."

"Hear me out," Erica says urgently. "He was crying, distraught—completely convincing—but I knew. He went away with the sheriff to be questioned and I was terrified. I thought they'd wear him down, that eventually he'd tell them about us, and they would think I was part of it.

"I went home and hid in my apartment. I kept asking myself how Patrick could have done that to his wife and unborn child. I thought I was to blame, that he'd done it to be with me. I was waiting for the police to come, to question me, and I was going to tell them the truth. That I wanted Patrick to leave her, but that I had no part in her death. But nobody came. I saw on TV that night that they'd declared it an accident. That he'd gotten away with it. I couldn't believe it—I was horrified. And then I was relieved, because I wouldn't have to go to jail. But I felt the most horrible guilt and remorse about Lindsey. I knew she was dead because of me.

"I didn't want to see him, I didn't want to talk to him. I didn't know how to act around him,

knowing what I knew. I was the only one who knew the truth. I was afraid he might call me, but he didn't. I didn't want to go near him, but I had to go to the funeral. It would look strange if I didn't.

"The funeral was a couple of days later. It was ghastly." She looks at the twins nodding off in their stroller, and Stephanie follows her gaze. "Everyone completely broke down. Patrick's grief was totally convincing and I even wondered if he had regrets, though he was now free and he'd gotten away with it.

"He tried to talk to me at the funeral. I turned my back on him. No one seemed to think that was strange—I was Lindsey's best friend, and it was his fault she was dead. Everybody was a mess. But I know Greg thought I was behaving badly. He came up to me and told me to get a grip, that everybody was hurting, not just me, and who the hell did I think I was to treat Patrick like shit at his wife's funeral? Of course, Greg didn't know anything." She pauses. "It was the next day that I found out I was pregnant. I was a few days late. I tried to ignore it, but after the funeral I got a pregnancy test from the pharmacy where I worked." She takes a deep breath, exhales. "Of course it was Patrick's. I wasn't with anybody else when I was with him."

"Where is the child now?" Stephanie asks.

Erica turns to her. "I gave him up for adoption. I never said I kept him."

Stephanie is silent. Her mind is tumbling over with confusing thoughts, like a dryer full of clothes.

"Why didn't you just have an abortion?"

"Maybe I should have." She pauses for a moment and then says, "The truth is I knew that if I carried the baby to term there might be some money in it. A private adoption. Yes, I'm greedy. But you know that."

Stephanie turns away; she can't bear to look at Erica any longer.

"He did it deliberately, Stephanie, I know he did," Erica says. She seems to consider something and then says, "I'll tell you why I came forward now, after all these years."

Stephanie turns back and stares at her, waiting. There's something more. There's always something more.

"I've been keeping an eye on Patrick all this time. I knew he'd remarried. When I saw that he'd married again, I looked into you."

"You looked into me? Why?"

"Because some men use wives like ATMs," Erica says. "And I saw that you were going to inherit quite a lot of money."

"How did you know that?" Stephanie asks. She's wondered about this for a while.

"Because wills that are probated are public information. I looked into your parents, saw that they'd been wealthy, that they'd died in a car accident. I

looked at your parents' wills. And I saw that they left you a trust, and that you would come into the money when you turned thirty." She adds pointedly, "Which was only a couple of months ago."

Stephanie looks back at her, shocked. She had no idea that kind of information was public. She thought nobody knew about her trust but her lawyers—and her husband.

"Tell me, did Patrick know about that when he married you?"

Stephanie remains silent.

"You have life insurance too? Let me guess—something you got when you were pregnant?"

Stephanie doesn't answer; she doesn't have to. The coldness in her heart spreads outward to reach all of her extremities. She wonders if Erica already knows her life is insured for a million dollars.

"So you see," Erica says, after a long pause, "regardless of what happens, I've done you a favor."

Stephanie slumps in her wicker chair on the porch, shaken. She remembers the fire, the frying pan left on the stove. She still doesn't remember putting the pan on the stove. Then she pulls herself together and reminds herself who she's dealing with. "Let's not forget why you're **really** doing this," Stephanie says coldly. "You looked into our financial situation, saw that we had money, and tried to blackmail us."

Erica nods. "Yes, well, I never said I was perfect."

"I think you should leave."

"Fine." She stands up. "But remember, just because I tried to blackmail you doesn't make it any less true that Patrick murdered his first wife."

She looks down at Stephanie, flicks a careless glance at the twins in their stroller, and says, "Be careful. After all, if he did it once, he could do it again."

Stephanie says emphatically, "Patrick would **never** hurt me. Or Jackie or Emmie."

Erica says, "I wouldn't be so sure."

# 24

As soon as Erica is out of sight, Stephanie brings the twins inside and lets herself fall apart. She rocks on the sofa, her face in her hands, sobbing. After a while, she pulls herself together, washes her swollen face, and resumes phoning the banks. Her heart almost stops when the woman at Hudson Valley Credit Union—the second to last one on her list—says, "No, your husband hasn't been in to the safety deposit box today."

She regrets having to waste the twins' naptime—she should be sleeping herself—but she quickly bundles them up and puts them and the double stroller in the car.

When she arrives at the bank, she wheels the twins up to one of the clerks at the counter. She takes the safety deposit key out of her pocket. "I'd like access to my safety deposit box, please," she says, showing her the key.

"Can I see some identification?" the woman asks.

Stephanie produces her driver's license and holds her breath.

"This way."

She leads Stephanie down a corridor—fortunately it's wide enough to accommodate the stroller—and unlocks a barred door that opens into a long, narrow room lined with numbered metal safety deposit boxes. Stephanie leaves the twins in the hall and keeps an eye on them. "What's the number on your key?" the clerk asks, pulling a card file.

"Two twenty-four."

The woman flips through the file and pulls out a card, asking Stephanie to sign. The clerk fingers her way down a row and finds the box. She inserts her key and asks for Stephanie's key, which she hands over. The clerk withdraws the box from the wall and leads Stephanie to an empty, private room with a table and chair. Stephanie follows her into the room with the stroller.

The clerk puts the box gently on the table. "There's a buzzer there on the wall when you're finished, and I'll come back," she says.

"Thank you," Stephanie says, waiting until the woman has pulled the door shut behind her. The twins are fast asleep.

She sits down and looks at the box for a moment, filled with trepidation. She can feel her heart pounding. What secrets are contained in it? She takes a deep breath and opens the lid.

The first thing she sees are the insurance papers. She looks them over, but they merely confirm what she already knows. Patrick got a $200,000 payout on the death of his first wife. She lifts the papers aside and reaches in for the next thing. Lindsey's death certificate, dated January 10, 2009. So far, no surprises. Stephanie swallows and lifts out the next item. It's a marriage certificate between Patrick Edward Kilgour and Lindsey Paige Windsor, dated August 12, 2008. Something doesn't feel right. For a moment, Stephanie blinks and can't put two and two together. She remembers Lindsey was eight months pregnant when she died—the newspaper accounts had confirmed that. Stephanie looks at the marriage certificate again and does the math. Lindsey must have been three months pregnant when they married in August. Why hadn't Patrick told her that?

WHEN PATRICK ARRIVES home from work, the twins are in the playpen and his wife is lying on the sofa in the living room, her eyes closed.

"Stephanie?" he whispers. If she's asleep he'll let her rest as long as she wants. But her eyes pop open and she sits up abruptly.

"When did you get home?" she asks quickly.

"Just now," he says. "Everything all right?"

"I was asleep. I shouldn't fall asleep when the babies are awake."

"Don't be so hard on yourself. They're fine in the playpen—you don't have to watch them every minute. Our parents didn't do that, and we survived."

"But I didn't even hear you come in." She brushes her hair back from her face.

He notices then that Stephanie seems agitated, even angry. "What's wrong?"

She looks up at him coldly and says, "I found a key. Taped to one of the drawers of your filing cabinet." She digs into the pocket of her jeans and holds it up.

He feels himself coloring. "What were you doing looking in my filing cabinets?"

"Can you blame me?" Her voice is sharp.

He realizes that she has a point. "No. I guess not."

"I FOUND YOUR SECRET safety deposit box," Stephanie says. She's furious at him and wants to hear his explanation. "I went through everything."

"Okay," Patrick says. "I'd forgotten about the safety deposit box. I got it long before I met you." He adds, his voice conciliatory, "I'm sorry I didn't tell you about it, but there's nothing in there that I don't want you to see."

She looks at him in disbelief. "Seriously? Then why did you hide the key?"

"If you remember, I had those filing cabinets before I met you. That key's been there for years."

She asks bluntly, "Why didn't you tell me that Lindsey was three months pregnant when you married her?"

He looks at her as if he's completely surprised. "What difference does that make?"

He says it utterly without guile, as if he can't see it at all. She can't believe his stupidity. "It makes all the difference in the world," she exclaims. "It looks like you married her because you **had** to, not because you wanted to. Did you?"

"Come on, Stephanie, that's ridiculous. How can you even say that? People don't get married anymore because of an unplanned pregnancy."

He seems to believe what he's saying. She's astonished. "Of course they do!"

"No, they don't. For Christ's sake! We were in love, she got pregnant, and we waited till August to get married, mostly because we didn't have the time. We weren't **ashamed** of it." He adds, clearly annoyed, "God, I can't believe you're so old-fashioned."

She raises her eyebrows at him, irritated. "I'm not old-fashioned."

"It sure sounds like you are."

She's livid all of a sudden. Patrick is certainly innocent in the death of his wife. But . . . surely anyone in their position would be concerned about how it looks? Stephanie says, "People will think that you married Lindsey because of the pregnancy, because you felt you had to, not because you loved her."

"That's not true," Patrick says stubbornly.

"It doesn't matter if it's **true**," Stephanie says, her voice rising. "For Christ's sake, can you just think about how it looks? Does Erica know?"

"No, I don't think so. We didn't advertise it. When we moved to Creemore at the beginning of September we were already married. Nobody asked us when the wedding was." He sounds angry now too.

"What if Erica looks up the marriage certificate?"

"For fuck's sake, Stephanie, she's telling nothing but lies!"

"It's not **all** lies, is it?" she shoots back, before she can stop herself. "You slept with her, you got her pregnant."

He takes a couple of breaths before he answers, his nostrils flaring. "Yes, I slept with her. But I'm not a murderer," he says lowering his voice and looking at her, almost coldly. "Maybe I should ask you what **you** believe."

Stephanie drops her eyes and avoids the question. She must tell him. "Erica was here today."

# 25

Erica sits on her sofa, eating take-out Thai food from cartons on her coffee table and thinking about her conversation with Stephanie earlier that day. Erica's annoyed. Stephanie isn't going to pay. Patrick would have, but she won't. And she's the one with the money. God, Erica hates stubborn people who can't see what's in their own best interest.

She remembers that Stephanie told her Patrick had seen her purse in Erica's apartment. She leans over and hauls the black bag up onto the sofa. She'll have to get rid of it. She'll throw it in the river.

This is all going to take a little longer than expected and require a bit of creative thinking. In the meantime, Niall has potential, and she has her part-time job at the hospital to tide her over. She likes working in hospitals, because hospitals have doctors. And doctors have money. And, in her experience, they have big egos, work long hours, and

are prone to having affairs. Sometimes they even have drug problems.

The world is full of opportunity, Erica thinks, if you keep your eyes open.

PATRICK IS CLEARLY shocked to hear that Stephanie has seen Erica. For a moment, he goes completely still. "What?" he says.

"She was here, waiting for me, when I got back from the park," Stephanie says. She doesn't tell him that Erica was inside the house. That she probably left the door unlocked again by mistake. "We spoke on the porch."

"And you're just telling me this now?" he bursts out. "Why didn't you call the police?"

"You didn't want to go to the police, remember?" she says with heat. "You wanted to wait and see if she'd just go away."

He runs a hand nervously through his hair. "What did she want?"

"Money, of course. I made it clear we weren't going to give her any." She adds, "And she wanted to talk to me. So we talked."

Now he turns worried eyes on her. "Jesus, Stephanie. You shouldn't have done that. She's dangerous. Devious. What did she tell you?"

"She said that the two of you were in love. That you weren't together only a couple of times, but a lot." She looks up at him from the sofa, where he's

standing in front of her, careful to watch his reaction to what she says next. "She said you used to go to her apartment at lunchtime and make love, and eat the lunch your wife packed afterward, in her bed."

She knows from the panicked look in his eyes that she's struck a nerve. She hadn't expected it. "It's true?" she gasps.

He shakes his head. He's gone pale, and when he answers, his voice is strained. "That only happened once, I swear. The only other time we slept together was before that, and we were drunk. I put an end to it after that." He adds, desperately, "It was nothing, Stephanie. I realized how stupid I'd been. She meant nothing to me, nothing at all."

She gives him a hard stare, less sure of things now.

"Erica isn't going to get anywhere with this, I promise."

She looks back at him, utterly exhausted. How can he not see what they're up against? How can he make that promise? How can he even say it? Maybe it's because he knows he's innocent. But even that is no guarantee. Innocent people get convicted of murder all the time. She feels her face begin to crumple. "How can you promise that it's all going to be fine? How can you promise anything?" she says plaintively.

"Where is this coming from, Stephanie? Don't you believe me?"

"Of course I believe you, but—"

"But what?"

"If Erica does go to the police—they might believe her."

PATRICK IS PRETENDING to sleep, but he's wide awake behind his closed eyes. Stephanie finally put the twins down and joined him in bed a few minutes ago. His back is turned to her, but he can tell by her breathing that she's fast asleep. He's been waiting, hoping that tonight she would drop off quickly.

Quietly, he gets out of bed, careful not to wake her. He pulls on his jeans and a T-shirt and creeps out of the room. Once she's asleep, she should be out cold until the twins start to cry around 6:00 a.m. He'll be back by then. With any luck, she won't even notice he's gone. And if she does, he'll say he couldn't sleep and went for a drive to clear his head.

He gathers his wallet and keys and sneaks out of the house, locking the door carefully behind him. He gets into his car, backs out of the driveway, and doesn't turn his headlights on until he's down the street. He takes the highway to Newburgh.

ERICA IS AWAKENED by the sharp sound of her apartment buzzer. She lifts her head and looks at her clock radio—it's 2:54 in the morning. The buzzer goes again, insistently.

She throws off her covers and pads in bare feet to her door. She speaks into the intercom. "Who's there?"

"It's me. I want to talk."

She recognizes Patrick's voice. Her heart begins to beat more rapidly. "Okay. Come in."

She wonders fleetingly if she should be afraid of him. She is, a little, but she thinks he's finally ready to talk business. This could work out well for both of them—maybe he's beginning to see that.

She's pulling on her robe when she hears his knock. She finishes tying her robe, then opens the door.

He stares at her for a moment before he brushes past her to enter the apartment. She closes the door, trying to gauge his mood. He turns around to face her.

"What brings you here in the middle of the night?" she asks.

"You need to stay the hell away from my wife!" His voice is threatening.

This is not exactly what she was hoping for. She was hoping he would realize that the death of his current wife would be in their mutual interest. Whether it's what he would have chosen or not. But instead he's being protective of her.

"Why would I do that?" she says, in an equally hostile tone. "She deserves to know the truth—to know what you're capable of."

"Cut the bullshit!" he thunders. Then he walks closer and lowers his voice and says venomously, "I've had just about enough of this—and just about enough of **you**."

She doesn't pull back; she pushes her face up closer to his. "Don't try to tell me you didn't have something in mind for her before I came along. You married a woman you **knew** would inherit a fortune. And now she has. And let's not forget the life insurance." She smiles coldly at him. "If I hadn't come along, how would this story have ended?" She sees the fury in his eyes. "Struck a nerve, have I? Ruined all your plans?"

"You miserable, lying bitch," he seethes. "You're so caught up in your own fantasies that you actually believe them!"

"In case you haven't noticed," she says, "I've got you in a tight spot. If your cheapskate wife dies now, before I go to the police in Colorado, no one has to suspect a thing, if you do it right. You'll be free of her, and you can split her money with me—there's plenty of it." He glares at her, speechless with rage. Erica says coolly, "The alternative is being investigated for the murder of your first wife. Once that happens, regardless of the outcome, you'd never be able to get rid of Stephanie, would you? You wouldn't dare." She waits a beat and adds cruelly, "And maybe she'd divorce you and take her money with her."

"You selfish, amoral, greedy bitch," he snarls.

His opinion doesn't bother her in the least. "So what are you going to do?" she asks.

He looks back at her, his face so close to hers. She can see a vein throbbing with tension in his temple. She waits for his answer.

"You're assuming I'm a killer," he says, in desperation.

"Aren't you?"

# 26

On Thursday morning, Hanna decides to invite Stephanie and the twins over for a playdate. She's grown increasingly concerned about her neighbor. Stephanie is clearly exhausted, and Hanna can tell she's finding it hard to cope. Who wouldn't, with colicky twins and no mother of her own around to help? Hanna is more grateful to her own mother, who lives nearby, than she ever thought she'd be, and Teddy is an easy baby.

It had been upsetting, the other day, finding Stephanie's door wide open and seeing her in such a state. Theirs is a nice neighborhood, but that doesn't mean you won't be robbed if you leave your door open. With the rise in internet shopping, there's been a rash of thefts of packages left on people's doorsteps, and probably more opportunists about.

There's something else that's bothering Hanna. A

couple of days earlier, she'd seen Stephanie talking on her front porch with the woman who'd looked at the house for sale two doors down. Hanna remembers her friendly chat with the woman when she first came by to check out the neighborhood. But from where Hanna was—glancing out her living-room window, while walking around and burping Teddy—it didn't look like she and Stephanie were having a pleasant conversation.

Hanna isn't nosy; she doesn't like to pry. And she's discovered that Stephanie is a private person, not quick to disclose personal information, so she's not sure she should bring it up. But if this woman is thinking of buying that house . . .

She picks up the phone and soon the two women and three babies are comfortably ensconced in her living room. Hanna notices that Stephanie looks worse than the last time she saw her.

"Don't take this the wrong way," Hanna says sympathetically, "but you look terrible."

"I feel even lousier than I look," Stephanie admits.

Hanna offers her a cup of coffee and asks casually, "Who was that woman you were talking to on your porch the other day?"

Stephanie averts her eyes, accepting the coffee cup. She takes a sip, and says, "Just an old school friend of Patrick's."

"Oh." Hanna considers the information and says, "Is she still interested in buying the house?"

"What house?"

"The one for sale two doors down from you. I spoke to her early last week, and she'd just been in to see it."

"Oh no, I don't think so," Stephanie says. Then she changes the subject.

Hanna thinks to herself, **Something here isn't adding up.**

NANCY TRIES TO LEARN everything she can about E. Voss. She does the obvious things—Google searches, Facebook—but she doesn't find anything helpful. She keeps an eye on the Tesla app. She'd seen her husband driving out to Newburgh when he was supposed to be working on Sunday afternoon, but she'd been trapped at a birthday party for one of Henry's little friends. She has taken to following her husband whenever she can—after all, Niall could be meeting this woman anywhere—but on a time lag. When she sees where he's gone and parked, she goes there later, sometimes with Henry with her in the car. So far he's only been to legitimate job sites.

But on Thursday afternoon, she sees the little blue dot on the move, heading to Newburgh. She's overcome with rage. At him, and at herself for not confronting him. At home they continue to act as if nothing is different. He's pretending he's not having an affair, and she's pretending

she doesn't know about it. They could both win Oscars.

She arranges for her mother to pick Henry up from afternoon preschool and keep him until she returns. And then she takes to the highway, seething. When she arrives at her destination, she parks across the street again, and then spots her husband's Tesla in the parking lot. She wants to take a sledgehammer to it.

Instead, she sits in her own car and waits, her eye on the front door of the building. Eventually, Niall comes out, alone. She waits for him to get into his car and drive away. She takes a deep breath and gets out of the car, walks into the building, and presses the buzzer for apartment 107. She wants to see this homewrecker for herself.

When Nancy hears a woman's voice on the intercom, she suddenly doesn't know what to say. What if she refuses to let her in? At that moment, a man comes out of the lobby and Nancy slips past him and inside, without speaking into the intercom.

Nancy walks down the corridor until she finds apartment 107. She stands there for a nervous moment. Will the woman who's sleeping with her husband answer the door, or look out the peephole and figure out why she's there—the angry wife? She steels herself and knocks.

The door opens. "Yes?"

Nancy stares at her. She's not as young as she was expecting, but she is certainly beautiful. Blond,

where Nancy is dark. Anne O'Dowd was blond too. Nancy wonders at her husband's sudden penchant for blonds. She feels envy, insecurity, and anger in equal measure, looking at the slim, shapely woman in black leggings and a clingy T-shirt.

"What do you want?" the woman asks.

"I want to talk to you," Nancy says firmly. "Can I come in?"

The other woman gives her a bemused look. "Who are you?" she asks.

Nancy glances past the woman to the barely furnished apartment. She pushes her way in.

"Excuse me . . . who **are** you?"

Nancy glances down at a small table piled with mail. She sees the name **Erica Voss** on one of the envelopes and looks up. "I wanted to meet you, **Erica**. You've been sleeping with my husband—I just saw him leave—and you are going to stop."

"Ah," Erica says, and smiles. "You're the neglected wife—I thought so. You've been following him, have you? How pathetic. And you think you can come here and tell me what **I'm** going to do." She adds, "How very . . . confident of you."

Nancy can tell that Erica thinks her confidence is misplaced. "Consider this a courtesy call," Nancy says in a hard voice. "I'm going to tell my husband that I know all about you and he will break it off immediately."

"What makes you so sure?" Erica asks, folding her arms under her perfect breasts.

Suddenly Nancy's not so sure. This woman is different from Anne O'Dowd. She's no pushover. "Just stay away from him," she warns.

"Or what? What are you going to do to me?" Erica looks at her, arching one eyebrow. Then she adds, "He's a big boy and he can make his own decisions."

Nancy throws her a look of contempt and turns away, reaching for the door. "You'll see I'm right."

"Drive carefully," Erica calls after her.

NIALL STAYS LATE at work to make up for the time he took in the middle of the afternoon to see Erica. He knows his wife won't be happy, but she doesn't complain too much about his working late. She knows he works hard, and she's proud of his success. They have a good lifestyle. Long hours are the price you pay for that.

When he gets home, he parks in the driveway and enters the house. Nancy doesn't greet him at the door like she normally does. Maybe she's in the kitchen, he thinks. She's probably kept something warm for him, she always does. He realizes he's starving. But the house is unusually quiet. He walks through the house on the way to the kitchen, calling, "Nancy, I'm home."

He stops suddenly when he sees her sitting quietly in the living room on the sofa. "Hey," he says.

But she's looking at him in a way that makes his

insides collapse. Her face is grim—reproachful, furious, hurt—and he knows she knows. She's found out about Erica, she must have. All at once **he's** furious. Has she followed him? Can he have no freedom at all? But those feelings are gone in an instant, a momentary burst of childishness, and then reality washes over him. He's been a fool. He's going to lose her. . . . He feels his face fall. Still, neither of them has spoken.

Finally he says softly, "Where's Henry?" He doesn't want their son to overhear what happens next.

"He's at my mother's," she says. "He's staying there tonight."

She's going to ask him to leave. He feels lightheaded with disbelief. How could he have been so stupid? He'd promised her. And he'd broken his promise. She won't give him a second chance. She already has, and he's blown it.

"Nancy . . ." he says, his voice halting. She's waiting for him to tell her, but he can't.

"How could you?" she hisses. "How could you, after last time?"

He comes slowly into the room, as if he's approaching his own funeral, and sinks heavily into an armchair across from her. "I don't know," he says. "I'm so sorry. Nancy, I love you. Only you. I've only ever loved you." He looks back at her, abject and pleading.

"That's what you said last time," she says angrily.

"I know. But it's true."

"I went to see her today," Nancy says.

He feels sick. He never meant for this to happen. It was meaningless, a bit of excitement. He didn't mean to hurt her. He doesn't want to lose everything.

"She's very attractive," Nancy says bitterly.

Oh God, not this again. "Nancy, please. You know how attractive you are. I mean, look at you! It's not about that."

"Oh no?" She waits a bit and then says, "Then why do you do it? Why do you sleep with other women? Why am I not enough for you?"

He almost wishes she would cry and throw things, but she's so angry, and so cold, he's certain that she's already made the decision to kick him out. He can't explain it. He'd tried, in marriage counseling, but had failed. He wants to explain it now, but he can't find the words.

"I've had enough, Niall. I think you should leave."

"No!" It comes out as a strangled protest. "No, Nancy, please. Please give me another chance."

"You can move into that cheap little apartment in Newburgh, with **her**. I'm sure you'll both be very happy. Or not. I don't care."

He lurches off the armchair and sinks to his knees in front of her. He's shaking his head. "I don't **want** her. She's nothing to me. I want to be here, with you. I love you, Nancy. I want to be here

with you and Henry. Please don't ask me to leave. I'll never see her again. I swear."

Then she begins to cry, and he does too. Afterward they sit in silence for a long time. Darkness falls.

Finally Nancy says, "I want you to call her, now, and tell her you'll never see her again."

"Sure, of course," he says eagerly. He takes his cell phone out of his pocket and calls Erica. His heart is pounding loudly. He holds the cell phone up to his ear.

Erica answers. "Hello."

"Erica," Niall says. "It's Niall. I'm sorry, but I'm not going to see you anymore."

"Afraid of your wife, are you?" her voice is scathing.

"I love her."

"Sure you do."

He disconnects the call. He can tell his wife has heard it all. He looks at her tentatively. "What now?" Niall asks.

"I'll think about it," Nancy says. She stands up and adds, "You can sleep in the guest room for now—until I decide what to do." She exits the room, leaving Niall holding his head in his hands.

ERICA WANTS to throw her cell phone against the wall. She stops herself just in time. She's just been humiliated. She didn't see that coming, not until

Niall's wife showed up at her door this afternoon. Of course she knew Niall wouldn't want to disrupt his family. What she hadn't expected was for his wife to find out about them, at least not so quickly. How had he let himself get caught? How had he allowed himself to be followed? How stupid can a man be? Did the idiot **want** to get caught?

Now she can't get money from him for her silence.

Lately, nothing is going the way she expected. She tells herself that she must have patience. These things take time. But patience has never been her strong suit.

# 27

Patrick keeps playing his last conversation with Erica—late that night in her apartment—over and over again in his mind. Sometimes, these days, his hands shake. Stephanie has noticed. She keeps asking him if he's all right, if he's keeping anything from her, if he's heard any more from Erica. But he hasn't, and neither has she. He's not foolish enough to think she's simply given up and gone away—not anymore.

Stephanie is a wreck too. Her face is drawn and she drags herself around the house as if every movement is an effort. He's seen her start at every unexpected sound, even something as innocent as the mail dropping through the slot at the front door. She'd told him what Hanna said—that Erica had been looking at the house for sale on their street. It has unnerved her. It has unnerved both of them, which he's sure was her intention, but they

both know she can't be seriously interested in the house—can she?

They're both going a little stir crazy. Patrick realizes that they haven't been out of the city much at all since the twins were born. Before Stephanie was pregnant, they used to hike the trails on the weekends and cycle regularly. Then, when Stephanie was pregnant, they'd talked about attaching baby seats to their bikes and cycling through the Catskills, as if having babies would be a mere hiccup. They'd had no idea how profoundly their lives would change. The idea of cycling with the twins in infant bicycle seats had been unrealistic. They hadn't realized what having twins would be like, and they hadn't expected colic, which has knocked them both sideways. Now all they want to do is sleep when they get the chance.

"Stephanie," Patrick says at breakfast on Saturday morning. "Why don't we pack a picnic and leave the city like we used to? It's going to be a gorgeous day. We can at least all get some fresh air and a change of scenery."

She tilts her head at him, considering it. He can tell she's torn: it sounds lovely, but she's likely thinking of the work involved—organizing the picnic, making the food—and losing the naptime because the twins will probably sleep in the car on the drive back.

"I'll do everything," he coaxes. "I'll pop into the deli and get everything ready-made." He smiles at

her. "Potato salad. Those Italian sandwiches you like. That fizzy lemon drink, and some cookies. We'll drive up to that spot in the mountains we used to go to—where we used to make out." He smiles at her, and earns a brief, weary smile in return. "We can relax a bit. And you can sleep in the car on the way back." Her face lightens a little, and she looks more like herself, he thinks, than at any time since Erica slithered into their lives.

"That sounds tempting," she agrees. "Okay. I'll pack a bag for the twins while you go to the deli."

"Great." He kisses her on the lips and grabs the car keys, humming as he goes.

STEPHANIE LEANS BACK in the passenger seat, lulled into a sense of ease as they leave the river behind and climb the road into the Catskills. With the deepening forest all around, she feels a familiar peace come over her. The sun is glorious. The twins are babbling happily in the backseat and Patrick, driving beside her, looks over at her and smiles. He reaches out his right hand and places it on top of hers. In a sudden burst of joy, she remembers how happy they are—just before memories of what they're facing flood back. Light and dark. Can you have one without the other? Looking at Patrick's profile, the sunlight flooding the car, the cooing of her daughters behind her—she knows what happiness is. With a jagged tug of fear, she

also knows that a dark shadow has been cast over their lives. She turns away from Patrick and looks out the window. She watches the landscape pass by, peering into the forest, thinking about all the fairy tales she looks forward to reading to the twins, the ones she loved so much as a child—"Little Red Riding Hood," "Hansel and Gretel," "Snow White and the Seven Dwarfs."

"Almost there," Patrick says, turning off the highway and onto a rutted road to the secluded spot they had discovered a couple of years ago and thought of as their own. They haven't been here since the twins were born, Stephanie reflects. Patrick pulls up and turns off the car. They're all alone up here; it's so quiet she can hear the ticking of the cooling engine. They get out of the car. Patrick comes close to her and they stand together looking down. From here the view is magnificent. Then Stephanie turns away and sets about laying the blankets on the grass while Patrick gets the infant seats out of the car.

Soon they each have a baby on their lap and they're enjoying their meal, drawing in lungfuls of fresh air. Their problems seem further away here, Stephanie thinks, as she bites into her sandwich and smiles down at Jackie, who is reaching for her hair. They're far away from everything. If only they could stay here, she thinks fancifully, where Erica could never find them.

"Do you want to go for a walk in the woods?"

Patrick asks after they've eaten. "I brought the baby carriers."

Stephanie, drowsy now after lunch, thinks about it and shakes her head. "I'd rather just sit here."

"Whatever you want," Patrick agrees. "This is your day." He leans over and kisses her on the mouth, and she kisses him back, hungrily, the way she used to.

After a couple of lazy, almost blissful hours, they pack their things and think about returning home. Stephanie notices that a cloud has passed across Patrick's mood. He seems to have become withdrawn, tense. Perhaps he's thinking about what's ahead. Their little escape is over. She imagines they're both worried about the same thing as they load the car. When will they hear from Erica again? What happens next? She appraises him as they finish securing the babies in the back. "You look really tired," she says. "Maybe I should drive."

He shakes his head. "No, I'm fine. I'll drive."

"You did all the driving up. I'll drive home."

He looks at her across the hood of the car. "No, really, I'm fine. You should nap on the way back."

But she won't take no for an answer. She walks around the front of the car to the driver's side and says, "I'm driving. Look, you're actually trembling. Believe it or not, I think you're in worse shape than I am."

# 28

A week has gone by since Patrick visited Erica's apartment in the middle of the night. Erica finds herself growing more and more impatient. Nothing is happening. Specifically—nothing has happened to **Stephanie**, and she doesn't like fucking around. She steps into the independent bookstore in downtown Aylesford. It's a charming place, but Erica didn't come here to be charmed. She knows what she wants. She spots the children's section and heads there.

It's time she brought a gift for the twins. She's spent so much time thinking about them, she feels like she's almost part of their little family now. She peruses the shelves, searching for something specific, something she remembers from her own childhood. It might even be her favorite story. For a moment she's worried she won't find it—that she'll have to order it online somewhere, and she

really wants to give it to the twins today. Patrick needs a nudge.

Ah—there it is. She recognizes the little book and plucks it from the shelf. She finds a chair and sits down and reads it all the way through. It's just as she remembered it, and in spite of herself she **is** charmed by it, finds herself smiling as she reads, enjoying the familiar words, the illustrations, the moral. It's perfect.

PATRICK SEES IT FIRST, the small gift-wrapped package topped with a bow, sitting at the base of their front door. They're returning from an evening walk around the neighborhood with the twins. He feels Stephanie come up behind him. She sees the package, wrapped in pale yellow paper dotted with little lambs, and gives a cry of delight.

"A present!" she says.

Stephanie has always loved gifts—choosing them, wrapping them, giving them, and receiving them. With a jolt, Patrick realizes that he hasn't given his wife any thoughtful gifts lately, not even flowers. He must make amends. He'll get her something soon.

Stephanie comes up the porch steps with him and reaches down to pick up the package, while Patrick unlocks the door. "Let's get the babies inside and see who it's from," she says.

They make their way in and set the babies down in the living room. "There's a card," Stephanie says. "To Jackie and Emma. I wonder who it's from?" Stephanie says, sitting down on the sofa and opening the card.

Patrick is about to sit beside her when she flings the gift away as if she's had an electric shock. She's still holding the card in her hand, looking at it with distaste. Patrick feels a terrible misgiving. "What?"

She hands him the card—he sees that her hand is shaking. "It's from **Erica.**" She says the name with revulsion.

He grabs the card from her and looks at it with alarm. Inside is written, "A little gift for you and the twins. Erica."

A feeling of dread sweeps over him. He looks at the package that Stephanie had thrown to the floor. It's small and flat, like a book.

"Don't open it," Stephanie says.

He hesitates. He doesn't want to open it either. Erica is sick and she's trying to fuck with them. But all the same, he needs to know what it is. He walks over to the gift and bends down and picks it up while Stephanie shrinks back into the sofa. He glances back at her, as if for permission. She doesn't say anything, so he rips the paper off. He lets his breath out in relief. He turns to Stephanie and says, "It's just a book. A picture book."

He comes back to the sofa and sits beside her, reading the title out loud. "The Little Red Hen."

Stephanie takes it from him and stares at the book. "I know this one. It's an old folktale. The little red hen has to do everything herself." She turns to the first page, and they glance through the book together, reading it quickly. It's about a little red hen who finds a grain of wheat, but no one will help her plant the seed. The goose and the cat and the pig say no. So the little red hen says she'll do it herself. When it comes time to harvest the wheat, no one will help her. She tells them she will do it herself. Finally, when it comes time to eat the bread that she's made from the wheat, everyone wants some, but she says that she will eat it herself.

Stephanie has flipped the pages to the end, as if expecting something more. But there's nothing else. She turns to him, her face grim.

"She's just trying to mess with us," Patrick says. But he knows what she's doing, and it chills him to the core. Erica is sending him a message, and it couldn't be more clear. **I'll do it myself.**

THE FOLLOWING EVENING, Wednesday, Erica is walking to work at Hillcrest Hospital in Newburgh, where she is an administrative assistant three days a week. She really should have gone back to school, settled into something worthwhile. But she's always been restless, not able to stick to anything long enough. Always looking for some quicker, easier way to make money. She's on the night shift,

and it's already dark. The hospital is not far from her apartment, and she enjoys being alone with her thoughts. She always has so much to think about.

Erica is walking along the edge of the service road that leads to the back entrance to the hospital—there's no sidewalk—and her thoughts turn to choices she's made. She has no husband to support her. She gave her only child up for adoption. It had been a practical decision, and a financial one, and not difficult to make. Erica had leaned on the eager, well-to-do couple a little. And then a little more. It was all done very quietly. They were happy to pay.

She wasn't ready to be a mother. How was Erica, just twenty-two, supposed to raise a child on her own? When in truth, she'd never really considered whether she even wanted children? She knows now that she doesn't—she's not the nurturing type. It surprises her a little, how little interest she has in her own child.

She walks briskly along the dark, deserted stretch of road with her head down, engrossed in her thoughts, earbuds in, listening to music. Suddenly she senses something, hears the sound of acceleration behind her. She turns to look and sees the dark, menacing shape of a car bearing down on her at high speed, its headlights off. Acting on pure instinct, she dives into the ditch at the side of the road, landing hard on her side and rolling, as she hears the car speed away.

She lies in the ditch, panting, her heart beating wildly. She sits up slowly, rubbing her shoulder. She's shaken but unhurt. **That was close.**

Maybe, she thinks, suddenly afraid, maybe she's pushed Patrick too hard. He's made his choice. She's fucking blown it.

# 29

It's late, and Stephanie has Jackie in her arms, the baby's face red and bawling and covered in mucus and tears. Her little body is hot, even in just a diaper and a light T-shirt. Stephanie is sweating, too, from holding her against her chest for so long. She talks to Jackie, jiggling her as she carries her around the living room, but the baby will not be soothed. If they try to put the babies down, they cry even more frantically, and neither she nor Patrick can stand it. Patrick has Emma in his arms and he's walking her around the hall and in and out of the kitchen. Night after night they do this, and it's wearing them down. They can't even speak to each other through the noise, but maybe that's a good thing. Stephanie doesn't want to speak to her husband right now.

She's angry. At him, at the situation. She's so tired she can't think straight. She's generally a very

rational person, but she hardly recognizes herself anymore.

She doesn't believe that Patrick killed his first wife deliberately. Stephanie **knows** him. It's an outrageous claim. If he really was in love with Erica, like she says, then why wouldn't he just leave Lindsey, like Erica claims she wanted? That's what anyone would do. There'd be no reason to kill her.

Except—there was going to be a baby, and supporting a young family you've left is very expensive. And there was that insurance money.

She goes wearily around and around the living room, the thoughts going around and around her mind, just as wearily. Erica is a blackmailer, a cold-blooded liar. But she's so persuasive, so believable. Still, even if Erica, with all her lies, is able to make the authorities believe that the affair was serious, that's not enough, surely, to prove that Patrick **murdered** his first wife? But then she remembers the money, and feels a wave of nausea sweep over her. Her knee bumps the sofa and she stumbles a bit. And then she remembers the warning that Erica had left her with: **If he did it once, he could do it again.** She closes her eyes for a moment and stands still. No. She will not go there. Erica was just trying to mess with her mind.

Stephanie bites her lip and resolutely refuses to allow her mind to go down that treacherous path.

She tries to stick to what she knows for sure. Erica knows they're not going to pay. She certainly won't get anything out of them once she goes to the police. She might go to the police anyway, out of spite. If she does, this thing is going to take on a life of its own. With any luck it will be dealt with quickly in Colorado and no one here will ever have to know.

But if it isn't—if it comes to the attention of the media, if she doesn't get some sleep—she's afraid that she's going to snap.

EARLY THE NEXT MORNING Erica drives to LaGuardia Airport for her direct flight to Denver.

She'd thought about it all through her shift the night before. Then she'd gone home and packed an overnight bag for Colorado. She's going to pay a visit to the Sheriff's Office. It's the best way she's got of protecting herself from Patrick.

She sleeps the entire flight, and once she's landed, she picks up a rental car—a convertible. She sits in the driver's seat for a minute, thinking of what's behind her, and now, what's ahead of her.

She used to live in Denver. Her son is here. She'd moved downtown—out of Creemore—after Lindsey died. But today she will go back to Creemore, where it all happened. She will visit the sheriff and tell him everything. She really hadn't

thought this would be necessary. She'd misjudged things.

But she's starting to consider another possibility. When one door closes, she thinks, another one opens.

STEPHANIE FUMBLES THROUGH THE MORNING, forgetting what she's doing, bumping into things, berating herself for not paying enough attention to the twins. She stands in the kitchen, her mind in a fog, knowing that she should get the girls ready for the stroller. But she doesn't have the energy to face it all, the enormous effort it will take. She reaches automatically for another cup of coffee, but the caffeine isn't helping. Maybe she should stop drinking it altogether. But then how the hell would she manage? It's not easy looking after twins all day and most of the night too.

She takes her coffee and her laptop into the living room. With one eye on the babies, she turns on her computer and googles sleep deprivation. What she sees disturbs her. There can be physical effects—clumsiness and being prone to accidents. She knows. But it's the psychological effects that are even more concerning. Forgetfulness. Yes. Emotional instability, mood swings. Yes, but it's hard to tell if that's from lack of sleep, considering the circumstances. Loss of perspective. Quite

possibly. Acting impulsively, uncharacteristically. Imagining things, hallucinating. Will all these things happen to her, if she doesn't soon get these babies to sleep on a schedule?

Are they happening already? In her darkest moments, she has actually imagined Patrick packing the snow deeper into that exhaust pipe, leaning on his shovel, taking his time, waiting for the carbon monoxide to work, to rid himself of his unwanted family. . . . She gives her head a quick shake, and then another. Tells herself to stop it.

She doesn't know if her wild imaginings are a result of not sleeping, or a legitimate response to what she's learning about her husband. When she's feeling awake, and lucid, she knows better. She knows Patrick would never hurt anyone, let alone someone he loved. She's beginning not to trust herself, her own thoughts. No wonder she's starting not to trust him.

And Patrick—he, too, is affected by the lack of sleep, and being under all this additional stress. They would both be handling things better if they were more themselves, and not trying to cope with this cycle of colic and exhaustion.

But she doesn't see any sign of the babies changing their routine any time soon.

She sits on the sofa, overwhelmed with fatigue, and she can feel herself starting to go down the rabbit hole. She stares at the pattern in the rug and can't seem to drag her eyes away, even if she moves

her head. Her mind shifts to Erica and what she might be doing now. Suddenly Stephanie gets up, knocking her coffee mug over on the floor at her feet, but she ignores the spill and rushes to the front door and looks out at the porch, to see if Erica is there. But the porch is empty. She locks the door and wanders back to the living room. Erica is the enemy, she reminds herself, the serpent who has intruded into their almost-perfect lives to destroy them. Her husband isn't guilty of what she accuses him of.

She thinks about getting the stroller ready and taking the twins out for their morning walk. But what if Erica is out there? Patrick says she's dangerous, possibly a psychopath. Patrick doesn't want her to talk to Erica ever again.

Stephanie sits on the sofa, almost catatonic, too tired and afraid to go out of the house at all, while the spilled coffee seeps into the rug.

# 30

Erica sets off on the hour-long drive from the Denver airport to Creemore. She skirts the city, and soon leaves it behind. Her route takes her into the Denver foothills; it's a beautiful drive, but she's not taken with the scenery. The familiar road unwinds in front of her.

When she arrives in town, she finds herself taking an unplanned detour back to where it all happened, to the residential street where Patrick and Lindsey had lived. She parks her rental car across from the old brick house where they had the second-floor apartment. She gets out of the car and stares at the front window on the second floor. That was their living room. Erica can still picture it perfectly; cheaply furnished, crowded with items—some new, some secondhand—for the expected baby. Erica turns and looks at the little cul-de-sac where their car was parked that day, the day Lindsey died. It's late August, and it's hard

to imagine, right now, this street buried in four feet of snow. She tries to remember exactly where Lindsey's body lay that day, but there's no snow-bank, so she can't be sure. Then she closes her eyes and suddenly she can see it all.

After a few minutes, she gets back into the car and drives to the Grant County Sheriff's Office. It's a large concrete-and-glass building set back from the road. She parks in the lot and takes a moment to mentally prepare herself. Finally she gets out of the car and strides up to the front doors and walks in. She approaches the uniformed woman at the front desk.

"Can I help you?" the woman asks.

"I'd like to speak to the sheriff, please."

"Can I ask what it's regarding?"

"It's about an old case," Erica says. "I have some important information."

The other woman studies her for a moment. "Wait here," she says, and leaves the desk. She soon returns and says, "Come this way, please."

They walk down a shiny corridor, their footsteps noisy on the floor. They arrive at an office, its door open. "In here," the woman says, and departs.

A tall, burly man wearing a dark uniform stands up from behind his desk and approaches her. He looks to be in his early forties, she thinks. "I'm Lorne Bastedo," the sheriff says, shaking her hand.

"Erica Voss," she says.

He offers her a seat and sits down behind his desk.

information," she says, "about a murder." As she speaks, he listens attentively. She sees his face grow more serious. Finally, when she's told him all of it—the affair, the pregnancy, the look Patrick gave her, the insurance payout—she waits for his reaction. She's told her story well. And she's confident that her actions since—staying away from Patrick, giving their baby up for adoption, coming forward now—will assure him that she had nothing to do with it. That it's only her conscience that's making her do this now.

"This is a serious allegation," the sheriff says pensively, sitting back in his chair. He studies her for a moment. "This case was before my time," he says finally. "Let me get the file." He steps out of the room and she can hear him talking to someone in the corridor. He comes back and sits down and soon after someone drops a file on his desk and leaves. He reviews the sparse-looking file silently, while she watches. She knows there's not much to it.

"It looks like there wasn't much of an investigation," he says, echoing her thoughts. He looks up at her, considering. "Leave it with me," he says.

ONCE ERICA VOSS DEPARTS, Sheriff Bastedo looks at the file again. Notes the name of the coroner, George Yancik. Yancik has been the coroner in Grant County for almost twenty years. It seems

that Yancik and the previous sheriff, Michael Be-
wdly, quickly agreed that this was simply a tragic
accident. On the face of it, that's certainly what it
appeared to be. But Bastedo's curiosity is aroused,
and he'd found the woman who just left to be
compelling. She spoke clearly and persuasively, and
what she said had the ring of truth.

But is there anything to what she's saying? It ob-
viously looked like an accident at the time. On the
other hand—if it **was** murder, he'd gotten away
with it. The perfect murder. If you had to get rid of
your wife and unborn child, it was an easy way to
do it. Brilliant, really.

He picks up the phone and calls George Yancik.
When he answers the phone, Bastedo asks, "Mind
if I pay a visit?"

"Sure, when?"

"Now," Bastedo says. "I'll be right over."

He hangs up, grabs the file, goes outside, and gets
in his black-and-white truck with SHERIFF em-
blazoned across the door and drives the short dis-
tance to the coroner's office. When he arrives, he's
met by Yancik, and they go to his office. "What's
this about?" Yancik asks when they are seated.

Bastedo places the slim file on the other man's
desk. "This case. Nine and a half years ago. A
woman died of carbon monoxide poisoning sitting
in a running car on Dupont Street while the hus-
band shoveled it out of a snowbank. She was eight
months pregnant."

Yancik's eyes sharpen. "Yes, I remember. It was tragic."

"I have some questions."

"Okay," Yancik says, "but it was a very straightforward case."

"Tell me what you remember."

The coroner settles back in his chair. "There was a big snowstorm. Record snowfall—everybody was digging out. The plows were running. If I remember correctly, they were going on a trip and the wife waited in the running car. She fell asleep. End of story. An autopsy confirmed she died of carbon monoxide poisoning. Very open and shut."

"And the husband? No one seems to have investigated him very thoroughly."

Yancik's eyes sharpen and he leans forward. "Sheriff Bewdly questioned him, and we spoke afterward. I found, based on what I had before me, that the death was accidental." He sits back again in his chair and asks, "Why?"

Bastedo tells him about the new information. As he talks, he sees Yancik's brow cloud over.

"We didn't know about any of this at the time," the coroner says. "Why didn't this woman say anything then?"

"She says she was afraid of being implicated," Bastedo answers, "and that now she wants to do the right thing. In any event," he continues, "we know about it now. The question is, what do we do about it?"

· · ·

YANCIK SITS BACK in his chair, thinking about the case. He feels uneasy. What the sheriff has just told him is disturbing. If what this woman said was true—if she was having an affair with the husband, if he told her that he wanted out of the marriage, if there was insurance money—they really should take another look. Just to be sure.

It will look bad to bring this up again, as if he hadn't done his job the first time around. There's been a lot of flak, recently, about the fact that coroners in Colorado are elected officials. Colorado is one of only sixteen US states that still elect coroners, the others having moved over to a system of qualified medical examiners. This will stir the pot, cause further scrutiny. It's the coroner's job to investigate deaths, to determine the cause of death and the manner of death—whether it be from natural causes, suicide, accident, or homicide. People will complain that he wasn't qualified for the job. The press will give him a hounding. He feels a bit indignant. He relied on the Sheriff's Office to investigate properly. The autopsy itself was performed by a qualified forensic pathologist. He didn't have any of this information at the time to help him in his determination.

There's a new sheriff now, sitting right across from him, and he's not afraid of past mistakes—he wasn't there. He's likely to want to fix them, to

make his mark. Yancik needs to get out ahead of this.

He knows the sheriff can undertake his own investigation, but the coroner can also decide to call an inquest, even this many years after the death. He can call witnesses, listen to evidence.

"Maybe I should call an inquest," Yancik says.

"I think that's a good idea," the sheriff agrees. "Hear what people have to say under oath."

# 31

Erica has booked a hotel room in downtown Denver for the night. After her visit to the sheriff in Creemore, she drives back to Denver and checks in. She's tired after a long day of traveling coming off a night working, but she has one more thing she has to do before she flies back to New York in the morning.

It's not sentimentality that sends her to Washington Park, one of the nicest residential areas of Denver. This is where families with money live. Erica parks her car directly across from a beautifully remodeled brick home. She knows this house, although she's never been inside. When she gave up her baby for adoption, the Mannings lived in another house, not quite as impressive as this one, in a less prosperous neighborhood. She's kept tabs on them over the years; they moved into this house when Devin was a toddler.

They've obviously done well for themselves. Erica is happy about that.

She sits in her rental car and waits. She'd gotten a convertible for a reason; fortunately, it's a nice day and she's got the top down. It doesn't look like anybody's home—there's no car in the driveway—but it's nearly dinnertime, and she hopes to see someone soon.

After almost an hour, a shiny white SUV pulls into the driveway. She watches Cheryl Manning get out of the driver's side while Devin jumps out of the passenger side and sprints to the front door. It's not the boy who holds Erica's interest; she barely gives him a passing glance. No, she stares at Cheryl, willing her to look over at her. She's rewarded—Cheryl glances up toward the street as she closes the car door, and freezes. She stares at Erica sitting in the open convertible. She gets a good look, while Devin calls to her impatiently to hurry up.

Erica waves casually at Cheryl, starts the car, and drives away.

CHERYL FEELS like she can't breathe. There's no doubt this time. That was Erica Voss, Devin's birth mother. Sitting outside their house, wanting to be seen.

"**Mom**," Devin calls again, sounding frustrated.

"I'm coming," she says, so flustered that she's

dropped her keys into the depths of her large purse and has to search for them again as she walks to the front door. She finally finds them and puts the key in the lock. Her hands are unsteady.

"Are you all right?" her son asks, looking at her curiously.

"I'm fine," she says, smiling at him.

"You look weird," he says.

She turns away from him and heads for the kitchen. "Shall we order a pizza tonight?" she says with false cheerfulness. "Dad'll be late."

"Sure." He heads up to his room, leaving her alone in the kitchen with her disturbing thoughts.

Cheryl lets herself collapse into one of the kitchen chairs. Her heart is beating furiously. So she wasn't wrong. It probably **was** Erica that she'd seen at the park not that long ago, with a camera around her neck. Gary thought she'd imagined it, had soothed away her nerves.

**Why? Why is she here, after all this time?**

Her first thought is that Erica needs money. Soon she'll be dropping by, like she did before, putting them in an uncomfortable position, giving them a choice. What will it be this time? And what will they do? Gary won't like it, not one bit. But really, what can she do to them? She's already given up all her legal rights to Devin.

Then her thoughts turn darker. What if it isn't money she wants? What if she wants a bigger role in Devin's life? They have an open adoption; Erica

had terminated all parental rights, and then had said she wanted no contact after all. But what if she's changed her mind about the contact part? She knows who they are and where they live. They haven't even told him he's adopted yet.

Devin is **everything** to her and Gary. They can't let Erica mess with that. Cheryl gets up and pours herself a glass of white wine.

Later that night, once Devin has gone to bed and Gary is finally home from a dinner meeting, Cheryl takes him down to the TV room in the basement and unloads all her fears. "I'm telling you, it was her!" Cheryl says to her husband.

"Keep your voice down," he tells her in a loud whisper.

"I don't think he can hear us down here," Cheryl says in a more normal voice.

"This isn't good," Gary says, looking worried. "I don't trust her. I never have."

GARY MANNING has been very successful, partly because he's smart and hardworking and partly because he can be quite ruthless—when he needs to be. He hadn't liked it when this Erica Voss had come into their house and told them to pay her a hundred thousand dollars or she wouldn't give them her baby. They could have told the agency what she was doing—but then she never would have let them have Devin. If it had been just him,

he might have told her to get lost. He wanted the baby; on the other hand, he didn't like being taken advantage of. But he'd taken one look at his wife, remembered everything she'd been through to get to this point, the years of frustration, anticipation, and pain—there was no question, it was all much harder on her than it was on him—and he gave in, just like that, and offered to write the woman a check.

He'd been more worried than he cared to admit that she might back out of the deal after she got the money. He hadn't liked it that she'd forced them to break the law—they would have no recourse if she double-crossed them. But he did it for Cheryl. And now . . . God, Devin is such a great kid, and they both love him to death. Devin is the best thing that ever happened to them. So he's never regretted it, not one bit. Devin is theirs, he was meant to be theirs, and he will always be theirs. So he doesn't know what this woman thinks she's going to do.

She has no legal rights to their son. And he doesn't think she gives two figs about him or she would have shown up before now.

He tries to tell Cheryl that she doesn't need to worry; Erica's not interested in her son. But he's plenty worried.

# 32

When Patrick gets home from work he finds Stephanie pacing the living room. Her hair is a mess, and she looks more distressed than he has ever seen her. "Was Erica here?" he asks suddenly, with a sickening feeling.

She looks at him, her eyes a little wild. "No. Why?"

"You look upset," he ventures.

"Of course I'm upset!"

"Have you been out today at all?" he asks, looking around the untidy house, the coffee mug on the floor, the fussing babies that smell like they need a change.

She shakes her head. "No. I don't want to run into her. I'm not going outside again in case she's out there."

Patrick's heart sinks. This is all his fault. His wife is in terrible distress, not herself, and he's to blame. Erica leaving that gift for the twins on their

doorstep seems to have pushed her over the edge. "Stephanie, you have to calm down."

"How can I calm down?" she asks, her voice rising. "Your ex-lover might be a psychopath and she's trying to destroy us. I can't leave the house because she might be waiting for me! I'm a prisoner in my own fucking house!"

She looks back at him wildly; he's never seen her like this. She's completely losing it. "Honey," he says, his voice breaking, "you just need to get some sleep."

"Yes, I need to get some sleep," she agrees. "But that's not going to make all of this go away, is it?"

He looks back at her in alarm. He needs her on his side. He can't do this alone.

Suddenly she says, "Patrick, why did you marry me?"

"What? What are you talking about?"

She repeats tearfully, her voice anguished, "Why did you marry me?"

"Because I love you. I fell in love with you the moment I saw you, you know that! This—this is—you're just overtired, Steph, you're not thinking straight."

The twins begin to cry and the din is soon overwhelming. Uncharacteristically, Stephanie plants her hands firmly over both her ears as if she can't stand it, tears spilling down her face. Patrick is appalled, utterly lost for a moment. He doesn't know

what he'll do if she can't cope. He can't manage the babies on his own. He can't manage any of this on his own.

He approaches her, tries to take her in his arms, but she thrusts him off and backs away.

"Erica said something to me when she was here." But then she stops, as if checking herself.

"What? What did she say?" Patrick cries.

"She said, **If you did it before, you could do it again**."

Patrick feels a colossal rage surging in his chest. That bitch. That interfering, lying bitch. How dare she tell Stephanie lies and make his own wife doubt him? He swallows, almost choking on his fury. "Stephanie. I didn't kill Lindsey on purpose. You must know that." She stares back at him, looking as if she's about to collapse. "You can't believe anything she says."

"I know," she says, sinking into the sofa and covering her face with her hands.

LATER THAT NIGHT, while Stephanie is walking with a crying Emma in her arms, and Patrick carries Jackie in a different orbit, careful not to cross paths, she thinks back to what they said earlier that evening. She'd thrown at him, **Why did you marry me?** But what she hadn't had the guts to say was, **Did you marry me for my money?** Because that's the elephant in the room—the fact that neither of

them has been willing to acknowledge. Only two months ago, Stephanie became the sole trustee of the trust that her parents left her when they died together in a car accident when she was a teenager. They'd left all their money to their only child, and she'd received all of it—worth over two million dollars—on her thirtieth birthday. No strings.

This has been preying on her mind, along with everything else. The seed of doubt has been planted by Erica, has taken root. Patrick had collected the insurance money on his first wife. Of course, that in itself doesn't mean anything. But now, with all these unwelcome revelations . . .

She's so tired it's making her dizzy; she lurches on her feet. She feels fat and sloppy and unattractive, so full of doubts about herself. A mother who can't even get her babies to go to sleep, as if she is defective somehow. She's not sure of anything. She thought Patrick loved her. But might he have married her for her inheritance? They have no prenup. They both thought the idea was ridiculous—they were so in love, after all. But it's a lot of money.

If she dies, according to the wills she and Patrick made after they were married, Patrick gets everything. And there's the life insurance—a million dollars.

In these dark, strung out, hopeless hours, it makes her think.

. . .

A FEW DAYS pass quietly and Stephanie is beginning to hope that Erica has given up after all. They haven't heard from her, not since she left her unwelcome "gift" for the twins. Maybe everything will still be all right.

Stephanie is at home when there's a knock at the door. She looks out the living-room window to see who it is. She's afraid it might be Erica, just when she's been thinking that she might be out of their lives. It's the postman.

She opens the door. He hands her a registered letter.

"Sign here, please."

Stephanie signs, and takes the letter. She closes the door and sees from the envelope that it's from the Coroner's Office of Grant County, Colorado. She sinks back against the door and slides to the floor, feels the tightness in her chest beginning. She takes several deep breaths, her eyes closed, but the tightness doesn't go away. Finally, she looks down at the envelope, trembling in her hands. It's addressed to Patrick but she rips it open. Her eyes blur, but she forces them to focus.

There's going to be an inquest into the death of Lindsey Kilgour.

"FUCK!" PATRICK SAYS when he comes home and sees the letter. He reads the whole thing through, swearing as he does, and then tosses it onto the

kitchen table. "I can't believe she's going through with it!"

The twins begin to cry, loud and insistent. Patrick ignores them. "This is—this is fucking outrageous!"

He closes his eyes and exhales deeply. Suddenly he's exhausted, as if he carries the weight of the entire world on his shoulders. He can't keep this quiet any longer. "I'm going to have to tell Niall about this. I can't hide the inquest from him. I'll have to be off work and it's probably going to be in the news." He opens his weary eyes and sees his wife's frightened face. Patrick adds bitterly, "I wonder how he'll feel when he realizes the kind of woman he's been sleeping with?"

"When will you tell him?" Stephanie asks.

He runs a hand anxiously through his hair. "Tomorrow, at the end of the day."

THE FOLLOWING DAY, Niall sits behind his desk, long after everyone else has gone home, overcome with shock and disbelief. He dreads facing his wife. He will have to tell her.

He knew something had been going on with Patrick—something more than just colicky twins. He was right—Patrick's being blackmailed, by the very woman Niall had been sleeping with. And now he has to tell Nancy—it's going to be in the news, their business will probably take a hit. And

Nancy still hasn't decided whether she's going to divorce him.

Patrick doesn't know Niall was sleeping with Erica, and Niall's going to keep it that way. He's horrified at the lies Patrick said she's telling about him. Erica is a blackmailer—maybe it's a good thing that Nancy discovered their affair on her own, before Erica had a chance to ask him for money to keep it to herself. All of it makes him terribly uneasy. Patrick and Erica had known each other all along and had pretended not to. And he'd had no idea.

Niall drives home and lets himself into the house. He finds Nancy in the kitchen, cleaning up. She turns around, and for the first time in days she actually has a smile on her face—until she sees him.

"What's wrong?" she asks quickly.

"We have to talk," he says, and sits down heavily at the kitchen table. She joins him, alarm in her eyes.

"I've had some terrible news today," he says. He tells her in detail about the pending inquest, that a woman has been trying to blackmail Patrick, making up lies, accusing him of murdering his first wife, a death that was clearly an accident.

"Oh my God," Nancy whispers, shaken. "Of course he didn't do it. He did the right thing to stand up to her." She brings a hand to her mouth. "Poor Stephanie."

Niall nods. "She's telling terrible lies—but what if they believe her over him?"

"They won't—of course they won't."

He hangs his head, takes her hand in his. "Honey, there's something you need to know." He can feel his face draining of color, he feels light-headed, as if he might be sick.

She looks intently at him. "What is it? Niall, you're scaring me."

"The woman who's accusing him—it's Erica Voss."

NANCY STARES BACK at her husband, speechless. She can't quite get her mind around what he's telling her. It takes her a few seconds to process what he's saying. But it must be true because Niall looks awful. "How is that possible?" she says stupidly.

"I didn't know, Nancy," Niall insists. "I had no clue about any of this! If I'd known what she was like, I would have stayed a million miles away from her!"

Nancy remembers then, her confrontation with Erica in her apartment, her sense that this woman was no pushover, like Anne O'Dowd had been. No, she's something else entirely.

Nancy is struck suddenly with a horrible, overwhelming fear that crowds out everything else. She whispers to her husband, "Do you think she

knows?" Her fear is enormous—she can see it reflected in his eyes, and she knows he's already arrived at the same terrifying thought.

"No. She can't. How could she?" he says. But he looks petrified.

# 33

## SIX WEEKS LATER

Cheryl and Gary have started to relax a little. They haven't seen Erica since Cheryl found her sitting in a convertible outside their house several weeks ago. Maybe they'll never see her again; that is what they both hope for.

In these last few weeks, Cheryl has begun to notice some subtle changes in Devin—moodiness, a certain self-centeredness that she's not used to. Kids go through phases, everybody knows that. But she's keeping an eye on it.

She takes the newspaper and her coffee into the living room. Gary has gone to work and Devin has already left for school. She sees an article on the front page of the Denver newspaper: INQUEST TODAY INTO DEATH OF PREGNANT WOMAN IN SNOWBOUND CAR.

She reads the article with interest. She remembers

the original story; it made all the Denver papers. It had resonated with her because the woman who died was pregnant. It was so sad. She's startled now to see that there are some questions about it, that it might not have been an accident after all.

How awful, she thinks.

She'll have to watch the news at six and get the details.

PATRICK IS WEARING a well-cut navy-blue suit, a white shirt, and a conservative blue tie. He has been advised by his lawyer on his attire, and everything else. He sits in the stopped taxi in front of the local courthouse in Creemore, Colorado, leery of the reporters standing nearby, waiting for him. The time has come. The air is brisk now; it's mid-October, and it's always cooler in the mountains. They arrived here last night, he and Stephanie, for what is expected to be a one-day hearing. The twins are staying in Aylesford with Stephanie's friend Hanna.

It feels strange to be back here, in Creemore.

It's been a hellish few weeks. The notification of the coroner's inquest, the meeting with the lawyer in Denver, his concern about Stephanie. The twins have finally and rather suddenly gotten over their colic—the only good thing that's happened in the last few shitty weeks. They now go down without too much fuss at around 10:00 p.m. and sleep

until about 6:00 a.m. The screaming and crying stopped without warning, just like the doctor said it would. They couldn't believe it, kept expecting the peace to end.

But it hasn't been the blessing they hoped for, because Stephanie seems to have lost the habit of sleep. She is now plagued with insomnia, all, no doubt, because of him. She lies in bed staring into the dark, or wanders the house in the middle of the night like some tortured Lady Macbeth. She looks worn out, her shoulder-length hair limp, her skin pale, her eyes puffy. She no longer wears makeup, although she has made an effort today. His attorney had impressed upon her how important appearances are at times like this—she must look well rested, confident, and supportive of her husband. She looks none of these things, he thinks, glancing sidelong at her. He hadn't wanted her to come. He thought it would be too much for her, and that she should stay home with the twins. But the attorney felt it was important that she be there.

And she'd wanted to come. In fact, she had insisted on it.

He desperately wants this to be over—for the jury to quickly find that the death was accidental so that they can go home and put this behind them. Stephanie will finally start to sleep again, she will regain her equilibrium, and things will go back to normal. And Erica won't be able to touch them.

They've sat in the cab for too long, and now

the reporters are swarming around the vehicle. Stephanie looks at him, tense.

"It's going to be all right, Stephanie," he says. "After today, this will all be over." He reaches out and tucks a strand of hair behind her ear and kisses her on the cheek. She nods at him and turns away to unbuckle her seat belt.

They get out of the cab and begin to walk. Television crews follow them, and reporters with large microphones. Of course. This is big news in this little town—and in Denver, and even across the state. He'd seen the paper at breakfast this morning in the hotel: INQUEST TODAY INTO DEATH OF PREGNANT WOMAN IN SNOWBOUND CAR.

He'd read the entire article and then passed it to his wife. It didn't say anything they didn't know already; there was nothing in the article about Erica and what she might say. The journalists shout their questions.

**Was it really an accident?**

**Mr. Kilgour, did you deliberately kill your wife?**

Why do they even ask such questions, Patrick thinks bitterly, striding forward, holding Stephanie's hand—do they expect him to answer?

**Do you know what new evidence has been uncovered?**

**Do you have anything to say in your defense?**

Stephanie stumbles twice, latching on to his arm for support. He helps her up the steps and inside.

Somehow they make it without Patrick lashing out at anyone.

It's a modern room with a dais at the front, a witness box, long tables for the lawyers. This is supposed to be a nonadversarial proceeding, a fact-finding mission, but to Patrick, it doesn't feel that way. His eyes shift over to the jury box, now empty. He shudders involuntarily.

The coroner's inquest is in open court, with the public and the media permitted to attend. And they've taken advantage; the place is almost full. The press is keen to hear salacious details about how he might have deliberately murdered his wife and unborn child. How they will love this, Patrick thinks, his bitterness growing. Patrick sits down in the first row of seats, with Stephanie rigid beside him. The sheriff who questioned him after the accident, and the coroner, will be called as witnesses. He and Erica will be called. There shouldn't be any surprises. He glances at Stephanie, tense beside him.

Patrick's gaze sweeps the courtroom nervously. Then, suddenly, he sees the sheriff, Michael Bewdly. Patrick almost didn't recognize him because he's not in uniform. He's in plain clothes now—he's not the Grant County sheriff anymore. Patrick's attorney, Robert Lange, has told him that the former sheriff will probably be adamant that they made the right finding. Next he sees the current sheriff arrive—his uniform gives him away—and take a

seat on the other side of the courtroom. He will be at the inquest to listen to the evidence, Lange warned, in case, after the jury returns its verdict, he needs to decide whether to move ahead with further investigation or criminal charges. Patrick looks at the sheriff and swallows, then turns away, his eyes searching the courtroom. He recognizes Lauren, Lindsey's sister, sitting toward the back, as if she doesn't want anyone to know she's there. Then— another face he recognizes, although the man is somewhat older. It's the coroner, George Yancik. He was there that day, leaning over Lindsey's body in the snow, studying the car in the snowbank. But it's Erica who worries him. It's her word against his. Where is she?

He hears a slight commotion behind him and turns to look. It's her, as if he'd summoned her somehow. She's in a charcoal-gray business suit, her hair up, makeup kept to a minimum. She looks professional, and he feels a tremor of fear run up his spine. He's afraid she will come across better than he will—it has been his fear all along that they will believe her over him. He feels Stephanie stiffen as Erica sits in the front row on the opposite side of the room without looking at either of them.

Lange comes up to Patrick then and leans in close. "You okay?" He glances quickly at Stephanie, as if worried about how she's holding up.

Patrick nods. "We're fine."

"Good, we're about to start." Lange moves away and sits at counsel's table.

Moments later, the six jurors file in and take their seats with a minimum of fuss. Patrick, unsettled, watches them come in. These six people might determine the course of the rest of his life. The idea frightens him. He has never thought of himself as a coward, but right now, he's scared. He feels himself clenching his jaw and forces himself to relax as the judge enters from a side door and sits at the dais. The jurors are sworn in. The coroner is represented by an attorney by the name of Susan Spellman. Patrick has elected to be represented by his own counsel.

They begin. The judge addresses the court with opening remarks. Coroner's counsel then addresses the jury and calls the first witness. Patrick knows that as each witness is called, Lange will have the opportunity to ask relevant questions of the witnesses and challenge them in cross-examination.

First the coroner's attorney calls the coroner, George Yancik.

# 34

Yancik walks briskly to the witness box. As he takes his place, Patrick notes that he seems slightly nervous as he's sworn in. That's not what they want. They don't want the coroner to be on the defensive. It makes Patrick anxious too.

Once they establish his credentials, the attorney asks, "Did you, as the Grant County coroner at the time, attend at 712 Dupont Street, Creemore, on the morning of January 10, 2009?"

"Yes, I did."

"Tell us about that morning, and what you found there."

The coroner says, in a clipped voice, "A 911 call had come in at eight twenty-nine a.m. I was notified of the sudden death of a woman and made my way there immediately. When I got there, a woman had been pulled out of a vehicle and laid

out on the snow." He clears his throat. "I observed the heightened color indicative of carbon monoxide poisoning and declared her dead at the scene."

"Can you tell us what you did then?"

"I spoke to the woman's husband, Patrick Kilgour. He was obviously distraught. I asked him what had happened and he told me that his wife had been waiting inside the running car while he shoveled it out. It had been snowing heavily for a couple of days before. I immediately examined the vehicle. It was parked at the end of a cul-de-sac, backed almost into a snowbank. The exhaust pipe was packed with snow. From this I determined that it was most likely the victim had died of carbon monoxide poisoning, but I ordered an autopsy, to be sure."

"And who performed the autopsy?"

"I contracted it out to one of the forensic pathologists we use, Karen Soley."

"Did you make any further investigations into the death of Lindsey Kilgour?"

Yancik shifts uncomfortably in his chair. "Well, as coroner, it is my responsibility to investigate deaths. I took charge of the scene, ordered the body to be taken away and autopsied. The sheriff at the time, Mike Bewdly, questioned the husband, Patrick Kilgour, down at the Sheriff's Office, as he appeared to be the only actual witness. The sheriff spoke to me afterward about that conversation."

"And what did the autopsy show?"

"The autopsy confirmed that the victim died of carbon monoxide poisoning."

"And was there anything revealed in the questioning of Patrick Kilgour, as reported to you by the sheriff, that led you to have any suspicions as to the manner of death?"

"No, not at all."

"And based on your observations, your investigation, and the autopsy, what was your conclusion?"

"I concluded that the death had been accidental."

"Thank you."

Patrick's attorney stands and says, "No questions, your honor."

The coroner leaves the stand and retakes his seat.

Susan Spellman says, "I call Michael Bewdly to the stand."

Michael Bewdly rises and moves heavily to the witness stand. Patrick watches him closely.

"You were the Grant County sheriff at the time of the death of Lindsey Kilgour, is that right?" the attorney asks, once the witness has been sworn in.

"Yes."

"Tell us what happened after the coroner arrived."

"The coroner arrived and took control of the scene, as was proper. Once that was done, I escorted Patrick Kilgour to the Sheriff's Office to speak to him about what had happened."

"And what did he tell you?"

"He told us—myself and my investigating officer at the time, Dan Abbott—that his wife had got in the car to stay warm until he'd finished shoveling. When questioned, he said he was unaware that the exhaust pipe of the car was plugged, and unaware of the dangers of such an occurrence." The former sheriff clears his throat and volunteers, "This happens every year somewhere in the United States after a heavy snowfall—people aren't as aware of the dangers as they should be."

"Did you have any suspicion at all that it might have been deliberate?"

"None at all."

"Did you ask him if he had a policy of life insurance on his wife?"

"No."

"Did you ask him about the state of his marriage?"

"No."

"Thank you."

Again, Lange stands up and says, "Why did you not ask Patrick Kilgour about his marriage, or about possible life insurance?"

"It—it was just so obviously a tragic accident, I didn't think it was necessary."

"No more questions, your honor," Lange says and sits down.

So far, everything is going their way, of course.

Patrick has nothing to worry about until Erica takes the stand. He tries to relax, but knowing she will appear makes that impossible.

Ms. Spellman says, "Next I'd like to call Ken Dingwall."

Once the witness is sworn, the attorney asks, "Mr. Dingwall, did you underwrite a life insurance policy on Lindsey Kilgour?"

"Yes."

"And what were the circumstances surrounding the purchase of that policy?"

"The two of them, Patrick and Lindsey Kilgour, came into the office in November of 2008. They explained that they were newlyweds—they were obviously expecting a baby—and wanted life insurance policies on both of them."

"And how much were these policies for?"

"One hundred thousand dollars each, with a further one hundred thousand each in the event of accidental death."

Patrick hears a buzz of excitement travel around the courtroom.

# 35

Stephanie hears the whispers and feels anger at everyone in the courtroom. They all want her husband to be guilty.

Ms. Spellman asks, "Is it . . . unusual to have an additional amount in the event of accidental death?"

The insurance professional is clear and confident. "No, not at all. Most young people are more likely to die from accidental death than from natural causes. So accidental death coverage is something we encourage."

Lange has no further questions, and the witness is sent back to his seat.

Stephanie feels her shoulders relax slightly. So far, it has gone well. But Erica hasn't given her evidence yet.

As if her mind has been read, Erica Voss is called to the stand, and Stephanie feels her heart begin to race. She watches Erica walk with noticeable poise

to the witness box, and then turns her attention to the jurors—how are they reacting to her? Everything boils down to whom they will believe—this woman, or her husband.

"Ms. Voss," Ms. Spellman says, "do you know Patrick Kilgour?"

"Yes, I do."

"Can you please explain the nature of your relationship with him?"

She nods. "I met Patrick through Lindsey, his wife. Lindsey and I were friends. In spite of that"— she hesitates and then says—"I had an affair with her husband, Patrick, in the weeks before her death."

There's a frisson of heightened interest in the courtroom. This is what they're all here for, Stephanie thinks bitterly. This much has been leaked; there had been mention of a possible affair in the newspaper. She has just confirmed it.

"A sexual affair?"

"Yes."

"Was this affair casual, or would you say it was serious?"

Erica appears to take a moment to compose herself and says clearly, "It was serious. We were in love."

Stephanie hears murmurs in the courtroom and several gasps. The jurors are looking at Erica with great interest. Stephanie glances at her husband

beside her; his profile is set, his jaw tight. He's staring at Erica as if he loathes her.

"How often did you meet?"

"It began one night when a bunch of us had gotten together for drinks. Lindsey had gone home earlier. Patrick and I both got drunk. We ended up back at my apartment, in bed. After that, we took every opportunity we could to be together, but it wasn't easy, because he was married, and Lindsey wanted him at home." She adds, "We would meet at lunchtimes during the week. His wife would make him a lunch to take to work, but he'd come to my apartment and we'd make love."

Stephanie hears the murmur of disapproval go around the courtroom.

"Did the two of you ever talk about being together, about telling his wife?"

"Yes. He told me he didn't love her, and he resented being tied down by her. He didn't want a baby at that stage in his life. They argued a lot. He said he wanted to be with me."

"Did you or he ever talk about making concrete plans to be together?"

Erica bites her lip. "Not in so many words. He said he wanted to be free of her. But I thought he was talking about divorce, not murder."

Another gasp around the courtroom; the judge bangs his gavel and everyone falls silent, riveted by her testimony.

"Tell us what happened on January 10, 2009."

"I got a phone call from Greg Miller. He was a friend of Patrick's, from work. We all used to socialize together. He called me and said there had been an accident. I got over there as fast as I could."

"Did you talk to Patrick?"

"No. I was in shock. He was hysterical, sobbing. But then, when no one was looking, he caught my eye, and—the look in his eyes was one of triumph."

"Triumph?"

"Yes. I knew then that he'd killed her on purpose, and that he thought he was going to get away with it." She pauses, looks suitably upset—the first break in her composure. "I think he expected me to be . . . glad."

Another murmur of shock makes its way across the courtroom.

"Did you speak to him after that?"

She shakes her head. "Not then. He tried to speak to me but I avoided him. I went to the funeral and I avoided him there too. I thought he'd killed her on purpose, because of me, but I was too afraid to say anything. I was afraid the police would think I was involved in it. I felt guilty—I thought he'd murdered her to be with me. I couldn't even look at him after that. I knew what he'd done." She pauses and then adds, "And by then I knew I was pregnant with his child."

More consternation in the courtroom. Stephanie tries to read the mood of the jurors, but she can't tell what they're thinking as they hang on Erica's every word, every gesture. She doesn't know if they believe Erica's story or not. It sounds so over the top.

"And what happened to that child?"

"I gave him up for adoption at birth. I don't know where he is."

"One last question. Did anyone else know about your affair? Can anyone confirm what you've told us?"

She shakes her head. "We didn't tell anyone. I've come forward now because I can't live with this anymore. I owe it to Lindsey to tell the truth. And I want the world to know what he did because I'm afraid for his current wife. I'm afraid he might do it again."

There is an audible gasp in the courtroom. Of horror? Or of disbelief?

"Thank you, Ms. Voss."

Stephanie watches anxiously as Lange stands up to cross-examine. He walks slowly toward the witness stand. "Ms. Voss. You say that you and Patrick Kilgour were 'in love.' Do you have any proof of that?"

"Well, no. We didn't tell anyone, and no one saw us, because we had to keep it secret."

"Right. So we only have your word for it. Do

you have any proof of the number of times that the two of you slept together?"

"I had his baby," she says, a little defiantly.

"You had **a** baby. We haven't determined that it was Mr. Kilgour's, have we?" He waits.

Finally she says, "No. But I know it was his."

"In any event, a single act of intercourse can result in pregnancy. Do you have any actual proof that the two of you slept together more than once or twice?"

"No."

"One more thing. Isn't it true that last August you approached Patrick Kilgour in Aylesford and attempted to blackmail him? Did you not threaten that if he didn't pay you money, you would tell his wife that you'd had an extramarital affair with him and that he'd deliberately killed his first wife— and when that didn't work, did you not threaten that you would try to have the investigation into Lindsey Kilgour's death reopened?"

Stephanie holds her breath.

Erica looks back at the attorney, perfectly calm. "Not at all. Is that what he told you? In fact, I approached him, in Aylesford, to tell him I was going to the authorities in Colorado with the truth. When I told him that, he tried to give me money. Cash. I refused to accept it and told him I couldn't be bought off."

Stephanie feels like she's had the breath sucked

out of her. She wants to leap up and yell, "She's lying!" But she's paralyzed. She looks at the attorney's face—he hadn't anticipated this, clearly, and is doing his best to recover. He'd expected a flat denial. Patrick has gone white.

# 36

Unable to shake Erica's story, Lange says he has no further questions. The judge calls a short lunch break, and when they reconvene, it's Patrick's turn to take the stand. Counsel to the coroner says, "I call Patrick Kilgour."

Stephanie can see that he's nervous. She squeezes his hand encouragingly as he rises, but he doesn't even look at her. He walks up and takes his place in the witness box as if he's going to his doom. At least, that's the way it looks to Stephanie.

Stephanie feels dizzy. She barely slept last night, plagued by insomnia, unaccustomed to being apart from the twins, worried about what would happen today. And she hadn't been able to get much food down at breakfast. Now she's feeling light-headed. Erica just perjured herself. Stephanie tries to focus on what's happening in front of her—it's so important, but her head is swimming, and the tightness in her chest is becoming unbearable.

Once Patrick is sworn in, Ms. Spellman says to him, "Tell us about the morning of January 10, 2009."

He has considerable poise, and Stephanie is relieved to see it. "We were going to Grand Junction to visit Lindsey's mother and sister. Lindsey was eager to go. It had been snowing heavily, so I didn't want to go, but she insisted. We did have a mild argument about that the night before, but I could see how important it was to her. It had been snowing since Thursday night, and I'd worked from home on Friday for that reason. By Saturday morning, the car was almost buried in snow. I went out to shovel out the car, turned it on to warm it up. She came out and got in the car to wait. I'd told her to wait in the house, but she was so eager to get going."

"Did you notice that the exhaust pipe was plugged with snow?"

"No. It didn't even occur to me to look. I didn't know that it could cause carbon monoxide to build up in the car. I blame myself for that every day."

Spellman asks, "Did you have an affair with Erica Voss before the death of your wife?"

Patrick takes a breath and says, "I did not have an affair with her. I slept with her exactly twice. Once at her apartment after we'd been drinking— that was the first time. And another time when she asked me to come over to her apartment on my

lunch hour to fix something. We wound up in bed together. I ended it after that."

"So you dispute what Erica Voss has said."

"I dispute it wholeheartedly. We had casual sex. Twice. That's it. We were not in love. She never indicated that she had any feelings for me. I loved my wife. I felt that Erica had deliberately seduced me both times. I was twenty-three years old. I'm not proud of cheating on my wife. I put an end to it. Quickly. I didn't want to jeopardize what I had with Lindsey."

"So your marriage was a good one?"

"Yes, absolutely."

"You didn't argue?"

"No. Certainly not much, anyway. We got along well."

"Did you try to talk to Erica after the death of your wife?"

"No. I'd been avoiding her since the second time in her apartment. I did approach her at the funeral—I tried to speak to everyone, to thank them for coming—but she turned her back on me. I was relieved, frankly. I didn't want anything to do with her."

"Did Erica Voss ever threaten you and demand money from you in return for her silence?"

"Yes, on several occasions, in August of this year."

"Did you ever pay her any money?"

"No."

"Did you ever offer her any money?"

"No."

"Thank you."

Patrick's own attorney stands and says, "No questions, your honor."

Stephanie watches her husband leave the witness box. He had conducted himself well. He'd been believable, perhaps even slightly more believable than Erica. But she doesn't know what the jurors are thinking. He sits down beside her and she clutches his hand and squeezes it fiercely. He squeezes her hand in return.

"Your honor, I call Dr. Karen Soley."

A heavy woman makes her way to the witness stand and is sworn in.

"State your name, please, and your credentials," Spellman says.

"My name is Karen Soley. I'm a forensic pathologist with Grant County."

"And did you perform the autopsy on Lindsey Kilgour?"

"Yes, I did."

"What were your findings?"

"I found that Lindsey had died of acute carbon monoxide poisoning. The baby had died in utero."

"Was there anything else of interest in the autopsy?"

"No, not at all."

Next, Ms. Spellman says, "I'd like to call Dr. Joseph Chang."

Stephanie feels Patrick start beside her. She glances at him, but he is facing forward. She wonders who this other doctor is. She doesn't have to wait long to find out.

"Can you state your qualifications?"

"I am an emergency doctor at Saint Brigid Hospital in Denver. "I've been there over twelve years now."

"And in the course of your work, did you ever have occasion to see Lindsey Kilgour in the emergency room at Saint Brigid Hospital?"

"Yes. I saw her late on the night"—he consults his notes—"of November 24, 2008. She had fallen down a flight of stairs and wanted the baby checked. She was about six and a half months pregnant at the time."

"She'd fallen down the stairs?"

"That's what she said."

A murmur runs through the audience.

"And did you examine her?"

"Yes. We performed an ultrasound and found that the baby was unharmed. But she—Lindsey— had fresh, extensive bruising along her back, as well as bruising and a contusion on the back of her head, under her hair—injuries consistent with a fall down a flight of stairs."

"And did you have any suspicions about this fall?"

"She insisted it was an accident. There was no reason—at that time—not to believe her."

# 37

Stephanie sinks back into her seat. She tries to breathe through the intensifying pain of a panic attack. She doesn't want anyone to see that she is in distress. Patrick is staring stoically straight ahead, but she can detect the tension in his clenched jaw. He looks stunned. She knows she shouldn't, but she dares to turn around and look at Erica. Erica's face shows shock. She didn't know about this, Stephanie realizes with a sickening feeling.

**What's going to happen now?**

As if in answer to her question, the judge bangs his gavel and says, "I'm calling a short recess. We'll resume in twenty minutes."

Stephanie and Patrick hurriedly retreat to a private room, ushered away by Lange, who closes the door behind them. His face is flushed. Stephanie is trying to make sense of what this might mean.

"Sit down," he directs them.

They both promptly sit. He remains standing, looking down at Patrick, his expression severe. "Why didn't you tell me about this before?"

"I don't like your tone," Patrick says, looking like he's spoiling for a fight.

"You have a lot more to worry about right now than my tone," the attorney replies sharply.

Stephanie watches her husband swallow; her chest is so tight it's almost unbearable. But they don't notice the distress she's in; she's become so good at hiding it.

"It slipped my mind," Patrick says sullenly.

"You expect me to believe that?" the attorney says angrily.

Patrick remains stonily silent, refusing to look at his attorney.

"Tell us what happened."

"She fell down the flight of stairs from the kitchen to the back door. She was tired and missed the top step when she was taking out the garbage."

Stephanie puts a hand to her mouth, feels the bile rising in her throat. He's never told any of them about this before. Why was Lindsey taking out the garbage? Why didn't he take the garbage out for her? She was six and a half months pregnant. Patrick always takes the garbage out for her. Did he simply **forget** that she had fallen down the stairs and been to the hospital a few weeks before she died? Did he not see how damning that might look? She wonders if he's lying.

"Where were you?"

"I was in the kitchen."

"Were you arguing?" Lange asks.

Patrick looks up at his lawyer coldly. "No. I wasn't anywhere near her. She fell on her own."

Stephanie looks at Patrick's attorney. He looks grim, and her heart sinks further. She knows, now, that they're in trouble. She feels as if she's floating up, out of her body. She knows tiredness can wreak havoc with her perceptions, and it's almost a relief, to feel as if she's floating away, away from what's going on here in this claustrophobic room in the courthouse. She wonders in a strange, detached way if they argued, if they **fought**, despite her husband's denials, and whether he pushed his wife down the stairs. She knows his lawyer is wondering the same thing. Patrick has never been violent with her. Was he violent with his first wife? Is it possible? The moment of silence seems to go on forever, as if they are all poised on the brink of disaster, and no one wants to move forward.

But finally the attorney glances at his watch and says, "You're going to have to explain."

Patrick nods.

"And you're going to have to be convincing."

WHEN PATRICK IS RECALLED to the stand, he rises and walks the short distance across the courtroom floor. He feels as if all his senses are heightened.

He reminds himself not to look angry. He must not show how angry he is to be here, defending himself against these accusations, no matter how justified that anger is. It should never have come to this. It's all because of Erica. How dare she lie about the blackmail? But he must not think about Erica, because she makes him angriest of all. He won't look at her when he reaches the stand, turns around, and sits facing the people in the crowded courtroom. He will look only at counsel asking him questions. He will keep his voice mild and even, and explain what happened. They will believe him. They must. They believed him before—he could feel it. He could sense in the courtroom, just a short while ago, that the jury was on his side, not Erica's. But this bit about the bruises has pushed them away from him, he knows it. He knows how it looks. His lawyer is worried, and his wife—he can sense that she has begun to doubt him, and it has unmoored him. This has upset her. He no longer knows what she believes.

He remembers that night. He'd seen Lindsey fall down the stairs, saw the whole thing happen as if in slow motion. He'd been afraid that some- one might dig up that hospital visit and try to make something out of it. But he didn't think they would.

The counsel for the coroner asks, her voice sol- emn, "Can you explain how your wife got these bruises?"

· · ·

CHERYL TURNS ON the evening news in the kitchen while she's preparing supper. She hears a reporter start talking about the inquest today in Creemore and turns to look at the television screen. She watches footage of a dark-haired, harassed-looking couple hurrying into the courthouse, and then of a blond woman following in after them. Cheryl's entire body tenses when she recognizes Erica Voss. What the hell has she got to do with this?

Cheryl turns up the volume and listens to the reporter give the highlights from the inquest. She hears it all. Erica Voss claims that she was having an affair with Patrick Kilgour, whose wife died in that car. She says Kilgour deliberately murdered his wife. She had his child. Cheryl works it out. That child is Devin. And his father is, quite possibly, a murderer.

THE EXCRUCIATING INQUEST is over. They have retreated to a nearby Italian restaurant for dinner. They've chosen a table at the back, which affords them more privacy.

Patrick had explained the fall down the stairs that night in a calm, convincing way. Lange seemed pleased with how he had handled himself, even patting him briefly on the shoulder when it was all over.

Stephanie orders a glass of white wine and tips almost half of it down her dry throat once it arrives. They now have to wait for the verdict. They're all nervous. Stephanie is so wrung out that she's simply glad the ordeal of the inquest is over. She can't think about what happens next. Lange wants to discuss where things might go from here. She wants to scream.

They order food, but she can hardly eat. Her mind drifts to Jackie and Emmie. She longs to hold them close to her, to smell them, to feel their skin against her face. She wants to be home. They're flying back first thing tomorrow morning, whether the jury has come to a decision or not, and regardless of the outcome.

She knows what the possibilities are. The jury might find that Lindsey's death was an accident. This is what they all clearly hope for. But she now thinks it's about as likely as winning the lottery. Erica was convincing, and there was that worrying fall. If they don't return a verdict of accidental death, the current sheriff would likely undertake his own investigation. He might even arrest Patrick immediately. She realizes, lifting her now empty wineglass, that she might be going home alone tomorrow. Would that be such a bad thing?

She feels a sudden lurch in her chest. She can't believe she's even thinking that. But that fall down the stairs—and the fact that Patrick had hidden it from them—has changed things for her. She puts

the wineglass down. She wants another, but she will resist. She feels like she's secretly just crossed some kind of line, and she's horrified at herself.

**Of course he didn't do it.**

She loves Patrick, she tells herself. He's the father of her girls. It's just hard to feel it in the same way as before, given all the strain they've been under. She doesn't believe for a second that he's a **murderer**. That's impossible. Too bizarre to seriously consider. He's never shown any tendency toward violence to her at all. Lindsey must have fallen, the way Patrick said. He didn't push her during an argument. He doesn't lose his temper easily—she's never seen it. He's not greedy, or selfish. He's not impulsive. He's kind and patient and generous. All this is Erica's fault. Erica is a vindictive liar, driven by her own selfish, twisted motives. She's got no conscience at all. She doesn't care who she hurts.

It's quite possible the jury will return a finding of "undetermined." That the jury will be unable to decide, on the basis of what they've heard, whether the death was accidental or intentionally caused. The jury can't assign blame. It would be up to the sheriff then. He might investigate, he might not. He probably would. Stephanie doesn't think she can live with this much uncertainty any longer without losing her mind. She needs to be a good mother to her children. She needs this to stop.

A cell phone pings and Lange reaches for his phone in his suit jacket pocket. She can tell by the

look on his face that it's what they've been wait-
ing for. She freezes, watching his face. "The jury's
back," he says.

They quickly leave the restaurant, the meal fin-
ished, and drive the short way to the courthouse.
They take their seats as the jury files in.

The judge asks the foreperson if they have
reached a verdict. They have.

Stephanie feels like she's going to pass out.

"What is your verdict?" the judge asks.

"Undetermined, your honor."

Stephanie looks at Patrick; she sees him actu-
ally flinch. She glances at Lange. His expression
is grim.

The ensuing silence is one laden with terror. It's
not over, not at all. It might be just beginning.
Stephanie stares at her husband. He's gone blood-
less. She realizes, watching him, that he expected
a different finding. He expected to be exonerated.

Finally Patrick says to his attorney, his voice
quaking, "What do we do now?"

"It's up to the sheriff," the lawyer says quietly,
"and the district attorney. You go home and wait."

# 38

That evening, Sheriff Bastedo sits at his desk in his office, in the dark, deep in thought. He's not particularly happy that this mess has landed on his desk. He knows it's an opportunity. And that's what worries him. It's an opportunity that could make or break him, and he would rather keep his head low. He's steady and methodical—that works for him—but he can already tell that this case has all the makings of a circus. But he can't just turn a blind eye. That's what the last sheriff did, and it might have resulted in Patrick Kilgour getting away with murder.

He had watched the inquest with great attention, taking careful notes. When it was over, he was just as unsure as the jurors. He's cautious by nature, but he's aware of the pressure on him to do something. He must talk to the district attorney first thing in the morning.

.   .   .

PATRICK STRUGGLES TO WAKE the next morning when his phone alarm goes off at 5:30. He'd only gotten to sleep after 3:00 a.m. He feels like shit. Stephanie stirs beside him.

"Come on, we have to catch a plane," he says and gets up and pads to the bathroom of their hotel room. He steps into the shower, letting the hot water wash away the cobwebs. But clarity is worse. He's terrified of what might happen next. He tries to remember what his attorney said last night, but he was so distraught that some of it hadn't really sunk in. His mind starts to spin out of control. If he's arrested, and the case goes to trial, he probably won't be able to get out on bail. He might have to spend months in prison, away from his wife and children. At trial, they would have to prove he murdered his wife beyond a reasonable doubt. But there is a lot of doubt in this case. There's no dispute about the facts; they don't have to worry about forensics. They know his wife got into the running car and that the tailpipe was blocked with snow. "They can't prove you stuffed the exhaust pipe yourself," the attorney said bluntly, "or that you let her sit in the running car knowing that it was blocked and that it would kill her." This is all about his intention, and surely there's no way they can prove his intention beyond a reasonable doubt. This is what Lange told him last night, trying to

reassure him as he felt his once-comfortable life slipping away from him on a tidal wave of fear. "They might feel they have to bring you in," Lange said. "But it shouldn't go to trial. They haven't got sufficient evidence."

But the stigma—everyone will think he did it. He will be tainted by this for the rest of his life. There is no way for him to prove he **didn't** mean to kill her.

No way to prove it—even to his wife.

This was not the result they'd hoped for. Stephanie won't be able to go home now and put it all out of her mind—she'll be waiting for the next thing to happen. There will be no chance for her to recover her equilibrium.

And Niall—his partner had been supportive when he heard about the coming inquest, but he hadn't liked the optics. Patrick told him that he understood. But there has been a deepening rift between the two men since Patrick had told him.

Patrick knows that anything less than a complete exoneration won't be good enough for Niall. And he didn't get that.

Now—will Niall want to dissolve the partnership? How would Stephanie take it? Not well, he suspects.

They might have to live for the next while on Stephanie's money. And the legal costs—they are going to be exorbitant, if this goes any further.

He goes back into the bedroom and Stephanie

is up, getting dressed. She doesn't speak. She's said almost nothing to him since the inquest ended. He wants to know what's going through her mind. "Steph?" he says.

"Yes?" she answers, her back still turned to him as she pulls a shirt on over her bra. She doesn't even look at him.

"Stephanie," he repeats, "look at me." She turns slowly around, standing on the other side of the unmade bed, across from him. "It's going to be okay. I didn't do this, and they can't prove that I did." She nods. He walks around the end of the bed and takes her in his arms. "Steph, I love you. You know that, don't you?" She looks up at him and there are tears in her eyes. One tumbles down her face and he wipes it gently away with a finger. "We'll get through this, I know we will."

She turns away.

"I CAN'T BELIEVE IT," Niall says. "I can't fucking believe it."

Nancy can't believe it either, but they were up early and they've both read the online news— everything they can find on the inquest in Colorado. Now Nancy looks up from the laptop at the kitchen table and says, "You'd better eat something."

He shakes his head, visibly upset as he leans back against the kitchen counter. She pushes back

her chair and walks over to the coffee machine, pours him a fresh cup and hands it to him. He turns to her in disbelief and says, "I mean, it must have been an accident. Patrick wouldn't murder his wife!"

The verdict wasn't what they'd been expecting. "She's obviously lying," Nancy agrees, but the information that had come out at the inquest had been rather shocking. She wonders how Stephanie is handling it all. She feels a terrible pity for her.

But what she feels most is alarm. "He certainly picked the wrong woman to sleep with," she says spitefully, "and so did you."

Niall closes his eyes and says, "Nancy, don't start."

She takes a deep breath. He's right. They have to stick together; they can't tear each other apart, not now. She says, more calmly, "You're going to have to cut ties with Patrick."

His eyes open. "Nancy, maybe we should wait and see what happens. They haven't arrested him."

"They haven't arrested him **yet**," she says. "You have to cut him loose. More importantly, we have to distance ourselves from Erica. As long as you stand by Patrick, if he's working with you, you'll be in her sights." She adds anxiously, "She keeps calling you—it borders on harassment." He nods back at her, looking troubled.

She knows she's right. He's as worried about Erica as she is.

"I just hate to kick a friend when he's down," he says angrily.

"You don't have a choice. You can end the partnership. Bring in someone else. But be kind about it; surely he'll understand."

IN DENVER, Cheryl paces the kitchen wringing her hands while Gary stares at the floor. The newspaper is spread out on the kitchen table. They're alone—Devin went to school early for soccer practice.

"She's obviously lying about the blackmail," Gary says eventually. "She did it to us—there's no doubt in my mind that she blackmailed him."

"Should we tell them?" Cheryl asks tentatively.

"We can't."

Cheryl puts her face in her hands and bursts into tears. "I can't believe this is happening," she sobs. She hears the scrape of a chair and then feels her husband's arms around her as he holds her tight. When she's cried herself out, she pulls back from him and says, "What kind of woman does this? She could be lying about everything at that inquest. She's Devin's **mother.** She could be some kind of sociopath. What if that's genetic?"

She can feel herself losing it. Her perfect child. Gary looks back at her; she can tell he's deeply unsettled by this too. She continues, "And what

if it's true that he killed his wife—his pregnant wife—on purpose? He can't be normal either, and he's Devin's biological **father**. I can't deal with this. I can't!"

Gary looks directly into her eyes and says, "Listen to me. Devin's a great kid. He's had a great upbringing. He'll be fine. You're such a good mother—he's turning out great, you know that. Please don't worry. He has us. He'll always have us."

SHERIFF BASTEDO MAKES HIS WAY to the district attorney's office. He'd had a quick conversation over the phone with the coroner, Yancik, early that morning. They'd discussed the verdict, what it meant.

"This is messy," Yancik said unhappily. "How did Mike miss this? It's making us all look bad."

Bastedo remembers how sheepish the previous sheriff had looked the day before in court, but isn't terribly sympathetic. He knows Yancik is feeling defensive; but none of this is making Bastedo look bad. He wasn't around back then. But he knows what Yancik means. There's enough pressure on the coroner's office these days without this kind of fuck-up. And he's right that it's messy.

"The question is what to do now," Bastedo said. He'd been thinking about it all night. "I'm seeing the DA this morning."

"What do you think she'll want to do?"

"I don't know. But I'll let you know what she says."

Now, as the sheriff arrives at the district attorney's office, he sees her nameplate on her door. Aurora Lydia Dominguez. There's not a lot of crime in their rural community, but this is rather huge. She will want to look at it carefully. She has her own position to consider too. Everyone has their own angle to consider, Bastedo thinks, a little cynically.

"Come in," Dominguez says when he knocks on her door.

She's in her late thirties. Her dark hair is in a tidy ponytail, and she's wearing a good suit, sensible shoes. He spots a pair of black heels in the corner. She's too smart to wear those all day. He trusts her to make the right decision on this. He doesn't know what the right decision is—he's hoping she does.

"Close the door," she says.

# 39

The flight home is a nightmare. Stephanie keeps seeing people glancing at her, looking again; they recognize her. The story is in the newspapers this morning, and their pictures too. They have been on TV, clips of them going into and out of the courthouse. Even though she's put her hair up and is wearing dark sunglasses, people know who she is, because Patrick looks just the same.

When they finally arrive home from the airport and park the car in the driveway, all Stephanie wants to do is drop their things and run across the street to Hanna's and get her babies. She doesn't wait for Patrick to accompany her; she'd rather he didn't. "Can you get things ready here, and I'll bring the twins home? They'll need to be fed."

With that, she walks across the street, her heart bursting with anxiety. How have the twins fared without her? She felt so bad leaving them. But she'd

left a bunch of breast milk with Hanna for them, and she'd trust Hanna with her babies over anyone else. But now, as she heads toward Hanna's house, desperate to see her daughters, she falters. How will Hanna react? It wasn't the verdict Stephanie had said they expected.

A few weeks ago, she'd told Hanna about the impending inquest. She'd gone over to Hanna's with the babies. She put the girls with little Teddy on play mats on the living-room floor. Stephanie had never said anything to Hanna about it before, but the date for the inquest was looming and she knew she had to tell Hanna the truth about why she needed her to watch the twins for two nights. It would be on the news. She would find out soon enough.

Watching the different emotions on Hanna's face as she stumbled through the story—disbelief, uneasiness—intensified the acute dismay Stephanie had been feeling over the last weeks. She knew Patrick had had a similar, difficult conversation with his business partner. He'd told her Niall took it well. She wasn't sure she believed him. But Hanna had been surprisingly supportive, once she'd gotten over the shock. Now Hanna feels like the closest thing she's got to a shoulder to lean on. Stephanie wishes again that she had family—that her parents were still alive, that she'd had siblings. She feels terribly alone in

the world. The one person she'd come to depend on was Patrick.

Hanna answers the door with a sympathetic frown on her face and immediately reaches out to hug her. Stephanie feels herself sinking into the comfort of Hanna's arms. The two women separate and without speaking of the verdict—which Hanna must already know from watching the news—Stephanie asks breathlessly, "Where are they?"

Hanna steps back and Stephanie can see her twins in the living room from here. She slips off her shoes and rushes to them. She sinks down on the carpeted floor and pulls her babies to her, breathing them in, feeling their warm bodies against her. She tries not to cry, but the tears spill forth anyway. And then she thinks, fuck it, what mother wouldn't cry on seeing her babies again after a whole day and two nights? She cuddles them, knowing that she would do anything for her children. They are the world to her.

She looks up as Hanna comes into the living room, smiling down at her. "They were great. Fed well and slept well. But they're obviously happy to have you back."

Stephanie regards her smiling, babbling infants, both of whom are starting to root for her breasts. She needs to take them home.

"I'll help you gather up their stuff," Hanna

says, beginning to pack toys and blankets into the baby bag.

"Thanks so much, Hanna. If there's any way I can ever repay you—"

"Oh, please don't worry about it. It was my pleasure."

"I know, but if you ever want to leave Teddy with us, we'd be happy to take him."

Stephanie notices something come over Hanna's face, but it quickly disappears. And she realizes that Hanna will never leave little Teddy with them. Because Patrick may have murdered his wife.

The chill Stephanie feels follows her all the way back across the street to her own house and settles in her heart, to make a permanent home there.

SHERIFF BASTEDO WAITS for the DA to sit down behind her desk and then settles himself heavily in the chair across from her.

"What a mess," Dominguez says. "A classic case of he said, she said. Who's telling the truth?"

"Or another way of looking at it," Bastedo says, "which one of them is lying?" He sees her eyebrows go up. He says, "One of them clearly is." He adds, "I'll have to bring him in for questioning."

She nods thoughtfully. "Yes, by all means, bring him in," she agrees, frowning. "But I don't want to prosecute something I don't have a good chance of winning." She leans forward, over her desk. "His

wife was in the running car, the tail pipe blocked with snow. Did he know? Did he do it on purpose? It will be practically impossible to prove the necessary intent for a murder-one conviction—unless he told someone what he was planning. And I'm sure he didn't."

"Maybe we could go after him on a lesser charge?"

She shakes her head, slowly. "No. He either did it deliberately, knowing what he was doing, or he didn't. If he didn't, it was an accident. We can't treat him differently from other cases like this unless he did it intentionally."

The sheriff nods. "I'll bring him in and ask him to take a polygraph."

She nods. "Try to wear him down. Maybe you can get him interested in a plea bargain."

PATRICK KNOWS NIALL isn't expecting him to come in to work today, but he wants to get this over with. He has to explain the unexpected verdict. Stephanie has a twin in each arm. "Why don't you try to rest," he says gently. "You look exhausted."

She nods absently. He kisses her on the top of her head and says, "Will you be okay if I go out for a bit?"

"Where are you going?" she asks, looking up at him.

"The office."

There's suddenly more tension in the room than

there was the second before. To each other, they had always pretended that only one verdict was possible—that it was an accident.

"How do you think he'll react?" she says now.

Patrick shrugs. "I don't know. None of us thought this would happen. We didn't really talk about it."

He turns to leave the room and says, "I won't be gone long."

STEPHANIE PACES THE LIVING ROOM, imagining what's going on at the office. Niall will want Patrick out. Anyone would. You can't have a business partner with a possible murder charge hanging over him.

She hears Patrick's car pull into the driveway. She stops and stands in the living room, waiting for him to come into the house. He enters, throws his keys on the table by the door, and turns to look at her. She can tell by the look on his face that the news is bad. "What happened?" she asks.

"He's going to dissolve the partnership."

"Can he do that?" she asks.

"Of course he can, according to the terms of the partnership agreement." He adds, "He'll buy me out."

She feels a stab of fury. "With friends like that," she says bitterly, "who needs enemies?"

. . .

ERICA SITS IN HER APARTMENT, nursing a cup of coffee.

**Undetermined**. Now the ball is in the sheriff's court. He will have to do something, after hearing the evidence. Patrick must be terrified. She thinks for a moment about his wife, Stephanie. She'd looked awful at the inquest. Thinner, but not in a good way. Her face was hollow. She must be going through hell, Erica thinks now. She tells herself that's not really her problem. She's doing Stephanie a favor. She should know what she married. She hopes they arrest him.

She tells herself that every cloud has a silver lining. She certainly thinks this one does.

# 40

For Stephanie, that first day back is a blur of fatigue, caring for the twins and worrying ceaselessly about the future. The weather has turned dark and wet, and people have begun preparing their yards for Halloween.

Stephanie can't stop thinking about the bruises on Lindsey's body. Did Patrick push her down the stairs? Could he have? She's seeing signs of stress in him, cracks in the façade that make her wonder. He'd snapped at her that afternoon for allowing them to run out of milk. She'd snapped right back.

Late that night, staring into the dark, she finds herself wondering what it was like for Lindsey, to marry so young, to be pregnant, to be alone all day in a place away from her family. They didn't have much money. Love flies out the window when the wolf is at the door. Did she know he had cheated on her? Did she suspect? Did she accuse

him? Maybe she did, and he didn't like it. Maybe that's why he pushed her down the stairs. . . . No. She can't think this way, she can't. It's just anger making her think like this, anger at him, at everything. Anger that he cheated on his first wife and brought all of this on himself, on her, and their beautiful daughters. They could lose everything because he slept with an attractive woman a couple of times when he shouldn't have. She's angriest of all at Erica—for sleeping with a friend's husband, for persisting with this crazy story about murder. For lying on the stand about the blackmail.

She tries not to blame Patrick for what he's done. Sleeping with his wife's best friend is unforgivable. So why has she forgiven him?

**Has** she forgiven him?

She still hasn't decided. She goes back and forth. He hasn't cheated on **her**, as far as she knows. Should she leave him anyway, on principle? Because once a cheater always a cheater? Even if nothing more happens with the case, and it all just goes away—the best they can hope for—people will look at her for the rest of her life and wonder if she's married to a murderer. She remembers the expression on Hanna's face when she offered to take Teddy.

If she left him now it would look like she didn't believe him, that she thought he was a murderer. She can't do that to him. And she has the babies

to think of—he's their father. They can't grow up thinking their mother believes their father murdered his first wife. Especially since it isn't true.

THE NEXT MORNING Patrick is out picking a few things up at the grocery store when the phone rings, and Stephanie reluctantly answers. "Hello?"

"May I speak to Patrick Kilgour?" a man asks. Immediately her body tenses. The voice is serious, authoritative.

"He's not here. May I ask who's calling?" she says, her heart racing.

"It's Sheriff Bastedo with the Grant County Sheriff's Office. Could you please have him call me as soon as he gets in?" He gives her a number, and she writes it down, her hand trembling, her mind panicking. When she hangs up the phone she walks into the living room and collapses onto the sofa. It's happening—they're going to arrest him. She feels dizziness wash over her. She puts her head down between her knees before everything goes black.

Moments later she hears Patrick return home. He must see her, she thinks, bent forward in what looks like a faint, but she can't lift her head.

"Stephanie, what is it?" Patrick cries. And then he's kneeling in front of her, his voice worried. "Are you all right?"

But she can't catch her breath. It feels like there's

a band across her chest and black spots are dancing in front of her eyes.

"Breathe," he tells her.

The moment passes. The black spots recede and she's able to lift her head and look at him. He brushes a lock of hair away from her face. "What's wrong, what happened?" he asks, his voice tense.

"You had a call," she says. "From the Grant County sheriff." She sees the fear settle on his face; they're both terrified. "He wants you to call him back. He left a number."

Patrick stands up quickly and looks down at her with frantic eyes. "What did he want?"

She looks back at him, frightened. "He didn't say. He just wants you to call back."

He begins pacing the room. "Fuck. **Fuck.**"

**There's no way out of this**, Stephanie thinks, starting to panic. They'll arrest him. He'll go to jail. He'll go to trial. She doesn't think she can survive a trial. The inquest was almost more than she could stand.

"I'm going to call Lange. Ask him what to do," Patrick says. She nods as he takes out his cell and makes the call.

Stephanie watches as Patrick talks to the attorney. It's a short conversation.

"What did he say?" she asks nervously.

"He told me not to panic," Patrick says with heavy sarcasm. "Easy for him to say. He wants me to find out what they want and call him back."

Patrick paces around the room a few more times, too agitated to phone the sheriff. She watches him go into the kitchen, hears him pouring himself a drink. He comes back into the living room with the glass of liquor and downs it in two gulps. He waits for a long moment and then says, "Where's the number?"

She finds him the piece of paper with the number on it. He swallows and then calls. She can only hear one side of the conversation, but it's easy to piece together what's happening.

"What does that mean, exactly?" Patrick says. "Are you arresting me?"

She watches as his face takes on a new pallor. "Fine, sure." He hangs up. Slowly, he turns to her. "They want me to do a polygraph test."

PATRICK STANDS COMPLETELY STILL, his cell phone still in his hand. He can feel the sweat at his hairline. He reaches up automatically as if to loosen the collar at his neck, but he's only wearing a T-shirt—he doesn't have to dress for work anymore—and he lets his hand fall.

His wife looks at him. "That's all right, isn't it?" she says tentatively. "They're not arresting you. They'll do the polygraph, and when you pass, maybe they'll drop the whole thing and leave us alone. They'll know you didn't do it!"

He turns on her, his voice tense. "It's not that simple, Stephanie."

She falters, her face pale and drawn, "What do you mean?" There's a long, fraught pause.

"Those tests aren't reliable. They aren't even admissible in court."

"Then why do them at all?"

He looks back at her, rage building inside him. **Those bastards.** He tries to remain calm. "I'll tell you why. The police can manipulate them. They'll make me come off badly."

"Surely they can't **make** you fail—not if you're telling the truth."

He turns away; he doesn't want to look at her. He turns to his cell. He needs to talk to his attorney.

# 41

The following day, Thursday, Stephanie wakes early. She looks over at her husband, still sleeping. The babies aren't even awake yet. She stares at his sleeping form, the familiar shoulder, his dark hair, his classically handsome profile. She thinks about how much she once loved him. It wasn't even that long ago. It makes her wonder if love is just an illusion, one that disappears when reality gets too dark. No, she decides. Love **is** real. The love she feels for her baby daughters is real. But romantic love—maybe that's all an illusion.

She must pack up the twins early and take them back to Hanna. They have a flight to Denver today. They will meet at Lange's office in Denver, and then together they will go to the Sheriff's Office in Creemore. She doesn't know what's going to happen. She finds the tension almost unbearable. There was an awful moment, booking the tickets online, when Patrick didn't know whether

to book two same-day return tickets or just one. Lange had warned him that he might not be coming back. In the end, a return ticket wasn't much more expensive than a one-way fare, so he booked himself a return ticket too.

She knows that she, at least, is coming home on the evening flight. She's assured Hanna of that. She'll be home late that night to take the twins off her hands.

Patrick had argued with her about whether she should go at all. He'd been quite insistent—even adamant—that she not go. There was nothing she could do to help; she should stay home and take care of the twins. It wasn't like the inquest, where appearances mattered. They were going to go to the Sheriff's Office, as requested, and whatever was going to happen would take place outside of the public eye. There was no need for her to be there, he'd assured her.

But she'd stood her ground. What he didn't seem to understand was that she **wanted** to be there. She wanted to hear for herself what the attorney had to say.

Most of all, she wanted to be there when Patrick took the polygraph at the Sheriff's Office.

She slips out of bed quietly and goes downstairs to put on the coffee.

The time goes by in a blur—she feeds the babies, dresses them, has toast while Patrick showers, and takes the twins across the street just before

they leave. They're in the car by 6:00 a.m. for their 8:35 a.m. flight. They don't speak during the entire long drive to the airport.

Stephanie spends her time leaning against the window, her mind blank. She'd told Hanna that they were going to see the attorney in Denver, and that the police wanted to question her husband. Hanna hadn't known what to say. She'd just given her a big hug.

The flight lands on time and soon they are in a cab on their way to the attorney's office. Stephanie stares stoically in front of her. She has no interest in Denver.

The law firm is sleek and modern and hums with a discreet energy. Lange meets them at reception. "How was your flight?" he asks. It's small talk and none of them are in the mood to engage. "Follow me," he says and directs them to his office. They were here before, to prepare for the inquest.

Once they're inside his office, settled in their chairs, he gets right down to business. "I'm sorry about this, but I'm not surprised. As I told you after the inquest, after a verdict of undetermined, they have to be seen to be doing something. Questioning you is the next step. They have to do it. And, in Colorado, it's pretty common to ask a suspect to come in and take a polygraph."

"What if I don't do it?" Patrick asks.

Stephanie looks at him in dismay.

"Then they might arrest you," the attorney says.

"I don't understand any of this," Stephanie says. "Why do the polygraph if they can't use it?"

Lange looks at her. "Let me explain about polygraphs. The way they work is by measuring various physiological changes—in heart rate, blood pressure, perspiration, breathing, and so on—when the examiner asks each question. Based on the results, the examiner may conclude whether the person is lying or not. They are often unreliable. And yes, for that reason, they're generally not admissible in court."

"Then what purpose do they serve?" Stephanie asks.

The lawyer says carefully, "Although they may not be admissible in court, the police think they provide valuable information."

"So the police believe them, they just can't use them in court," she says, reading between the lines.

Without answering, he turns to her husband. "If you pass, that will probably be the end of it. It usually is. And it would be next to impossible to prove murder at trial."

Stephanie glances at her husband, who has his attention fixed on the attorney.

The lawyer leans forward at his desk. "Let me tell you something else about polygraphs. They are very risky. We never let our clients take a police polygraph without doing one with our own examiner first." He lets that sink in, regarding them both with a serious expression. "In any event, agreeing to

come in and take a police polygraph test amounts to the same thing as giving an interview to the police. You may be manipulated or tricked into giving incriminating information—because although the results of the polygraph aren't admissible in court, the questions and the answers you give are. Sometimes it's better not to talk to them at all. It's an important decision, not to be taken lightly." He adds, "In most cases, a police polygraph is not helpful, but sometimes it can be."

There's an uneasy silence, into which Patrick says, "So what are we going to do?"

"Like I told you on the phone, we're going to get you hooked up to the machine and do a polygraph right here," the attorney says. "Sit tight, I'll be right back."

Patrick hadn't told her that they would do a polygraph at the law firm first. Stephanie sits in her chair, reeling. The attorney doesn't seem to think Patrick will pass the polygraph. Fair enough—most of his clients are probably guilty; they probably routinely fail. But surely Patrick didn't murder his wife. This is going to help them. It has to.

She looks at Patrick, sitting nervously in his chair; he refuses to meet her eyes. A chill creeps over her, like cold fingers running over her body.

When the attorney returns, he's accompanied by a man carrying equipment. They quickly get everything set up on a table in the corner of the large office. Soon Patrick is sitting across from

the examiner. He has two rubber straps across his chest and a clip on his index finger.

Stephanie and the attorney watch from the side. "Just relax," Lange tells Patrick. "Roddy here is one of the best in the business, a retired police officer. He knows what he's doing." Her husband flicks a nervous glance at the examiner. "Roddy is going to ask you a series of questions that we have prepared. Just answer yes or no," the attorney says.

The examiner nods at Lange, and the attorney says, "Okay, let's begin."

The examiner, when he speaks, has a calm, measured voice.

"Is it the month of October?"

"Yes."

"Are you going to answer all my questions truthfully?"

"Yes."

"Have you ever lied to get out of trouble?"

A slight hesitation. "Yes."

"Were you living in Creemore, Colorado, in January 2009?"

"Yes."

"Before your wife, Lindsey Kilgour, died on January 10, 2009, did you know that it is dangerous for a person to be inside a running car if the exhaust pipe is blocked with snow?"

"No."

"On the day that your wife died, did you tell her to wait in the car while you shoveled it out?"

"No."

"Before your wife died on January 10, 2009, did you know that the exhaust pipe of your car was blocked with snow?"

"No."

"Do you currently live at Seventeen Danbury Drive, Aylesford, New York?"

"Yes."

"Did you ever push your wife Lindsey Kilgour down the stairs?"

"No."

"Did you intend for your wife Lindsey Kilgour to die by having her stay in a running car with the exhaust pipe blocked with snow?"

"No."

"Before January 10, 2009, had you ever heard of an instance where a person died inside a running car because the exhaust pipe was blocked by snow?"

"No."

Finally, the examiner turns off the machine and looks up at Lange. He shakes his head, his mouth turned down.

Stephanie sees black spots dancing before her eyes.

# 42

Patrick, stunned, remains seated in the chair, bolt upright, arms on the armrests, his heart hammering. No. This can't be what it looks like. But Lange is standing beside the examiner, studying the results. His face is serious.

Suddenly he hears Stephanie gasping. She's sucking in air, her hand clutching at her chest, and everyone's attention is pulled toward her. He watches her, unable to move. Lange bends down toward Stephanie. Patrick's still hooked up to the equipment, as if he's already in the electric chair. He watches his wife in disbelief; she's having one of her panic attacks.

The attorney is telling her to breathe; her head is bent forward, down to her knees. This is what she does, Patrick thinks, when things get rough. He knows about the panic attacks. She's told him all about them, described what they feel like. He

knows he has failed the polygraph—he can tell by the reaction of the examiner and his attorney.

They are all focusing on his wife. What no one seems to realize is that he's in just as much shock as she is.

Gradually, the distressed noises coming from his wife subside and she starts to breathe more regularly. "That's it," Lange says, his voice steady. Patrick feels the examiner's hands on him, undoing the equipment. Patrick wants to speak, but he can't seem to make his voice work.

The mood in the room has shifted, he can feel it. He stares at his wife. He hadn't wanted her to come. She should have stayed home, like he told her to, he thinks, and she would have been spared this.

Lange stands up straight, his hand on Stephanie's shoulder. She's still bent over, probably so that she doesn't have to look at him. Her worst fears realized, Patrick supposes. How wrong she is.

Lange turns his attention to Patrick, exhales deeply, and says what they all now know. "I'm afraid you failed the test, Patrick."

Patrick shakes his head. "No. That's impossible. The test is wrong!"

Stephanie slowly sits back up, but she seems to have turned to stone. Why does she believe the machine over him? He's told her how unreliable these tests are.

Freed now from the wires, Patrick finds himself

stumbling over to his wife, kneeling down beside her. "Stephanie, you know how inaccurate these tests are. It was an accident!"

She doesn't even look at him.

Lange says, "Look, we have to make some decisions." He nods to the examiner, who is quietly leaving the room with his equipment. "Thanks, Roddy." He turns to Patrick. "Sit down," he says, moving back behind his own desk. "We've got work to do."

Stephanie faces the attorney. Patrick doesn't like the expression on her face. He can imagine what's going through her mind. She thinks he did it. Maybe it's all over between them now, Patrick thinks numbly. She won't trust him after this. She won't love him anymore. He wonders how long it will be before she leaves him. The thought renders him frightened and hollow.

"We're expected at the sheriff's. Here's what I suggest," Lange says. "We know they will ask you to take a polygraph. You will, on my advice, decline. They will probably, in that event, arrest you on the charge of first- or second-degree murder. It will depend on the level of premeditation they think was involved." Patrick can only stare back at the attorney, frozen in disbelief. "You will then be in custody. You don't have to talk to them. I will be there with you. I suggest we allow a brief interview in which you deny the charges unreservedly.

You explain, again, that it was an accident. And that's it. I won't allow them to question you any further. It is up to them to prove their case beyond a reasonable doubt at trial. We don't give them anything to work with, got it?"

Patrick nods, unable to speak.

"You won't be going home tonight." The attorney glances over at Stephanie, and Patrick dully follows his gaze. "I don't think there's anything to be gained by your going to the sheriff's with us," he says.

Patrick has to agree with him. Stephanie looks like she thinks it's a foregone conclusion that her husband will be convicted of murder. He wants her to go home. She's certainly not helping.

The attorney turns to him, and he must look as frightened as he feels because Lange says, "Chin up. It's up to the state to prove it was murder, beyond a reasonable doubt. You sit tight. The burden is on them. And honestly—I don't think they'll go through with a trial."

Patrick wonders if his own lawyer thinks he's guilty. Does Lange care? To him Patrick's just another client.

Lange comes from behind his desk and helps Stephanie up with a hand at her elbow. "I'm sorry, but I think it's best if you just go to the airport. I'll have my secretary call you a cab. Let's go see her."

Patrick watches her leave the room with his

attorney without a backward glance. He feels terribly alone, and despite his attorney's reassurances, what he's facing terrifies him. And it's all because of that treacherous bitch Erica.

STEPHANIE WANDERS AROUND the airport, killing time until her scheduled flight. How strange, to be in an unfamiliar airport, drifting in and out of shops, while her husband is at the Sheriff's Office, being charged with murder.

Finally, exhausted, she stops at a Starbucks and sits at a little table with a coffee. What she needs is someone to talk to. Someone she can trust. She has so much turmoil inside her, and no one to unburden herself to. She thinks about Hanna. Can she trust her? Can she tell her what happened at the attorney's office today? No, she decides. She can't.

She can hardly come to grips with it herself.

He hadn't passed the lie detector test. What does that tell her? He did it. He killed his wife and unborn child on purpose.

She wrestles with the information, trying to get hold of it in some way that makes sense. Polygraphs can't be counted on. Everyone knows that. He didn't mean to kill her. He couldn't have.

But the police believe in polygraphs. They will believe that her husband is guilty, if they ever find out about the test. The lawyer had turned to her,

outside of his office, and assured her in a low voice that the police will never learn that he failed the test. The information is privileged.

Maybe she wants them to know.

It was a strange, surreal moment.

She's the only one, besides Patrick and his lawyer—and the examiner—who knows. It's such a heavy burden to bear. But she knows she can't tell anyone. She must keep it to herself.

And now, she must decide what to do.

# 43

Patrick stands up straight and walks toward the building that houses the Sheriff's Office.

He arranges his face into an expression of resolution. He is an innocent man, unfairly treated, doing as his attorney is advising him to do.

"Ready?" Lange says, beside him.

As they walk up the steps, Patrick thinks back to the last time he went up these same steps, the morning that Lindsey died. It was winter then. He can't believe he's back here. He feels sick to his stomach. He was sick that day. He threw up in the snow.

They are expecting him. He is taken into an interrogation room, Lange close beside him. The sheriff and a uniformed police officer are there. This is all just a formality. It's what comes after that is terrifying him. The nights spent in jail. The trial. He's projecting into the future, barely able to pay attention to what's happening in the here and

now. He hears his attorney explain that, on his advice, he will not be taking a polygraph, as they are unreliable and inadmissible in any event. Patrick sits up straighter then and meets the sheriff's eyes firmly, unwilling to look guilty. He sees the sheriff's knowing smirk and realizes then that the sheriff assumes from this that he's already taken one and failed. He feels like he's been punched in the gut. Suddenly his situation seems much worse. The sheriff sitting across from him already thinks he's guilty.

"We'd like to ask you a few questions, if that's all right with you," the sheriff says.

"He'll make a statement, but that's it. Patrick?" The attorney sits back and waits for him to say his piece. They'd discussed this—what he was to say—in the car on the way up.

Patrick clears his throat and speaks in a firm voice, with conviction. "I did not intend to kill my wife. It was an accident. I didn't know that the exhaust pipe was plugged, or that she was in any danger."

"Anything else you'd like to add?" the sheriff asks after a moment.

Patrick shoots a nervous glance at Lange.

"No, I think that's it," the attorney says smoothly.

The sheriff stands up and says, "Patrick Kilgour, you are under arrest for the murder of Lindsey Kilgour on January 10, 2009. . . ." Patrick's mind goes blank and he doesn't hear the rest. Then someone is nudging him. "Please stand up."

Patrick stumbles to his feet, blood rushing from his head.

"Hands behind your back, please," the uniformed police officer says quietly.

Patrick puts his hands behind his back, feels the cuffs go on. And just like that, he's arrested for murder. He's going to jail.

STEPHANIE APPRECIATES the anonymity of the plane ride home without her notorious husband by her side. He's handsome, recognizable; on her own, she's able to pass as a tired, ordinary woman. No one bothers her or looks at her twice, not the way they had when they'd traveled back from the inquest. Patrick had attracted a few curious looks, and because of that, she had too. She knew what people were thinking when they looked at her: **Who could possibly marry someone who had murdered his first wife?**

They'd read the newspapers, seen the coverage on TV, and assumed he was guilty. And now she knows something they don't. She knows he failed the polygraph. Now she wants to scream, **I didn't know about any of it. I didn't know!**

She wants to weep against the window of the airplane, but she doesn't allow herself. She will weep tonight, at home, alone, after the twins are asleep. She will let it all out in a way she had never felt able to do when Patrick was in the house. Perhaps

it will be cathartic, and then maybe she will finally be able to sleep. And to think clearly about her situation.

She's had a text from the attorney telling her that things went as expected, that Patrick has been arrested and is now in the county jail. She won't be hearing from Patrick directly anymore, unless he calls her from a phone at jail. She pictures him in a cell, wearing some kind of jumpsuit. She imagines they have taken away his belt, his shoelaces—anything he might use to kill himself. But she can't imagine what's going through his mind. Because she doesn't have any idea of what's in his mind at all. She shudders to think that a machine might know him better than she does. Did she ever know him at all?

Maybe she's safer with him in jail. She and Emmie and Jackie. If he really is a murderer, they're all better off with him locked up, far away. She thinks with horror about the fire in the kitchen. She still can't remember putting the pan on the stove that day. Could Patrick have done it? Was Erica right? Did Patrick want to get rid of her and the twins, so he can have her money—over three million dollars altogether?

She can't believe it. She can't believe that she could have been so terribly mistaken about someone she loved. But she has just enough doubt left to make her utterly miserable.

She doesn't know what is true or how to act

anymore. Patrick's lawyer expects her to be supportive, to rally around him. But can she do that? Should she? What if he did it, and he gets away with it, and comes home? Surely he wouldn't . . .

But he could be innocent.

**How will she ever know for sure?**

By the time the plane lands, it's already late. She retrieves the car from the airport parking and drives the hour and a half home, her eyes burning with fatigue. The house is dark; she wishes she'd thought to leave the porch light on. Finally, she gets the door open and enters the house nervously, all her senses on alert. Being alone in the house at night frightens her. She's used to having Patrick here—he used to make her feel safe. Now every little noise startles her, every shadow jumps out at her. She wonders if she will ever feel safe again. But then she tells herself to snap out of it.

She quickly turns the heat up a bit, flicks on lights all over the house, slips into some sweatpants, and then grabs her keys and hurries across the street to pick up the twins. She thinks about what to say to Hanna. She must not tell her about the polygraph, no matter how much she longs to confide in someone.

When Hanna opens her front door and smiles a welcome at her, Stephanie surprises herself by bursting into tears. Hanna hugs her and then pulls her from the chill of the doorstep into the warm house. She looks at her sympathetically. "Come on,

the babies are all asleep upstairs. I'll get you something to drink."

"Are you sure? It's so late," Stephanie says.

"I'm sure."

Feeling too weary to protest, and utterly alone in the world, Stephanie follows her toward the kitchen. She wants to see her girls first, though. "I'll just tiptoe up and look in on them, okay?"

"Of course," Hanna says, changing direction. "We'll be quiet, though—let's not wake them."

The twins' playpen is set up in the nursery next to Teddy's crib, with her two girls fast asleep. Stephanie creeps into the room and peers down at them. The nightlight casts a soft glow. They are on their backs, their heads turned toward each other, little fists curled, knees bent, chests rising and falling. They're so innocent. Her heart breaks a little, looking at them.

"Okay?" whispers Hanna.

Stephanie nods, and they quietly exit the room and go back downstairs. Stephanie follows Hanna into the kitchen. She's startled to see Ben, Hanna's husband, there. But of course, he lives here. She's the interloper, relying on the kindness of strangers.

"Don't mind Ben," Hanna says. "He's watching something in the basement."

Ben nods cordially at her, having the grace not to stare as he grabs a beer from the fridge. He probably expects to hear it all later, Stephanie thinks

cynically. But she shouldn't be cynical about them, she tells herself. They have been good to her. She can't let what's happening to her color her view of everyone else.

Ben retreats downstairs with his beer and Hanna asks, "Tea? Or something stronger?"

"Do you have any wine?" Stephanie asks.

They sit down in the living room with a bottle of red and two glasses, the lights low, and Hanna asks, "What happened?"

"They've arrested him," Stephanie says bluntly.

Hanna's expression is a mix of shock, compassion, and dread.

"What are you going to do?" Hanna asks quietly.

"I don't know."

LATE THAT NIGHT, in his cell, Patrick lies on his bunk, his mind racing. He imagines Stephanie lying awake in their bed, staring at the ceiling. Or is she wandering around the house, the way she's been doing since all this started, thinking about him? Does she think he did it? Does she believe the polygraph? Or has she calmed down now and seen sense?

The fucking polygraph. She shouldn't have been there. Still, he expected to pass it. It had been a terrible blow when he hadn't.

# 44

Cheryl feels like she's trapped in a living nightmare. Now that she knows more about Devin's biological parents, she finds herself studying Devin and wondering about every little thing. She's seen behaviors in him lately that she'd perhaps been blinding herself to. Sometimes Devin puts himself first, before his friends. He has considerable charm, which he uses to get what he wants. She's never worried about that before. She'll hardly admit it to herself, but she's looking out for sociopathic traits.

Gary tells her she's imagining things, looking for problems that aren't there. He assures her that love is enough; love can solve anything. They've brought Devin up properly. They're good people. They're going to get through this.

. . .

ERICA VOSS is in her apartment the next morning scrolling through the news feed on her phone when she stops suddenly. **Arrest Made in Kilgour Case.** Her adrenaline surges; she taps the link and races through the short article. Then she sits back in her chair, a slow smile playing about her lips.

Serves him right. That's what happens when you fuck with her.

She picks up her cell phone and calls the Manning residence. She's already planned what she's going to say.

"Hello," Cheryl's voice comes over the phone.

"Hi, Cheryl," Erica says.

"Who is this?"

Erica can hear the suspicion, even fear, in the other woman's voice. She'd prepped her with that visit to her house. "It's Erica, Devin's mom." There's a long, fraught silence.

"What do you want?"

"I don't know if you've been following the news . . ." Erica says, and waits.

"You mean about the inquest," Cheryl says, her voice uneven.

"It must have been quite a shock," Erica says, "learning all that about Devin's father."

"Tell me the truth," Cheryl says harshly. "Did he really kill them?"

"Of course he did."

"What do you want?" Cheryl asks again.

"I'd like to see more of my son," Erica says.

"He's not your son. He's ours. You terminated all your parental rights when we adopted him."

"I don't care about **legal** rights," Erica says. "You're welcome to him. But I think he should know where he came from, don't you? I could meet him, tell him he's adopted—I bet you haven't even told him he's adopted, am I right?—and I could tell him about his father, why I had to give him up, even though I didn't want to." She waits a beat and says, "Did you see that Patrick was arrested this morning?" There's an audible gasp from the other end of the phone. "For murder."

"I'm hanging up," Cheryl says.

"No, you're not," Erica replies. "You're going to listen to me. You're going to tell Gary that I want another hundred thousand dollars, or Devin will soon find out things that I don't think you want him to know. You can't watch him every minute of every day. I'll call you back in a few days. In the meantime, get the money together." She adds, "When Patrick goes to trial, I really don't want to tell them I actually know where my son is, and put you through the whole paternity testing thing. It would be so hard on Devin to learn the truth that way."

STEPHANIE PICKS UP the newspaper from the front step and carries it inside to the kitchen. The day

is cold and wet. She sits down at the kitchen table and leafs through the paper, looking for any mention of the arrest. She finally finds it, buried in the back of the front section. At least it didn't make the front page here. She wonders how much longer she's got before the local press is all over this.

She presses her palms against her burning eyes. She'd spent longer than she'd planned to at Hanna's last night and had more wine than she should have. It felt good to lean on Hanna, to dwell in her comfort and normalcy. She'd wanted to confide in her. Now she's afraid she'd let slip a bit too much—about her doubts. But she hadn't said anything about the polygraph.

She goes back to the front page of the newspaper. She has a few minutes, the babies happy in the living room before she gets them ready to go out. They will walk to the grocery store this morning, pick up a few things. She hopes she doesn't run into anybody she knows, although she probably will. She always does.

An article on the second page catches her attention. It's a lurid story about a man in Albany who has killed his two children, his wife, and then himself. She tells herself not to read it, but of course she does. She can't help herself. There are always stories like this, and she always reads them. The man smothered the two young children before his estranged wife returned home from work. When the mother arrived home, he stabbed her several

times in the chest. And then he calmly got into his car and drove off a bridge.

She sits back, her head swimming at the horror of it.

These sorts of things happen all the time. And no one ever seems to see it coming.

The phone rings in the kitchen, making her jump. She glances at it, reluctant to pick it up. Whoever it is, it can only be bad news. She can't imagine anything else these days.

She picks it up. "Yes?"

"Hello, Stephanie, it's Robert Lange."

Her heart sinks. **What now?** "What is it?" she asks.

"I wanted to let you know that Patrick will be going before a judge this morning for the arraignment."

She can't think of anything to say.

"If they do go ahead with this—and I still don't see how they can, realistically—we'd be probably looking at a trial date sometime next spring or early summer."

She closes her eyes, and leans against the counter. "Okay."

"I'll need a retainer."

SOMEHOW, THE DAYS crawl by. Even when everything is falling apart, the sun still rises and sets, Stephanie still needs to eat and sleep. The babies

need to be taken care of—fed and dressed and changed. She has to answer the phone when Patrick calls from jail.

Their conversations are false, stilted, unnatural. How could they be otherwise? The time apart is quickly making them grow more distant, as they share less and less of the day to day. It's always that way when couples are apart, Stephanie thinks; it's much worse when one of them is in jail on a murder charge, and the other one isn't entirely convinced he didn't do it.

"Stephanie," Patrick always says, "you must believe me. I didn't do it."

"I know," she says automatically. She knows she doesn't sound especially convinced. She sounds detached, dismissive.

"They'll have to drop the charges. I'm going to get out of here and come home," he says.

"I know," she repeats tonelessly, staring blankly out the window. She doesn't feel anything when she talks to him.

"Lange says that if they can't find any other evidence, it won't be enough to go to trial—it will be her word against mine about the affair, and an affair isn't sufficient proof that I killed my wife. Neither is the insurance. They have no direct evidence that I meant to kill Lindsey."

She isn't really listening.

Suddenly Stephanie remembers something Erica said to her, that day on the porch. That her

neighbors might have seen him coming and going from her apartment, might have heard them in bed, through the wall. If they find just one neighbor who saw him there, she thinks, on more than two occasions—that would prove he was lying. Patrick said he'd only gone to her apartment twice.

"Stephanie, you have to be strong for me, okay? For me and for the twins."

She can hear a note of desperation in his voice now; his mask has slipped a bit. He's scared. Of course he is. "Lange wanted a retainer," she says.

"Yeah, he told me he called you."

"It's a lot of money."

"I know. And I'm sorry." He sounds contrite. "When this is all over and I'm back on my feet, it won't matter, Stephanie. It's just money. I'll start my own firm, earn it all back. People have short memories. A few years from now this will all just seem like a bad dream."

AS SHERIFF BASTEDO drives his truck down Creemore's main street, he reflects that they haven't gotten a damn thing out of Kilgour—his smart lawyer has seen to that. And if Kilgour doesn't talk, they aren't going to have enough to proceed to trial.

Even so, Sheriff Bastedo parks his truck in front of the K & R Pharmacy. This is the place where Erica Voss worked back then. It's a family-run

business. He makes his way to the back of the store, where he finds an older man behind the counter. The man looks up and he flashes his badge. "Are you the owner?"

The man nods and says, "What can I do for you, sheriff?"

"I'd like to ask you a few questions about a former employee of yours, Erica Voss. Remember her?"

The man gives him a knowing look. "I was wondering when you were going to show up."

Bastedo nods. The story is all over the news; he'd be interested to know what this man thinks of it all. There's no one else within earshot. "What can you tell me about her?"

"She was an excellent employee," the pharmacist says. Then adds, "As far as I know."

"What do you mean?"

"She was very smart, reliable, good with customers. Picked things up fast. Ambitious."

"I'm sensing a 'but,'" Bastedo says.

The pharmacist gives him an appreciative look. "We had a couple of break-ins back then. Drugs taken. Oxycodone mostly. Stuff you can sell on the street. You guys never caught who did it."

"And?"

"And I can't prove anything. But I always thought it was her, or that she was involved somehow. I mentioned it to the sheriff at the time as a possibility, but they didn't find anything. Like I said, she was smart."

"Did you let her go?"

"No. How could I? I couldn't fire her without some proof, and I didn't have any. But I did ask her, point-blank. She denied it. She was either telling the truth or she's a very good liar."

"So what happened?"

"She left town—not long after that terrible thing with the Kilgour family." He adds, "My wife and I were glad she was moving on. We didn't have any more thefts after that." He raises his eyebrows at the sheriff. "You know what I think?"

"What?"

"I wouldn't believe a word she said."

"Thanks for your time."

"You're welcome."

Sheriff Bastedo drives back to the station, his mind turning over what he's just heard. He'd better check it out.

THAT EVENING, ERICA CALLS. Gary feels sweat collecting in his armpits and down the center of his back. Cheryl is watching him anxiously from across the room. They knew she would call again; they've been waiting. They've gone downstairs to the basement so that Devin can't overhear them, just in case he isn't asleep.

"Hi, Gary," Erica says. "I assume you know I spoke to your wife the other day."

"I'm having trouble coming up with that much money," Gary blurts out.

"Right," she says, as if she doesn't believe him.

"It's true." It **is** true, which is why he's sweating so profusely. They've taken a hit on a couple of commercial properties over the last two quarters. "I'm overextended at the moment."

"Bullshit. I don't believe you."

"Why don't you believe me? This is America. Everyone's overextended!" He takes a deep breath. "Look, you'll get the money. I just need more time. We don't want you talking to Devin, ruining his life. Ruining our lives. You know that." He waits a long moment while she seems to consider.

"Fine. You can have more time. I'll call back in a few days."

# 45

The sun finally comes out again after days of relentless rain. Patrick has been in jail for the better part of a week. It's Tuesday morning, and Stephanie has arranged to meet Hanna and Teddy later in the morning, and go to the park together, and then to a coffee shop afterward. She feels safer going out and about with Hanna by her side, now that the news is generally known that Patrick has been arrested. Hanna has become her protector of sorts—her buffer against the world. Stephanie has been bothered by the press, but at least they aren't camping outside her door.

The twins are in their high chairs, and Stephanie is spooning pureed peas into their mouths, her thoughts going round and round, the way they have ever since Patrick failed the lie detector test.

If he really did it, if he killed his first wife in cold blood . . . she has to face that her husband might

be a murderer. How profoundly her thoughts have changed since this all began. At first she'd thought he'd been briefly unfaithful, and that Erica was simply trying to shake them down for money. Stephanie had lost weeks of her life in a blur of paranoid panic about her husband being wrongly accused. But now . . .

What does she hope for? Does she want them to let him go? Does she want him to be convicted? What if he comes home?

She stares at the wall and thinks, **Even if he gets away with it, it doesn't mean he didn't do it.**

There are too many things that make her doubt him. The fall down the stairs. The polygraph. She can't keep deluding herself—if he **is** a murderer, she can't endanger herself and the twins. She decides, **He can't come back here.**

She's finally admitted it to herself. She doesn't believe her husband is innocent.

PATRICK IS ESCORTED into the room that prisoners use to consult with their attorneys. He feels like he's aged years in the days he's been inside. How do people do this for twenty years? For life? Whenever he thinks of it his stomach lurches, and he sweats with fear. He and his prison clothes stink. He's not coping as well as he thought he would. But how does anybody know how they'll cope with prison,

with a murder charge, until they've tried it? It's a foreign country. One he doesn't belong in. He's not like the other men in here, mostly hardened criminals, uneducated toughs. He stands out. He still wrestles with disbelief every day. He wonders if it will ever really sink in.

"Patrick," Lange says, standing up.

Patrick shuffles over and sits down heavily as the guard retreats and closes the door behind him. His attorney is looking at him with concern, which Patrick appreciates. Patrick gets the sense that his own wife doesn't care that much, that she's going to bail on him. He wouldn't really blame her, given how things look.

"How are you doing?" Lange asks, worry evident in his face.

"How do you think?" Patrick says. Then he relents and says, "I'm scared shitless, if you want to know. I hate it in here. You have to get me out." He knows he sounds desperate.

The attorney nods, tries to reassure him. "That's what we're going to do, Patrick. You just have to hang on. Are they treating you all right?"

He nods wearily. "I guess."

"In case they proceed with this—we have to go over everything, anything that could be harmful to you. If there's anyone, anyone at all, who can harm you, I need to know about it now. We can discredit witnesses if we know what to expect, but I can't have surprises. Do you understand?"

Patrick looks back at him, feeling aggrieved. Lange thinks he did it.

"What about your friend Greg Miller?" the attorney presses.

"What about him?"

The attorney leans toward him over the table. "Look, a murder trial is a very different thing from a coroner's inquest. The gloves come off, you understand me? He knew you then. Is there anything he knows that can hurt you? Did you ever say to him, even as a joke, that you'd like to get rid of your wife?"

Patrick is taken aback. "No, of course not."

"Nobody lurking in the shadows who's going to pop up and say you tried to hire them to bump her off? Because shit like that happens."

Patrick sits, the sweat oozing out of him. He's drowning in his own stench. He's not worried about anything like that. But the truth is, although it wasn't the grand love affair Erica claims it was, he **had** minimized the number of times he slept with her to Stephanie, and then he'd had to do it again at the inquest. He's a liar. And Erica knows it.

He shakes his head. "No. I swear. Nothing like that."

"SO, KEVIN," SHERIFF BASTEDO says to the wiry man in unwashed jeans in the interview room. They've

been interviewing every drug dealer and former dealer in the area known to them.

"How about you tell me why I'm here? I haven't done anything wrong in years."

"You're not in trouble with us. We just want to talk to you."

"About what?" the man says nervously.

"You were active in the drug scene around here ten years ago."

"Yeah, and I done my time. I'm working now. Clean. Ask anybody."

"We did, and we know. You're not in any trouble. We just want to talk to you about Erica Voss."

The man goes still. Thinks about it. Swallows. "Okay."

"You know who we're talking about."

"Yeah, sure. She's in all the news about that man who killed his wife in the car."

"What we're interested in," Bastedo says, leaning toward the man over the table, "is what she was up to back then. Tell us about the drugs."

Kevin swallows again. "I already done my time. Nothing I say here is going to get me into trouble, right?"

"That's right. You're free and clear. You're just here helping us out."

"Okay, yeah, she was involved, in a small way. Just for a short time."

"Dealing?"

He nods. "She was dealing oxy. I got some from her."

"Where did she get the drugs?"

"She stole it. She worked at a pharmacy. That's where she got it."

# 46

The DA slaps the manila folder down on her desk the next morning in disgust.

"We're going to have to let Patrick Kilgour go," Dominguez says. "We were never going to win this one, not unless he broke down and confessed."

Bastedo nods. "Yeah. And his bloody lawyer won't let him talk. Haven't been able to get a peep out of him."

"And our only witness has been accused of stealing and dealing opioids." She thinks for a moment and then says, "Too bad the statute of limitations means we can't go after her for the drugs."

"Look on the bright side," Bastedo says after a moment, with a world-weary expression. "Think of all the money it will save the state not to have a trial, not to have to pay for him to serve a life sentence."

She snorts derisively. "Yeah, but I have a feeling the bastard did it."

"Me too." He gets up to go. "I'll have them drop the charges and release him."

ROBERT LANGE GETS a call on his cell phone. They're dropping the charges against Patrick, letting him go. About time. Lange heads to the jail to tell his client the good news.

When Lange gets there, Sheriff Bastedo meets him in the front area. Together they go to an interview room, where Patrick is brought in. He seems wary, frightened, when he sees his attorney there with the sheriff. It's unexpected; he looks like he's assuming the worst.

Lange hastens to reassure him, smiling at him. "Patrick—good news. They're dropping the charges. You're free to go. You're going home."

PATRICK HEARS THE WORDS, but he doesn't really take them in. His attorney steps forward and embraces him. Then it hits him, and the relief is overwhelming. For a moment he sags against Lange. He thought he would die in here. Despite the reassurances of his attorney, he was terrified that he'd go to trial, that he'd be convicted, that he'd never see the light of day again.

"We're really leaving? Now?" Patrick manages to say.

"Yes. I can get you back home tonight. There's room on an afternoon flight—I already checked."

It's starting to sink in. The shock is subsiding, replaced by elation. He can't wait to tear off his smelly prison clothes, to scrub the prison stink off his skin, to sleep in his own bed again.

"Let's get you processed."

Patrick wonders how Stephanie will react to him coming home so unexpectedly.

As if reading his mind, the attorney says, "We'll call your wife with the good news."

STEPHANIE SITS ON the living-room sofa, stunned. She's just spoken to Patrick on the phone. He's on his way home. She can't believe it. She thought he was in jail, that he was facing a murder trial. Now they've let him go, dropped the charges. He'll be home later tonight.

She thought she'd have more time to figure things out. She doesn't know what to think, what to do.

**Erica is a liar.** Stephanie knows for certain that she lied at the inquest about the blackmail.

**Her husband is a liar.** That's what the lie detector said.

Who is she supposed to believe? She wants to

be rid of both of them. She thinks uneasily about Patrick. She hasn't seen him since he failed the polygraph. When trust goes, how quickly love disappears and self-preservation takes over.

She could leave him. She could leave now, take the twins and be gone before he gets back, and not tell him where she's gone. She sits, trembling, on the sofa, thinking it through. She doesn't have much time, and the pressure makes it hard to think. If she ran away, he would find her eventually. And he would have the law on his side—she doesn't have the right to take his daughters away from him and run. In the eyes of the law, he is an innocent man. With rights to his children.

She thinks of the twins, her heart in her throat. **Her little birds**. She feels a dread creep over her. If it's true that he murdered his first wife—and his unborn child—if he was capable of that . . . **if she tried to take the girls and leave him—would he kill little Jackie and Emma? Would he kill her?** Her head begins to spin and she feels overcome with nausea. Lately she's been thinking a lot about the man in the news who smothered his two children with pillows and stabbed his wife to death. . . . It's something she has to consider.

Was Patrick violent before they married? Did he push his first wife down the stairs? Had she and Patrick been living a lie together before all this happened—and all along he's been someone

capable of **murder**? Parents—usually fathers—have been known to kill their children to get back at their estranged spouse. And then they kill their spouse. No one ever seems to see it coming. And he might have already done it once.

And he's coming home tonight.

# 47

Patrick fumbles with the key in the door. She's left the porch light on for him. It's late, after eleven. He's had a long trip home—he'd rented a car at LaGuardia rather than have Stephanie wake the twins and drive all the way to the airport to get him. He's had plenty of time to think. The earlier elation—Lange had driven him directly to the airport in Denver, and they'd celebrated with a drink in the bar, before Patrick boarded the flight home—has subsided as he thinks about what's to come.

But at least it's all over. For good. Nothing can change that now. Erica can't do anything to him. They don't have enough to proceed to trial and Erica has been completely discredited besides. She's a liar and a criminal. He's free—of her, and of the past.

He has to convince Stephanie that everything is going to be all right from now on, that they can

start over, and that none of this has to hurt them. They're free! He's been exonerated—it will be in the news that charges against him have been dropped. He'd had no idea about Erica dealing drugs back then. He'd hardly known her really—except in the most carnal of ways. He will rise above it all, start over. He'll start his **own** firm—show Niall what he can do. Niall will be sorry he dropped him. And he'll show Stephanie that she has reason to be proud of him.

But now he must talk to Stephanie, to explain. He tries not to feel irked by her apparent doubts— even though it was perfectly clear to Stephanie that Erica lied at the inquest.

He can explain about the lie detector test. He knows that Stephanie stopped believing him in the attorney's office that day. He can still see it— her reaction when she realized he'd failed the test. It had played over and over in his mind, while he was in jail. She thought then that he'd deliberately killed his own wife. She probably thinks so still, even though they've let him go. He must change her mind. He hopes that she will forgive him and they can move on. She loved him once, and it wasn't so long ago. They have the twins to think of. They have a life to build together.

He opens the door. There's a faint light coming from the living room. The twins must be asleep upstairs. He places his keys on the side table, takes off his coat, hangs it up, and walks slowly through

to the living room. His wife is waiting for him, sitting on the sofa in the semidarkness, and when she looks at him, she doesn't move. She doesn't run to him and throw her arms around him. He hadn't really been expecting her to, but he feels disappointed anyway.

He stands still as they stare at each other. He doesn't like the expression on her face. She looks wary, almost as if she's frightened of him. **Is this how he should be greeted, after being exonerated? After all he's been through?** He's never given Stephanie any cause to be frightened of him. His attorney had been happy for him. His lawyer knows polygraphs are meaningless. She should be happy too. She's his wife—she should give him some credit, or at least the benefit of the doubt.

"Stephanie," he says, his voice breaking. He steps farther into the room. "I'm here. It's okay. Everything is going to be all right now. It's all over. She can't do anything to us anymore." His wife stares at him, eyes wide. He must make her listen, understand. He takes another step forward. "Erica is a liar," he says, his voice becoming more forceful. "You know that. She wanted money, she wanted to hurt me, that's all. They let me go because they have no case. They know she made it all up. She's not credible and she can't be trusted."

"What happened?" she asks, her voice raw.

He explains. "They found out she stole drugs from the pharmacy where she worked and sold

them. They have proof. Witnesses." He sees the shock on her face at the news; she clearly wasn't expecting this. "She'd do anything for money," he adds bitterly. "She doesn't care who she hurts."

She remains silent, as if she can't grasp what he's saying.

"It's good news, Stephanie," he says, trying not to feel too disappointed by her reaction.

"You failed the polygraph, Patrick," Stephanie says at last. "What was I supposed to think?"

He feels a surge of annoyance. How many times has he gone over this? He moves over to her now, sits down beside her. "I know. And I can explain about that." He brushes the hair away from her face in a familiar gesture and she actually moves away from his touch. His heart sinks. He pulls away from her a little, gives her some space.

"No one was more shocked than me when I didn't pass the polygraph," he says. He looks at her and waits until she lifts her eyes and returns his gaze. "But innocent people fail polygraphs all the time." He pauses and then continues. "Maybe I failed it because I was nervous . . . because I lied to you about something else, Stephanie, about the extent of the affair with Erica." He closes his eyes for a moment so that he doesn't have to look at her face, but then opens them again, to gauge her reaction. "I told you I only slept with her twice, when in truth, it was more than that." She looks

like she's going to be sick. He presses on, feeling as if he's poised on the edge of an abyss. Everything depends on whether she believes him now. "I didn't want to lose you—you and the twins are everything to me. I know I'm not a murderer, but I thought if you knew how often I'd slept with Erica, you would leave me, and that you might not believe me about the rest. And once I told you I'd only slept with her a couple of times, then I had to say the same thing at the inquest."

Unnerved by the way she's looking at him, he gets up suddenly and starts pacing back and forth in front of the sofa, the way he has so often since Erica came back into his life. "Then they wanted to do the polygraph, and I was terrified. I was so nervous. I think that's why I failed the test." He turns to her, desperation in his voice. "But it wasn't like she said. We weren't **in love**. It was always just sex, that's all. I was twenty-three. My wife was pregnant—we weren't sleeping together anymore. It's inexcusable, I know. But there is no way in hell I would deliberately kill Lindsey. Not for Erica, not for anything. I'm not a murderer! The idea would be laughable if it weren't so damn terrifying!"

She looks up at him, appalled. "You lied at the inquest," she says. "You **perjured** yourself."

He nods. "I know, but it's over now. They'll never know." And they won't, he thinks, unless she tells them.

Stephanie stares at him, her eyes large. Finally she asks, her voice a harsh whisper, "Did you push her down the stairs?"

He looks at her in dismay. "No! No, how can you think that? I loved her!" He says, his voice breaking, "I'm sorry, Stephanie. I'm so, so sorry, for everything I put you through. I promise, I will spend the rest of my life making it up to you."

He watches her, his eyes pleading. So much depends on what happens next.

# 48

Stephanie looks into the eyes of her husband and asks herself if she is looking into the eyes of a killer. His words seem meaningless to her. He keeps telling her he's told her everything—he's said that all along—but there's always more. What more can there be after this? Will he stand over her with a knife in his hand some night and say, just before he slits her throat, **Oh yes, one more thing, I stuffed that exhaust pipe full of snow myself, and waited for her to die?**

She feels a shudder go through her body. She grips the edge of the sofa to ground herself. She finds herself unable to speak.

"Stephanie, say something, please," he begs, his voice breaking.

"I don't know," she says finally, woodenly. "I don't know what to say." But she's thinking about how easy it is for him to lie. He lied to her, he lied on the stand—he committed **perjury**, and even

that doesn't seem to have made much of an impression on him. She looks up at him. "You've been lying to me all along," she says finally, her voice becoming more animated. "Why should I believe you now? How do you expect me to feel?"

That actually seems to surprise him. Why should it surprise him? Did he think she would believe him? Just because Erica has been shown to be a liar, it doesn't make him any less of a liar. They're like two peas in a pod, Stephanie thinks. Two of a kind. Maybe they deserve each other. Maybe they **were** meant to be together.

"You have every right to be upset," Patrick says.

"Upset!" she cries. Then she lowers her voice. "I'm a little more than **upset**, Patrick." She wonders how far she can push him, this possibly murdering husband of hers. Wonders how far she dare go, to test him. To find out for sure. To see how angry he can get. Will he push **her** down the stairs? Maybe she should find out, she thinks recklessly. It's so important for her to know. To know what really happened all those years ago in the snow. She feels closer now to Lindsey than to anyone else—closer to his dead first wife than to her own husband. She's been manipulated by both of them—Patrick and Erica—all along.

"Is there more going on here than I'm getting, Patrick?" she asks suddenly.

"What?" he asks. "What are you talking about?"

She feels physically and emotionally exhausted,

too confused to think clearly. Everyone is after money. Her money. Are they after her money together? Her thoughts fall over one another in paranoid succession. Are Patrick and Erica still in love? Or maybe they're incapable of real love, capable only of self-interest, two psychopaths, in this together. No—they can't be working together. The idea is insane. She must pull herself together, stop this. She must deal with what's right in front of her, not imagine the unimaginable.

"What's wrong?" Patrick says urgently.

"Nothing. Everything."

He sits down beside her again, cautiously pulls her to him. "It's going to be okay, Stephanie."

She lets him pull her into his chest, wrap his arms around her. He holds her for a long time. She can feel his heart beating. She can feel his lips kissing the top of her head. He probably thinks that she'll forgive him. But she's not going to forgive him. She's trying to find a way out.

THE NEXT MORNING Stephanie is in the kitchen with Patrick and the twins, having breakfast, pretending that everything is normal even though it isn't, not for her. She can't imagine things ever being normal again. Patrick seems to think they might be. Stephanie is pouring herself another cup of coffee when the doorbell rings. She looks up from the coffee maker, looks through the vestibule to the

front door, and sees the distorted shape through the rippled glass. She thinks it might be Erica. Her heart skips a beat.

"I'll get it," Patrick says, and pushes his chair back. She fights a spell of dizziness, as the twins babble in their high chairs, oblivious.

Stephanie watches the door open, fighting panic, then sees Hanna's familiar face, gaping now in shock.

"Patrick!" Hanna says.

Stephanie recovers and hurries to the doorway. "Hi, Hanna," she says quickly. Hanna must guess that she won't necessarily be happy about Patrick's return.

"You're back," Hanna says to Patrick, trying to recover her footing.

Stephanie detects something in Hanna's voice besides the obvious surprise—nervousness, maybe, or dismay.

"Yes," Patrick says smoothly. "They dropped the charges yesterday. I came home last night. I've been completely cleared," he says, "just as we expected."

Stephanie's stomach clenches a little, at how he explains it. **I've been completely cleared**. That's what he will be telling everybody. But that's not really true, is it? They just won't ever be able to prove he did it. Hanna glances at her, standing behind him, as if to silently get her take on it. Stephanie steps forward. "Do you want to come in for coffee?"

Hanna shakes her head. "No, I don't have time. Ben is watching Teddy for a minute before he goes to work. I just popped over to invite you and the girls for a playdate this morning. Maybe ten-ish? I'm going to make muffins."

"Sure, I'd love to," Stephanie says, summoning a smile. She's eager to get out of the house. Away from Patrick, if only for a couple of hours. She can't think straight around him. She feels she must be constantly watching, evaluating. It's exhausting to have no downtime. She has to act normal, but she doesn't even know what that is anymore. There is no normal, not here. She needs to be with someone she can relax around, even for a short time.

She and Patrick had spent last night in the marital bed, her back to him, his body curved around her, his arm draped over her. She'd hated it. He'd quickly fallen asleep, but she'd remained awake for a long time. As soon as he started to snore, she removed his arm from around her waist, and inched farther away from him on her side of the bed.

ERICA FINDS OUT the way she seems to find out everything—from her news feed. She's having a late breakfast in her apartment when she sees the story on her phone. The charges against Patrick have been dropped. No explanation is given.

She calls the Sheriff's Office in Creemore. It's barely 8:00 a.m. in Colorado. She's in luck; the

sheriff is in. She waits impatiently to be patched through.

Finally, he comes on the line. "I was wondering if I was going to hear from you," Sheriff Bastedo says.

He explains that they don't have sufficient evidence to proceed. Then her blood runs cold as he tells her that they've uncovered her past as a small-time drug dealer. She thought that was dead and buried. That nobody knew.

"None of that is true," she protests.

"Right."

She hangs up the phone without another word. Then she storms around her apartment, furious at the turn of events. She grabs the pillows from the sofa and throws them across the room. She's so enraged that she overturns her coffee table and everything on it. Books, magazines, a dish of candy go flying. Then she collapses onto the sofa, tries to calm down.

It doesn't really matter whether Patrick goes to trial or not. It would have been nice to see him squirm. But financially speaking, it makes no difference. The Mannings still won't want her hanging around their son, telling him the truth. They'll still pay her. And keep paying her.

STEPHANIE IS ON her way out to Hanna's place with the twins when Patrick stops her in the doorway for a goodbye kiss. She lets him kiss her on the

mouth, even though his touch is distasteful to her. She can't help it—she thinks of him kissing Erica. She tries not to show her revulsion. She doesn't want to let him know how she feels, what she's been thinking. She needs more time.

Just because Erica is a liar doesn't necessarily mean she's lying about Patrick. And she's not satisfied by his explanation about the polygraph. She does now know, however, that he fucked Erica many, many times and lied to her about it. And that he perjured himself.

If she left him, she doesn't know how he'd react. He's seemed more possessive since he came home, always trying to touch her. Maybe she didn't notice it before because it didn't bother her. Maybe it's just that he missed her in jail. Or maybe he can sense that she's pulling away from him. If she tried to leave him, how would it end?

**Would he be violent?**

He would certainly be angry. She doesn't know what he would do. If she left him and tried to take the twins—and her money—with her . . . she doesn't really know what he's capable of.

**Stay or go?** She can't decide. Maybe over time the path will become clearer, more obvious.

She'd lain in bed last night awake until almost dawn, thinking how all her problems would be solved if he were to be killed in a car accident, perhaps hit by a drunk driver. But those things don't just happen when you want them to. And it always

seems to be good people who are taken too soon that way.

She's trapped.

Stephanie remembers all this as she stands on Hanna's doorstep, almost swaying with fatigue, and rings the doorbell. Hanna opens the door and invites her in. Stephanie settles the twins on the living-room floor, and Hanna retreats into the kitchen to make coffee. Stephanie can smell the muffins. She closes her eyes for a moment, fighting tears. She can remember when life was simple. She and Hanna getting together, talking about the babies—coffee and muffins and milestones. How did it all go so wrong? She hears Hanna coming back into the living room and opens her eyes, blinking away tears.

"Coffee will be ready in a jiffy," Hanna says, then looks at her more closely. "Tell me what's going on," she says.

Stephanie doesn't know what to say. This is something she thought about last night too. What to say to Hanna. Does she pretend everything is okay? Or can she be honest with her? She's not ready for that. Finally she forces a smile and says, "Everything is fine." She explains why they dropped the charges. She tells her about Erica, her criminal past.

Hanna looks back at her, concerned. She's not fooled. "But what do **you** think?" she asks finally.

Stephanie swallows. "He cheated on his first wife. I know that. I've managed to forgive him for

that—I think. But Erica is clearly a liar. She was telling nothing but lies about the accident. Everybody knows that now. It was just a terrible, tragic accident." She pauses, then adds, "But Patrick knows that if he ever cheats on **me**, I'll leave him."

Hanna continues to look at her uneasily, but Stephanie smiles back at her. "I don't think I have anything to worry about anymore. It's all good. And I'm dying for one of your muffins."

# 49

Nancy gathers up her purse and a jacket and leaves the house for her exercise class. She's opening her car door when she sees a woman approaching her from a car parked across the street. She immediately recognizes Erica and feels her insides turn to jelly. **Why is she here?** Nancy wants to get into her car and speed off, but she suddenly can't move. Instead, she watches Erica come swiftly up her driveway, the wind blowing her blond hair around. How could a woman who looks so angelic be so hideous?

"Hello, Nancy," Erica says.

"What the hell do you want?" Nancy asks nervously.

"Your husband isn't returning my calls."

"Of course he isn't. I told you that he'd drop you the minute I told him I knew. He never wants to see you again. He doesn't want to lose **me.**"

Erica gives her a skeptical look, which infuriates

Nancy. She now knows what this woman is made of—she hadn't known before, when she confronted her at her own apartment—and she's terrified. She just wants her out of their lives. How can she get rid of her?

"If you're so sure, then why are you so nervous?" Erica needles her.

"I'm not."

"What are you afraid of?" Erica asks slowly. "What are you hiding?"

"Nothing," Nancy says too quickly. She recovers herself and says, "Why is it so hard to believe that a man might want to end a stupid affair and stay married?"

"Tell him to call me," Erica says.

"Just get the hell out of our lives!" Nancy shouts.

Erica smiles and says, "Just have him call me, will you?" She turns on her heel and walks back to her car. Nancy watches her drive away, and then, shaking visibly, slams her car door and heads back into the house.

She locks the door behind her and collapses onto the couch, curling into a fetal position. Fear and dread envelop her. She's so frightened that Erica will find out what she and Niall have been hiding for the last six years. She doesn't want to think about it but guilt and fear pull her into the past.

It happened on a rainy night in late November. She and Niall had decided to go to dinner at a restaurant in Westchester County, a little over

an hour's drive from Aylesford. It had been a cel-
ebratory affair, because Niall had had an excellent
write-up in an architectural magazine—and they'd
had a lot of wine with dinner.

"Are you okay to drive?" Nancy asked as they got
their coats.

"Yeah, I'm fine," Niall said. And he seemed fine.
He certainly didn't seem drunk. But then, she'd
been drinking, too, and perhaps her judgment had
been impaired.

Soon after they started off it began raining heav-
ily. Niall was hunched forward over the steering
wheel, peering into the night. The car was warm.
The sound of the wipers sweeping noisily and me-
thodically across the windshield was hypnotic, lull-
ing Nancy to sleep.

Suddenly a loud **thud** shook her violently awake.
She felt the car swerve and then right itself back
into the center of the lane. "What was that?" she
cried. She looked over at her husband, who seemed
to be in a daze.

"I don't know. Maybe I hit something. I didn't
see anything."

He kept going, his knuckles tight on the steering
wheel. It was on the tip of her tongue to suggest
they stop, but she didn't. She persuaded herself it
was nothing. And once they'd driven on for a few
seconds, it became impossible to go back.

"It was probably just a rabbit," Niall said, after a

minute. But they both knew a rabbit wouldn't have sounded like that.

They arrived home and didn't mention it again. They fell into bed and slept in.

Nancy got up the next morning and picked up the newspaper from outside the front door. She saw a small story at the bottom of the front page, and her life changed forever. A young man, walking along the side of the highway in the rain on the edge of Westchester County, perhaps hitchhiking, had been struck and killed instantly the night before. The car had fled the scene. There was no camera footage, no witnesses. The police were appealing for anyone with information.

Nancy read the article twice, an awful certainty overtaking her. She went into the kitchen and approached the door to the attached garage with dread. It took her several minutes to build up the courage to open it. She thought about getting Niall, but she wanted to see it for herself first. In the garage, she bent down, freezing in her nightie and bare feet, and studied their car. There was some damage to the passenger side front bumper, but it wasn't too noticeable.

She rushed upstairs then and shook Niall awake, thrusting the newspaper in his face. "Could we have done this?" she asked in fear. She watched him read the article, saw the same horror overtake him.

He looked up at her, clearly shaken. He shook

his head back and forth. "I don't know. I thought it was nothing."

"But the location—that's just about where we were when you hit something," she persisted.

"So what do you want me to do?" Niall said, turning to her.

"I don't know."

"The harm's done," Niall said in a shaky voice. "A man is dead. If I hit him—my God." He got out of bed and started pacing the bedroom. "I was probably over the limit. I fled the scene. I'll probably go to prison."

"No, no, no," Nancy cried, tears running down her face. "I'll call my father. He'll know what to do."

"No," Niall said. "Keep him out of this."

"He can help us, Niall! He's a judge. He'll know what to do."

"He'll want me to turn myself in," Niall protested.

"Only if that's what's best. I'm calling him."

Niall sat by helplessly, his head in his hands, as Nancy called her father. She told him only that it was an emergency. He showed up less than an hour later, without her mother, as she requested.

"What is it?" he asked in his direct way. "What's the matter?"

They told him everything. Showed him the newspaper account. The judge's demeanor darkened. "How could you drive when you'd been

drinking?" he said to Niall in disgust. "How could you leave the scene? What were you thinking?"

"Dad, you have to help us," Nancy pleaded. She could see the conflict behind her father's eyes. He was wrestling with what to do. They all knew Niall should turn himself in. But what she really wanted from her father was his permission not to. To help them with that. She waited.

"Let me see the car."

They trudged out to the garage, and he looked at it for a long while without speaking. "You'd think there'd be more damage if you hit a person," he said finally.

Nancy let her breath out at last. "Maybe someone else hit him."

The judge turned around and went back into the house, his head down. Once he was back in an armchair in the living room he said, "I can't tell you what to do. The only way to be sure is to turn yourselves in," the judge said, looking directly at Niall, "and let them look at the car." He added, "The waiter at the restaurant would be able to say how much you'd had to drink. You'd probably be looking at jail time."

Nancy began to weep again.

The judge waited a long moment before he spoke again. "I can also tell you that the solve rate for hit-and-runs is laughably low." He added, "There's no footage, no witnesses." He was silent for another long moment and then finally said, clearly

unhappy, "Whatever you decide, I won't say anything."

Nancy shot a look at Niall. What would he want to do? She wished her father would be clearer about what they should do.

"What do we do about the car?" Niall asked at last.

"Nothing," the judge said wearily. "Don't take it to a shop to get it fixed. It doesn't really need it, and they'll be watching for that. No one's going to notice anything about your car."

And no one had. For a long time Nancy woke every day hoping that they would catch who'd done it, and that it would be someone else, with a badly damaged car—proof positive that it wasn't them. But it didn't work out that way. The case quickly disappeared from the news.

Now, Nancy, curled up on the sofa with her knees to her chest, has to resist the urge to telephone her father.

# 50

Patrick takes some satisfaction in the shocked look on the receptionist's face when he walks into the office. "Patrick!" she says.

"Hey, Kerri," he says with a triumphant smile. "Is Niall around?"

Niall must have heard him because he strides into the reception area.

"Patrick!" he repeats, sounding just as taken aback as their receptionist.

It's an awkward moment. The last time they spoke, Patrick had been anticipating arrest, and Niall had told him he was dissolving the partnership; it had been acrimonious. Niall still looks very much on his guard. Fuck him, Patrick thinks. Why can't he be happy for him? Does he have any real friends at all? "I have good news. The charges have been dropped. I've been completely exonerated, just as I expected," he says.

"That's terrific! Really good news!" Niall says, clearly relieved, but with less enthusiasm than Patrick would have liked.

"Do you have a minute?" Patrick asks.

"Of course, come into my office."

Patrick follows the other man and sits down in the chair he used to sit in, almost daily, for four years. He reflects for a minute that this time yesterday he was still in jail, thinking he might die in there. How quickly things can change, for better or for worse.

"So, tell me what happened," Niall says, sitting back in his chair.

"They had no evidence. None at all. And once they did some actual investigating, they found out that Erica Voss is a criminal and a liar." He explains what they learned about Erica's past. Patrick shakes his head. "She told all those lies; she could have put me in prison for life."

Niall has gone awfully pale. "Wow," he says. He asks, "Can they charge her with something?"

"I don't know," Patrick says. "But I'm free and clear of her. I'm ready to come back to work—no distractions." Niall looks uncomfortable. "What?" Patrick asks, confused. "I've been cleared, Niall. Completely. They realized they never should have arrested me at all. They even told me as much," he lies.

"I think there's been a misunderstanding," Niall begins.

"What do you mean, a misunderstanding?"

"We already agreed to dissolve the partnership, Patrick. You're getting paid out."

"But that was before. Everything's different now," Patrick protests. "You can't still want to dissolve the partnership!" But that's exactly what Niall wants to do, Patrick realizes, adrenaline shooting through his system.

Niall flushes. "Don't get me wrong, Patrick. I'm so glad—so happy and relieved for you—that this has worked out. That woman should rot in hell for what she did to you. But—the optics aren't good. I mean, you're all that people in this town have been talking about. It's—quite a scandal."

"And now they'll be talking about how they had to let me go. I didn't do it, Niall!"

"I know, and I'm sorry. But to be absolutely honest, I had been thinking about making a change before that. You'd been slipping for months, Patrick, you know that, you can't deny it."

"That was because of the twins! I hadn't had any sleep in months! They had colic, but they're over it now. Everything's back to normal. I can come back to work and give a hundred percent. A hundred and ten!"

"I'm sorry to tell you this," Niall says, averting his eyes briefly, "but I've already found another partner."

Patrick glares back at Niall in disbelief. "You son of a bitch."

"No need to get nasty, Patrick," Niall says, bristling.

Patrick wants to punch his former partner—former friend—in the face. So this is how it ends—four years of building a business together. He realizes he has nothing to lose now. He says, his voice accusatory, "You've been sleeping with her yourself, admit it." Niall's face pales further and he suddenly looks very distressed. "Made you feel good about yourself, did it?" Patrick says. "Let me give you a word of advice—stay away from her. She's dangerous—you have **no idea**."

Niall says, his voice trembling, "I didn't know what she was doing to you. Nancy found out about it and I broke it off. And then, when you told me about the inquest—and Erica's role in it—I was sickened by it all. Nancy had already threatened to leave me. I wanted to distance myself from both of you." He sinks in his chair in shame.

"You fucking coward," Patrick says. He tamps down his rage. He decides to take the high road. He'll make it on his own. He gets up and leaves, refusing to look at Kerri as he passes by reception, slamming the door on his way out.

# 51

An uneasy couple of days go by in the house on Danbury Drive. Patrick behaves affectionately toward Stephanie and the twins, pretending that everything is the same as it was before. But for Stephanie, nothing is the same.

Stephanie has been unable to make a decision. It's as if she's paralyzed, so she takes the path of least resistance, which is to do nothing. She focuses on the twins—feeding, bathing, dressing, changing. She takes them on outings, reads them stories, plays counting games with their toes.

It's like she's suffering from some kind of internal collapse that has sucked out all her energy. Or maybe it's just that she's finding it so hard to sleep. She's back to her old habits, wandering around the darkened house at night, brooding, staring at the sleeping babies, thinking the worst of people, imagining things. Awful things.

It's time for her to cut her losses and leave him.

But she's afraid. She's afraid for the twins, mostly. The twins need a strong mother. She must survive, whatever happens, and take care of her babies. She must protect them. She's tormented by images of her and her babies dying in a house fire. She thinks about the pan on the stove. She doesn't know who put it there. It might have been her. It might not.

Patrick breaks into her morbid thoughts. "I'm going out for a bit," he says.

She's so caught up in her own thoughts that she barely even acknowledges him.

ERICA HAS JUST LEFT her apartment and is on her way to her car when her cell phone buzzes. She looks down at it and sees who's calling. It's Patrick. She hesitates, and then accepts the call.

"Erica," he says in a low voice.

He's breathing heavily, as if he's walking quickly. Her heart speeds up and, involuntarily, she looks over her shoulder and around the parking lot outside of her apartment. He's not here. No, wait. Her heart spikes. She sees him, across the lot, walking toward her. She tries to keep her voice steady, put her old confidence into it. "What are you doing here?" As he gets closer, she disconnects and drops her cell phone into her purse. He comes closer still, until his face is mere inches from hers. It's the first time they've laid eyes on each other since the inquest.

"Why the **hell** did you go to the coroner?" Patrick hisses at her furiously. "I thought we had an understanding."

She looks back at him in surprise. "So did I— until you double-crossed me. What did you expect?"

"What the fuck are you talking about?"

He's staring at her. She can smell him—slightly sweaty, so familiar. She sticks her face right up to his and hisses back, "Someone tried to run me down. Don't pretend it wasn't you." She puts all her fury into her voice. "You were supposed to kill **her**, not me." She's breathing heavily now. She spits out, "Of course I went to the police—it was the only way to protect myself."

His face twists with rage and agitation. "Bullshit! I didn't try to run you down! Just stop with the fucking lies, can't you? You didn't give me enough time. I needed to be sure I wouldn't get caught. Now, thanks to you, I can **never** get rid of Stephanie—and it's all your fault—going to the fucking police! You've screwed us both."

She says bitterly, "No—**you've** screwed us both. I hope you have a miserable life with your stuck-up, controlling wife. If she even keeps you." She shrugs past him, gets into her car, and drives away.

PATRICK STRIDES ANGRILY BACK to his own car. As he drives back to Aylesford, his mind returns to the

turmoil of those days after Erica had given him a stark choice: kill his wife, or she'd go to the authorities. He'd been almost paralyzed by his situation, unable to think at all because of sleep deprivation and fear. He was living in a fog of indecision.

The day of the picnic with Stephanie, he'd been agitated, undecided. Over lunch he'd developed a half-formed plan to drive back, Stephanie and the twins asleep in the car, twist the wheel suddenly—he would claim that he'd fallen asleep, lost control of the car—and go off the road at a spot he knew and plunge into the lake. He wouldn't help Stephanie or the twins out of the flooded car—he would prevent her escape if he had to—but he would make it look like he'd tried to save her. But then Stephanie had insisted on driving back. He tried to protest, but it was as if she had a second sense, as if she knew. In the end, he'd been relieved. He probably never would have gotten away with it. It had been a desperate idea, born of a desperate situation. By the time he decided it would be a much better idea to get rid of Erica—the source of all his problems—she'd already gone to the coroner.

He'd always planned to get rid of Stephanie someday, somehow—but Erica had forced his hand.

He thinks back to how it all began—clumsily bumping into Lindsey at the top of the stairs while her back was turned. He made it seem like an accident but he knew exactly what he was doing. She went careening down the stairs to the floor at the

bottom, and he thought it was done. She lay still for a moment by the back door, but then she began to stir. And . . . she was **fine**. He remembers his disbelief, his crushing disappointment. But he'd quickly realized what he must do and dashed down the stairs to help her up, exclaiming how sorry he was. Fussing over her, making a big show of concern. She hadn't suspected a thing. She was only worried about the baby and insisted on going to the hospital for an ultrasound. They'd taken a cab to the hospital and he'd brooded in the waiting room at the ER, wondering how he could ever get rid of his wife and her child.

It wasn't until weeks later, during that snowstorm, lying in bed the night before their trip to her mother's, that he thought of it. The exhaust pipe. How perfect it was. How pleased he was with himself for thinking of it. How easy it had been to do, and so low risk. He remembers the look Erica had given him at the funeral. As if she **knew**. But how could she know?

He's been afraid of her ever since.

# 52

When Patrick returns, Stephanie is in the driveway, buckling the twins into the backseat. Through the rear window, she sees him drive in and park his car beside hers. She wonders where he's been for the last couple of hours.

"Hey," he says, getting out of his car and coming up behind her. She's still got her head inside the car, settling the twins. He sounds conciliatory. She doesn't care. She doesn't know what he expects from her. He's turned their lives upside down, their marriage into a fraud, and it doesn't seem to have registered that it's **all his fault**.

"Where are you going?" he asks as she pulls her head out of the car and turns to face him.

"Grocery shopping."

"You don't have to take them. I'm home now. You can leave them with me."

"No, I've got them all settled now. It's fine." She notices that he seems upset, although he's trying to pretend he's not. His eyes are cold, distant.

"No. Leave them with me. You always complain about grocery shopping with the twins, what a hassle it is."

She does. But she doesn't want to leave them at home with **him**. It's the first time she's really had that thought crystallize in her mind, and it gives her a start. She's afraid to leave the babies in his care. "I know," she says, turning away, "but it's good for them. They need an outing and they go to the park every day. The grocery store is different. I let them feel the oranges, the bags of rice. They love it." **And people always stop to tell me how adorable they are**, she thinks, **and I need that right now, it makes everything easier to bear.** Whatever she does, whatever she decides, it will be for them, for Jackie and Emma. Maybe she'll get in the car now with her twins, her diaper bag, and her purse, and just keep driving. . . .

"Do you want me to come?" he offers.

She manages to smile at him. "No, that's okay. I do this all the time."

"Okay, fine." He looks at her for a second and then turns away and goes into the house.

She drives to the grocery store, her mind in a tumult.

. . .

LATER THAT NIGHT, after a strained evening meal, after they have put the twins to bed, Stephanie takes her laptop to the living-room sofa and watches Patrick go upstairs to their bedroom.

Stephanie sits on the sofa dry-eyed. All her tears have been shed. Tears are a sign of weakness, she thinks. What she feels now is a coldness, a resoluteness, a resolve that she didn't have before. A kind of strength that comes from having no option but to face your situation head-on and deal with it.

It's late, nearly eleven. She closes the laptop, leaves it on the coffee table, and makes her way slowly upstairs. She's so tired; exhaustion makes it feel like she's climbing a mountain. She pauses at the top. For now, she's still sleeping in the same bed as her husband. Should she move to the bed in the guest room? She would like to. Does she dare?

She walks slowly to their shared bedroom, the carpet softening her footsteps to nothing. She gets to the bedroom door and stops. Patrick is at the closet. He has his back to her but at a slight angle, so that she can see what he's doing. He's holding his gun in his right hand, as if he's checking it. Her heart begins to beat wildly. **How had she forgotten about the gun?** It's always been there. Locked away, in the safe. Patrick keeps it there in case anyone breaks into their house while they're sleeping—it would take him only seconds to access it.

She stares, unable to move, her heart knocking at her ribs. The safe where he keeps the gun, on the

closet shelf, is open. She knows there's ammunition in there. Has he loaded the gun? Is this it? Is this how it all ends? He doesn't know she's there; he seems to be completely oblivious to her. She makes a quick calculation—she can't turn and run, she could never get to the twins and get them out of the house fast enough. She's glued to the spot.

He places the gun back in the safe, locks it, and turns around, startled to see her there. He must notice her pallor, because he says, "What's wrong?"

"Nothing," she says. "I'm just not feeling that great. I thought I'd go to bed."

He studies her. "Yeah, you don't look too good," he agrees.

She walks to her side of the bed, grabs her nightgown from beneath the pillow, and turns her back to him. She starts stripping off her clothes. She doesn't want to provoke him. She doesn't dare move to the guest room. She crawls into bed without bothering to wash her face or brush her teeth, and turns on her side facing the wall. She tries to fall asleep, but her heart is racing.

As Patrick joins her in bed and the long night stretches on, she can't sleep, because she's thinking about the gun.

# 53

In the dark, Patrick stares at his wife's back, which is all she offers him these days. She's pretending to sleep, but he's not fooled.

The look on her face when she saw him with the gun—Christ, it was like she expected him to shoot her. The situation is worse than he thought.

If it weren't for Erica fucking Voss, Stephanie would have no idea. She'd be happy and unsuspicious, with sleeping twins and an investment portfolio with over two million dollars in it. And now he might lose everything.

He can feel himself unraveling. He's incandescent with rage at Erica. He's furious with Niall, and disappointed in Stephanie. He thought he'd beat the polygraph. He'd studied how to do it, how to bite hard inside his mouth for a spike of pain to throw off the test. He thought it would work. It should have worked.

If Erica hadn't come back into his life, if she hadn't come to Aylesford . . .

He remembers how he hooked up with Erica, that first time. They were out at a bar after work on a Friday night, he and Greg. Lindsey had joined them, bringing along her friend Erica. Greg's girlfriend had been there too. Lindsey said she was tired and went home early after a couple of mocktails, waddling out the door, heavily pregnant. She left behind her best friend and her husband, not worried at all, because why should she be? She'd told him, in front of everyone, to stay and have a good time because after the baby came he wouldn't be able to do that anymore. He'd smiled at her, but the permission, and the warning, left a bad taste in his mouth.

He was twenty-three, in his first real job, and he wasn't ready to be a father. He watched his wife make her ponderous way across the bar and out the door, wondering if he should walk her home, but was soon distracted by something Erica said. He'd met her before, though he'd never really spoken much to her. But that night, beer had loosened his tongue, he felt reckless, and after Lindsey left, Erica seemed to be flirting a little with him. He was enjoying it, and it all seemed harmless. After all, she was a friend of Lindsey's.

They'd decided on just one more, and he'd tried to persuade Greg to stay, but he and his girlfriend

wanted to go. They didn't seem to think anything of leaving Patrick and Erica there together to have one last drink.

Once they were alone, though, the dynamic changed quickly. He realized that she wanted to sleep with him, that ending up in bed with her was actually possible. He wrestled with himself a little. She was his wife's best friend. Another drink, and it became probable. She whispered that Lindsey would never know. And then it was inevitable.

They left the bar, and once outside, she took his hand and dragged him around the corner of the building. She leaned against the wall in the dark and pulled him to her. It was like . . . skydiving. That kind of daring, that exhilaration. He was harder than he'd ever been with Lindsey. He wondered how he'd ended up with Lindsey, about to become a father, when he should be fucking women like this one.

She took him back to her place. It was a short walk away—everything in the small town of Creemore was a short walk away. He kept his eyes open for people he knew who might see them together, but no one was around. When they got to her building and into the elevator, alone, he almost unzipped. But there wasn't time. The door slid open and he imagined slipping into her.

Once inside her apartment—it wasn't much, none of them had much in those days—she led him to her bedroom. Soon, everything was a blur

of pounding excitement and a loss of boundaries. Afterward they lay on her bed, exhausted, and he stroked her hair and told her she was amazing.

She'd smiled at him and said, "I know," and they both laughed.

She hadn't said the same about him. "Lindsey can't find out about this," he said, turning serious. He didn't need the grief. He looked at her lying naked beside him, her pale, slender body, and a vision of his wife popped into his head. It was wrong to compare them, it wasn't Lindsey's fault that she was bloated, stretched, darkened, and marked with veins—she was about to become a mother. But God, how he wanted more of this, the perfect woman lying right beside him.

"No," she agreed. "It would kill her."

Was she waiting for him to say something? "Will we do this again?" he asked.

She didn't answer him. She just smiled and said, "You'd best be getting back to your wife."

That was what she was like. She liked to be the one in control. She hasn't changed. He'd gone home feeling like he'd been dismissed, wondering how the hell he would be able to act normally around Erica and his wife when they were all together.

But then she'd called him at work that Monday— she was all he'd been able to think about—and asked him to come over to her apartment on his lunch hour. And that had been their routine. A

pleasurable, exciting, but meaningless affair—for both of them.

He lies in bed, awake, staring at Stephanie's back, thinking about the past and everything that has led to this moment. He'd never loved Erica—there was something inherently unlovable about her. Perhaps it was that she herself seemed incapable of loving anyone. She frightened him a little, even then.

And now, it's ten years later, and Erica has wrecked everything. His once-adoring wife believes he's a murderer. He's afraid she'll leave him and take her inheritance with her.

# 54

The next morning Stephanie stumbles out of bed and robotically goes through her morning routine. She'd felt her husband's eyes on her back during the night, as she feigned sleep. She wondered what he was thinking, while she was thinking about the gun.

This can't go on.

She's coming up with a plan. It frightens her, but she needs a way out. She'd thought of it in that darkest hour right before dawn, when the mind turns to things that shouldn't survive the cold light of day.

But now it's morning, the sun is streaming through the windows, and she's still thinking about it.

Hanna has invited her over again today. Stephanie hasn't asked Hanna over to her place because Patrick is home and she can tell that Hanna

no longer wants to set foot in her house. Hanna thinks Patrick is guilty, regardless of how much Stephanie has pretended otherwise. She'd let her guard down that one time, after the arrest, and now she's afraid Hanna knows what she really thinks.

She will go to Hanna's this morning because she wants to—she's desperate for normalcy—and also because Hanna is now part of Stephanie's plan, although she does not know it.

She takes the twins over in the stroller and knocks on Hanna's door. She lifts the twins out of the stroller and carries them into the house. She puts them on their play mats on the carpeted living-room floor. Hanna has taken to baking comfort food for each of these visits—today Stephanie can smell chocolate chip cookies, and she is absurdly grateful for Hanna's attempts to make her feel better.

"Here, have one," Hanna says when she comes back into the living room with a plate of cookies fresh from the oven. "I've just put the coffee on."

"You're a godsend, Hanna," Stephanie says, meaning it. There's no one else she can turn to, or even comfortably hang out with. She never realized, before, just how isolated she's become. She hadn't made enough of an effort to keep up with people from work when she went off on maternity leave, she thinks. She'd let the women in her moms' group fall away, not up to making the effort with everything that has been going on. She wonders

what they think. Like Hanna, they probably think her husband is guilty. They all know he cheated on his first wife and how she died. She's sure they must ask themselves why she stays with him. Stephanie wonders if Hanna discusses her situation with the other moms in the neighborhood. She probably does, she realizes, finishing the cookie and reaching for another. She must.

They talk about the babies, what they've been doing, how they've been sleeping, little Teddy's latest visit to the pediatrician. But then there's a pause, and Hanna looks at her expectantly.

There's a long silence broken only by the sound of the babies babbling. Stephanie screws up her courage and says, "I'm going to leave Patrick." Hanna doesn't look surprised—she looks more relieved than anything. "I've realized that it's over for me, even if it isn't for him," Stephanie says. "I don't trust him anymore. He cheated on Lindsey. The whole world knows it. And all this about the accident—it's damaged us, Hanna, more than anyone knows."

"I understand completely," Hanna says. "I think you're doing the right thing. When trust is gone—"

Stephanie clarifies, "I don't believe he killed Lindsey on purpose—the idea is ridiculous. I'm not afraid of him, Hanna, but—I don't love him anymore." She adds, "I resent him too much for putting me through all this, even though it's not entirely his fault."

"He picked the wrong woman to have an affair with," Hanna acknowledges.

"He certainly did. And now we're all paying the price," Stephanie says bitterly. "I'm going to make an appointment with a divorce attorney on Monday. I have to figure everything out before I tell him."

"When **are** you going to tell him?" Hanna asks, her voice worried.

Stephanie takes a deep breath in. "As soon as possible. After I see the attorney, I guess. I just need this to be over."

"Like I said, I think you're doing the right thing," Hanna says firmly. "You know I'm here for you, right?"

Stephanie smiles sadly at her. "I know. And I appreciate it. I don't really have anyone else I can talk to. This is so hard." She puts her hands up against her face. "I'm worried about Patrick," Stephanie says, "about how he'll take it."

"He might see it as a betrayal," Hanna says uneasily.

"Maybe. And he's already really depressed. It's all been so horrible, Hanna." She bites her lip so that she won't cry. She pauses and grabs a tissue from her diaper bag. "It was so awful when he was arrested. He won't even talk about it." She pauses to gain control of herself. "I thought that when the police let him go, he would get past it. But Niall dumped him. He doesn't have his business, and

how is he supposed to start over? His reputation has been destroyed, even though they dropped the charges." She knows how bleak she must look. "It's so unfair. And when I tell him I'm going to leave him—"

Hanna looks back at her helplessly and says, "Stephanie, God, I don't know what to say."

Stephanie continues, "He's not himself."

"What do you mean?"

"He blames himself for everything that's happened. He's moody, depressed, he says things."

"What things?" Hanna says, leaning forward anxiously.

"He says we'd be better off without him." She turns worried eyes on Hanna. "I'm afraid that if I leave him he might do something. Something drastic, harm himself."

Hanna says urgently, "Forget about him. I'm worried about **you**. Stephanie, you should leave him. Take the twins and move out. **Now**."

Should she tell Hanna about the gun? No, that would be too much. She shakes her head. "I'm going to see the divorce attorney first."

"That's good."

"That might make things clearer," Stephanie agrees.

"But what if he—what if he hurts you, and the twins?" Hanna says, clearly worried.

Stephanie shakes her head. "He would never do anything to hurt me or the twins, I know that."

She adds, "But if I tell him I'm leaving him, he'll feel utterly abandoned. I feel so guilty. I—I'm not sure I can do it."

"You have **nothing** to feel guilty about, Stephanie," Hanna says strongly. "You have to do what's right for you and the girls."

Stephanie looks back at her only friend. Hanna thinks her husband is a murderer. Hanna is right. She probably thinks that if her husband were to kill himself, it would be the best thing for all concerned. She's right about that too.

Hanna looks back at her anxiously. "Seriously, Stephanie, I think you have to leave him, if that's what you want, regardless of how depressed he might be, or how he might take it. Think of yourself for a change. Think of your babies." She glances anxiously at the twins on their play mats. "What if he's dangerous?"

Stephanie shakes her head again. "He's not. We'll be fine. He loves me and the kids. He won't do anything to us. It's him I'm worried about."

PATRICK SLUMPS AT the kitchen table while Stephanie is at Hanna's with the twins. He drinks cup after cup of coffee, thinking. He's told Stephanie that he had an extended affair with Erica, that he didn't love her, that what happened to Lindsey was an accident. He doesn't think she believes him.

He'd been lucky enough to meet a woman who

had inherited a lot of money. If Erica hadn't come back into the picture, things would be very different.

When he thinks about Erica his entire body tightens with rage. He realizes that he'd gladly kill Erica Voss. He should have done it when he still had the chance, before she went to the police. But he hadn't acted decisively, he hadn't had time to come up with a sufficiently good plan, one that he was sure he could get away with.

But now, the damage is done. There's no point in killing her now, and besides, everyone would think he did it. They already think he killed his first wife. Even if he made it look like an accident the knives would still be out for him. Making it look like an accident is his modus operandi, they'd say.

And Stephanie would know what he'd done.

Stephanie is going to leave him. He's sure of it. He can tell that she's afraid of him. Her leaving him is the worst possible thing that can happen to him now.

Everyone will think she left him because he killed his first wife.

He needs to see a lawyer. He needs to know what his rights are. How quickly can she divorce him? If they're separated, but not yet divorced, would he still get her inheritance if she were to die?

He broods into his coffee. But he can no more kill his wife than he can kill Erica. He'd never get away with it. Not now.

# 55

Later that day, Stephanie stands in front of the bedroom closet. She has to think, to plan. Her mind works feverishly all the time. She's thinking about it when she feeds the twins. She's thinking about it when she changes diapers, when she's cooking. How will she get rid of the gloves?

She has decided that her husband should kill himself. It's the only way out of this mess. And he's not going to do it himself. She's going to have to do it for him.

It's come down to this, in the space of a few short months. They've gone from being a happy, well-off couple to being a pair of cold-blooded murderers. How quickly things change, she thinks. How crazy and unpredictable life is. It's like a circus—high-wire acts and people hiding behind clown masks. How little control we have, she thinks; so much is out of our hands.

But not everything. She can do this. She can take control again. She can protect her daughters. She's doing this for them.

**We don't always get to choose.**

But sometimes you can, she thinks.

She doesn't love him anymore. She's not willing to spend the rest of her life with him, and to share her inheritance with her cheating, lying husband who murdered his first wife. She's not willing to live in fear, waiting for him to kill her and the twins someday. He already got away with it once.

If only she could just leave him. But she doesn't see that as a viable option. Best case—in the eyes of the law, he's an innocent man. He has rights. Rights to see his children. He would always be part of their lives. But she knows what he's done. Worst case—he might be so angry if she leaves him that he comes after her and kills her and the twins. Like that man who smothered his children with pillows and stabbed his estranged wife to death. Like all those men who kill their families. There are so many of them. Angry, thwarted men who kill their wives and children.

So she has to figure out this glove business, how to get rid of them quickly. And also, it bothers her about the ammunition.

She stares at the open bedroom closet. Patrick has gone out, and she's alone in the house. She spins the dial on the combination lock and opens the safe. She's wearing the latex gloves she bought

for just this purpose. She looks at the Glock 19 9mm handgun that she'd last seen in Patrick's right hand. She knows the gun has his fingerprints on it, his finger was even on the trigger. It's like a gift. But now, as she inspects the gun, she sees that it isn't loaded. She will have to do that—that's not a huge problem because she's wearing gloves and she knows how. She's fired a gun before. But she worries that the bullets might not have his fingerprints on them and the gun will. Is that a problem? Her other worry is that he might check on his gun and find that it's loaded before she gets a chance to use it. So she will have to do this very soon. The sooner the better. She loads the bullets into the gun.

ON MONDAY MORNING, Stephanie tells Patrick that she's taking the twins out. She has a story ready if he should ask where, but he doesn't.

She's going to visit a law firm that specializes in divorce. She doesn't have an appointment, but she figures if she shows up and says it's urgent, someone will see her. She considered leaving the twins with Hanna, but Hanna has done a lot of babysitting for her, and she has been unable to return the favor.

She pushes the double stroller into the elevator and takes it to the top floor. She's done her research and Thompson Doyle is the best divorce firm in Aylesford. She apologizes for showing up without

an appointment but tells the receptionist that she needs to see a divorce attorney. The young woman asks her to wait. Stephanie takes a seat. The waiting room has a splendid view of the river, but she barely takes it in. She focuses on keeping the babies from fussing, and on what she's going to say.

"Gabriel Thompson can see you," the receptionist tells her after a few minutes.

She's ushered into his office. She takes one look around and she knows this is going to be expensive, but she doesn't care. She can afford it.

"How can I help?" the attorney asks, when she has wheeled the twins in and taken the seat in front of his desk.

"I want to divorce my husband," she states baldly.

"Then you've come to the right place," the attorney says dryly, with a kind smile. He's an older man, dressed in a sober suit and tie, with tidy silver hair.

"My husband is Patrick Kilgour," she says.

The attorney's eyebrows go up and he leans forward attentively. Stephanie wonders how closely he followed the case. She hesitates for a moment, swallows.

"I see," he says. "I'm somewhat familiar with the case." He looks at her encouragingly.

"It has put a tremendous strain on our marriage." She falters and takes a moment to compose herself. "Everyone knows he cheated on his first wife. He's admitted it. I don't know if he's cheated on me."

She adds, "In any event, the marriage is over, and I need to know what I can do."

"Of course."

"I came into a large inheritance on my last birthday. He doesn't have any rights to that, does he?"

"None at all. In New York, inherited property does not go into marital assets to be divided when a marriage ends. You have no worries on that score."

"Good."

He gives her a frank look. "Do you have a will?"

"Yes, everything I have goes to Patrick on my death, as things currently stand."

"I think we need to change that," he says. "Any life insurance?"

She's beginning to think this man had followed the case rather closely. She's not surprised—it was a cause célèbre in Aylesford, as well as in Colorado. "Yes."

His face is serious, his voice concerned. "Are you worried about your personal safety?"

She remembers what she came here to do. "No, not at all. But I am worried about how Patrick will take the news of the divorce. He's very depressed already, after everything that's happened. It's been a difficult decision, but I have to do what's right for me—and for the twins."

"Of course," the attorney agrees sympathetically. "Let's do this as expeditiously as possible."

# 56

That evening, after the twins are asleep, Stephanie tries to coax her husband into having a couple of drinks with her. It will help if he has some whiskey in him. And she needs something to steady her nerves.

She needs to get him into the kitchen. In a straight-backed chair with a glass of whiskey in front of him.

"I need a drink," Stephanie says, and gets up off the sofa. He lifts his head. "Care to join me?" He looks almost pleased to be asked. She should feel bad about what she's going to do, but she doesn't. Because it's not just for her. It's for Emma and Jackie. They deserve better than to grow up with a father who is a liar and a cheater and a murderer.

"Sure," he says, and follows her into the kitchen.

She sits in the chair she always sits in at meals, the one facing the entry to the kitchen, leaving Patrick his usual chair, with its back to the door.

She watches him open the kitchen cabinet where they keep the liquor. He takes out two glasses. "What do you want?" he asks.

"I'll have what you're having." When he looks back at her, surprised, she says, "I could use something strong."

He nods. Usually he drinks whiskey neat. He pours them each a generous amount. She's thinking it's good that he's handling the bottle, the glasses. She's thinking that when it's over, she'll wash her glass thoroughly and put it back in the cupboard if there's time before the ambulance shows up. Better if he was drinking alone, she thinks, while she was in the shower. She's lucky that the twins are so young that they are safely contained in their cribs. It would be much trickier to pull this off if they were older.

They won't even remember their father, they're too young. She can control the narrative, make it what she wants. She'll have to move away, though, start over somewhere else, but not too far away. Maybe she will go back to using her maiden name. Yes, she will.

"Stephanie," he begins, sitting down at the table, across from her. "You know how sorry I am."

She nods without meeting his eyes. She doesn't want to hear his apologies, his explanations all over again. It's too late for that. What do they say? By the time most couples make it to marriage

counseling, usually one of them has already decided it's over.

"I've been thinking about the future," he says finally.

She'll play along, to keep him at the table, drinking. She no longer cares what he says. She's found her own solution.

"Maybe I should start my own architectural firm."

She nods. No one else will have him; he doesn't have much choice. She sips her drink. It goes hot down her throat, steadying her nerves. She needs the whiskey—just enough to give her courage, but not enough to make her careless.

"It will probably take a lot of money to start, before it becomes profitable."

"There's a surprise," she says. She can't help it.

He bites his lip, as if hurt by her tone. Then he picks up his glass and finishes it off in one go. He reaches for the bottle and pours himself another.

Good, she thinks. He's completely oblivious to what's going to happen next. There isn't going to be any new firm. She has to turn her eyes away as he talks. She decides to play along. What difference does it make? None of this is ever going to happen. She pretends to consider what he's saying. She takes another sip of her drink, watching his face lighten a little at the prospect of getting her on board. At least he'll be happy when he dies.

He leans in closer, across the table, telling her more about his plans, but she's only pretending to listen. She must be pretending pretty well because he won't shut up about it. He pours himself another drink. She'll never get a better opportunity.

"Hold that thought," she says. "I have to pee. I'll be right back."

# 57

She hurries upstairs. She feels her face change as soon as she leaves the kitchen. She's cold, purposeful, remorseless. She walks quickly to the bathroom and closes the door, loudly enough, but from outside, in the hall. She hurries quietly into the bedroom, where she strips off all her clothes and drops them on the bed. Once she's naked, she grabs the latex gloves from her nightstand and puts them on. She goes to the closet and turns the combination to the safe with trembling hands. The door swings open and she grabs the gun. She returns to the bathroom, opens the door very quietly and steps inside. She catches sight of her reflection briefly in the large mirror over the vanity. She hardly recognizes herself. She's completely naked except for the pale blue latex gloves from the grocery store. And she's holding a gun in her right hand. She flushes the toilet, runs the tap; she wants everything to sound normal to Patrick.

She doesn't want to arouse any suspicion when he thinks she went upstairs to pee.

She moves quietly down the carpeted stairs. She prays he doesn't turn around when she gets to the kitchen. He shouldn't—why would he? She arrives at the entrance to the kitchen silently in bare feet. His back is to her and he doesn't seem to be aware that she's there. She remembers to angle the gun slightly upward in her hand and then in one fast movement she steps forward and pushes the muzzle firmly against the right side of his head and pulls the trigger. It all happens so quickly.

She's expecting the kick from the gun but somehow the shot is louder than she anticipated. He falls forward, slumping on the table. There's a bright red spatter of blood and brain matter across the table, floor, and against her white kitchen cupboards. She fights a sudden urge to vomit as she stares down at him, blood from the exit wound beginning to pool on the table. He's clearly dead. She hears her heart pounding in her ears and starts to panic. She takes some deep breaths to regain control. She looks quickly at herself and doesn't see any obvious blood on her. No backspatter on her hand holding the gun—she'd been careful to push the muzzle of the gun hard against his skull. She checks her feet. All clean. She must not track anything upstairs. She places the gun on the floor to his right-hand side, leaving the casing where it landed.

Then she flies up the stairs as fast as she can, peeling off the gloves, and flushes them down the toilet one at a time. She turns on the shower and steps in quickly, soaping herself well, shampooing her hair, as fast as she can.

When she gets out, dripping wet, she pulls on her robe without toweling herself dry and hurries downstairs, trailing drips of water behind her. She reaches the kitchen, picks up the phone, and dials 911.

"What is the nature of your emergency?"

"My husband shot himself! Please hurry!"

"What is your location ma'am?"

"Seventeen Danbury Drive."

"Can I have your name, ma'am?"

"Stephanie Kilgour."

"Is your husband breathing?"

"I-I don't think so."

She needs to deal with the glass. "Please hurry!"

"Emergency personnel are on the way, ma'am. Please remain calm and stay on the line."

Stephanie is barely listening to what the 911 operator is saying to her. Stephanie keeps repeating, "Oh God, oh God," into the phone as she stares at the carnage. She needs to remove her glass from the table to wash it. But then she realizes she probably shouldn't open the cupboards and disturb the mess there, and she doesn't want the operator to hear her washing the glass. She sobs, "Please hurry!" and disconnects the call. She rinses the glass and

slips it into the dishwasher. Then she turns around and surveys the scene. Patrick is slumped over the kitchen table with a gaping wound in his head. His eyes are wide open. On the table is the bottle of whiskey and a single glass—and his fingerprints are all over both. She was in the shower when she heard the gun go off. It's okay that she's been in the kitchen, that there's blood on the bottom of her robe. Any wife would look.

She stares at her husband until she becomes aware of flashing red lights in the dark outside, through the wavy glass of her front door, and hears heavy steps coming up the walk. She somehow makes her way to the front door and opens it wide. Police and ambulance personnel have arrived at the same time; they spill into the vestibule.

Now that she's done it, shock sets in. She begins to shake uncontrollably as she points them toward the kitchen. One police officer and the paramedics enter the kitchen; another police officer remains beside her, near the front door, watching her. Stephanie lets herself fall apart. She thinks she's convincing. She just has to be careful what she says.

The officer helps her—crying, incoherent—into the living room and onto the sofa. "Put your head between your knees," the woman says. She sits beside Stephanie, solicitous, concerned, one hand lightly on her back.

Stephanie keeps her head down and tries to

listen. It's quiet in the kitchen. There's nothing they can do for him. More arrive; suddenly there are many people in her house, and she can't keep track of anything. There's too much going on, too much noise. She can't think straight. She has to pull herself together. She must be careful now, not make a mistake. She can hear murmured voices, the sound of photographs being taken.

She's still slumped on the sofa; she doesn't know how long she's been sitting there—time has stopped—when she sees them wheel in the gurney with a body bag to take her husband away. It's sinking in. She's rid herself of him and all his baggage. He can't ruin her life anymore. And she's still here, she and the twins. She still has the house, her money. Everything is going to be fine, as long as she keeps her nerve.

The police officer who has been in the kitchen approaches. He sits down in an armchair across from her, and leans in.

"I'm so sorry for your loss," he says. He looks weary, and he seems to mean it.

She looks at him and swallows. Her focus is coming back. She's starting to recover from the shock of what she's done.

"Can you tell us what happened here tonight?" he asks.

She takes a deep breath. Clutches the tissues in her hands that the woman officer beside her provided her with at some point. "I was in the

shower." She pulls the robe more tightly around herself, as if embarrassed that she is naked underneath. Her hair is still damp and tangled down her back—it has soaked through her robe, and she's cold. "Patrick was drinking in the kitchen when I went upstairs. I was just finishing my shower when I heard the shot. I ran down to the kitchen and—I found him—" She breaks down, sobbing, and it's heartfelt, it really is. She's been through so much, lost so much.

"Take your time," the officer says, and waits patiently.

Finally she pulls herself together and tells them, "He's been under a lot of stress lately." She stops. They probably aren't aware yet of who Patrick is.

"What kind of stress?"

She says, her voice bleak, "I told him, tonight, after supper, that I was going to divorce him." And then she tells them everything, who he is, and the same lies she told Hanna and her attorney about his state of mind. When she finishes, the man is watching her as if he, too, is overwhelmed by their troubles. Finally he asks, "Do you know where the gun came from?"

"It's probably his gun," she whispers. "He keeps it in a safe upstairs in our bedroom closet."

"Can you show us?"

She gets up off the sofa and leads them upstairs to the bedroom. She points at the closet—the door

is open, and on the shelf, on Patrick's side, is the safe, wide open, the way she left it. They look at it.

When they go back downstairs, the body is being removed from the kitchen on a gurney, in a zipped body bag.

The officer glances at the empty baby swings, looks at her then and says, "Have you checked on the children, ma'am?"

And suddenly she's so deep in her own lies, her fantasies, her fears and justifications that she panics about the twins. She feels her face go white. She races up the stairs to the nursery and flings open the door and turns on the light. The twins are there, in their cribs, untouched. Of course they are. The officer is standing close behind her, his breath coming rapidly; she can feel it warm against her neck.

"They're fine," he says, clearly relieved.

# 58

On Thursday, November 1, the medical examiner determines that Patrick Kilgour's death was suicide. It's in all the news. Along with a recap of the death of Lindsey, the inquest, the arrest—everything. It's all fresh in the public mind again, on everyone's tongue. But that's fine, Stephanie thinks; everyone believes he killed himself. Soon it will die out for good. It will all die with him.

Stephanie hadn't really expected there to be any question, but nonetheless, the relief she feels at the official determination is profound. It's over. She can move on. Still, since she did it, she feels shaky, unmoored, not herself. Her mind is not quite right. She could never have predicted any of this. It's all bound to have an effect, she tells herself, staring catatonically at the twins. It will take some getting used to.

The evening it happened, the police were in

the house most of the night. The kitchen was off-limits. They suggested she go stay with family, but she had no family to stay with. Hanna, like most of the neighbors, had been drawn out onto the street by the flashing lights and emergency vehicles. They finally allowed Hanna into the house. Hanna insisted she gather up the twins and come home with her, and Stephanie was glad to have somewhere to go.

Once they were finished, by the next day, the special cleaners came in and did their job. Stephanie was relieved that she wasn't expected to clean it up herself.

That night she was back, alone in the house with the twins. She forced herself to go into the kitchen and make herself some tea. Everyone had gone, leaving an unnerving silence behind them. She wandered around the house until the early morning hours like she had before, unable to sleep.

It was the same last night, too, but now she no longer tortures herself with doubts about Patrick's guilt. She no longer thinks endlessly, obsessively, about what she should do. It's done. But she keeps seeing it, over and over, the moment she pulled the trigger. The way she shoved the gun into his hair against his skull, and the rain of blood and gore that blew out the other side. She can't believe she did that. It's as if it were someone else.

Hanna comes over to check on her. No need to stay away now that Patrick's gone. She has Teddy

with her in the stroller, and lasagna she's made her-
self. She stands on the doorstep with her offering,
obviously concerned about Stephanie's well-being.
Stephanie hesitates, because she's keenly aware
of her kitchen right behind her. The professional
cleanup team has scrubbed and scoured and it's
perfectly presentable. You can't even tell something
awful happened in there three days ago. But still,
it's going to be weird, having Hanna in the kitchen.

"I can come back," Hanna says, "if this isn't a
good time."

But Stephanie shakes her head and says, "No,
come in. I'm glad to see you. Nobody else has
come."

Who was she expecting? Niall? His wife? They've
stayed away. So have her friends from work, where
she'd spent four years of her life before going on
maternity leave. Really, there's no one but Hanna,
and right now she's grateful for her.

"I'm so sorry," Hanna says awkwardly, once she
gets inside with Teddy. She stands there with her
baby on her hip, as if uncertain what to do, what to
say. Stephanie has the tray of food in her hands and
turns and takes it into the kitchen. Hanna follows
tentatively. She knows he did it in the kitchen; she
was here, that awful night, sitting with Stephanie
in the living room. Stephanie turns to find Hanna
staring, uncertain where to sit.

"You can put Teddy in the living room with the
girls," she says. And Hanna pivots as if relieved and

goes into the other room. Stephanie starts making coffee. She finds her hands trembling slightly as she measures out the coffee grounds. It's important what Hanna thinks. She worries now: had she been too obvious when she told Hanna that she was worried about Patrick, that he might harm himself? Had she laid it on a little too thick? Should she have said nothing, allowed it to be more of a surprise? She's glad, now, that she hadn't mentioned Patrick's gun.

She takes a deep breath and tells herself to relax. Hanna isn't going to suspect the truth. She was here that night, saw how distressed she was. She's not going to think Stephanie is capable of holding a gun to her husband's head and blowing his brains out. Hanna is perceptive, and she might suspect that Stephanie is secretly relieved—even glad—that her husband has removed himself from her life this way, but she's not going to think that Stephanie pulled the trigger herself.

She brings the coffee through to the living room. They sit in silence for a bit, neither one of them knowing how to begin. They talk about the babies to break the ice. Finally Hanna gets up the nerve to ask, "What happens now?"

Stephanie exhales. Puts her coffee down. "There's the funeral, tomorrow morning. It's going to be private. Please don't feel you need to come." She's going to have him cremated.

"I'll come if you want me to," Hanna offers.

"I'd rather you didn't," she says. "In fact, I was hoping you'd watch the twins for me."

"Sure." Hanna is obviously relieved not to have to go to the funeral, and eager to do something useful to help. "You know I'm here for you, right?" she says, putting out a hand and laying it gently on Stephanie's arm.

Stephanie nods gratefully. She doesn't need to worry about Hanna. Even though they both know, now, that all of Stephanie's problems are solved.

# 59

Erica did not attend Patrick's funeral. But the following day she sits in her car outside of the house on Danbury Drive. None of this has gone the way she planned. You can never really predict how things are going to go. There's always a wild card in the pack somewhere.

She knows Stephanie is home. It's lunchtime, and the double stroller sits empty on the front porch. She's inside, probably in the kitchen, feeding the twins. Erica gets out of the car.

She walks purposefully across the street and rings the doorbell. She doesn't have to wait long before Stephanie answers the door. When she does, Erica can tell that the sight of her on the doorstep is a shock. Stephanie looks awful, besides—her hair is limp, she's not wearing any makeup, and her clothes are unwashed. She looks exhausted, wrung out. Erica hopes she's taking better care of the twins.

"What the hell are you doing here?" Stephanie says.

"Can I come in?"

STEPHANIE LOOKS BACK in dismay at Erica on her doorstep. She never wanted to see her again. "Why the hell would I let you in my house?" she says, her voice strident. "You're nothing but bad news." Her heart is beating fast and she moves to close the door in Erica's face. But Erica is too quick for her and blocks the door with her body.

"Calm down. I only came to talk," Erica says.

Stephanie glares at her, breathing rapidly; she can't get Erica out of the house without becoming physical, and she doesn't want to do that. She suspects Erica is much stronger than she is. She silently considers calling 911, but something stops her.

"So, that's where it happened?" Erica says, looking over Stephanie's shoulder into the kitchen and gesturing with her chin to where the twins sit in their matching high chairs.

Stephanie says nothing as Erica brushes past her and makes her way into the kitchen. She closes the front door behind her and follows.

"Just like that," Erica says, turning around to face her, "all your problems are solved."

"You've got a lot of nerve," Stephanie says acidly.

"I'm just speaking the truth, and you know it,"

Erica responds. "You're rid of your cheating, murdering husband."

Stephanie averts her eyes. Erica makes her nervous. She has a sick feeling in the pit of her stomach.

"Personally," Erica says, "I don't care. Good riddance to Patrick. He got what was coming to him, the bastard. The world is better off without him in it, wouldn't you agree?"

Stephanie can't read her. Why is Erica here? "What do you want?"

Erica says, "I just came to say **well done**."

Stephanie feels her stomach drop. "What do you mean?"

"I mean," she smiles a little smile, "if **you** killed him, you have my blessing."

"What the hell are you talking about?" Stephanie says. "He killed himself. I'd told him I was going to divorce him and take the twins and my inheritance with me. I'd already seen a divorce attorney."

Erica looks back at her through cold eyes. "Let's not kid ourselves," she says. "Patrick was not the suicidal type." She lets the silence lengthen, enjoying herself. "Don't worry, I'm not going to say anything. Not yet." Then she smiles again and says, "I'll let myself out."

After she goes, closing the front door behind her, Stephanie turns to the kitchen sink and throws up violently until there's nothing left in her stomach. Then she rinses her mouth, and ignoring the

twins, who have begun to fuss and cry in their high chairs, she starts to pace back and forth across the kitchen floor.

**Erica knows. Erica knows. Erica knows.**

She stops in her tracks. She should have foreseen this. Why didn't she foresee this? She'd thought Erica was out of their lives—Patrick released, Erica discredited. She had done her worst and failed. Stephanie had been so focused on getting rid of Patrick. . . . The babies are crying loudly, but she continues to ignore them.

Erica wants her money. Erica will try to blackmail her. She will do to her what she did to Patrick. Erica dealt drugs, she sold her own baby for money. Of course Erica will try to make her pay.

Finally Stephanie wears herself out. She slumps in the chair in front of the twins—the chair Patrick was in when she pulled the trigger—and picks up the spoon that she put down when Erica arrived at her door. Emma and Jackie are both red-faced and squalling from being ignored, their distressed faces covered in tears and snot and baby food. She lifts the spoonful of pureed carrots to Emma's eager, open mouth. But then her eyes go past Emma's face and fix on the white cupboard behind her. She remembers the blood spattered there. She closes her eyes. The babies clamor.

Then, with a great strength of will, she opens her eyes again and focuses on her babies. She takes some wet wipes from the table and wipes up first

Emma's face, then Jackie's. She puts on a cheerful expression and uses her singsong voice. She must be a good mother. She must be there for her girls. She will figure something out. "There we go! Time for carrots! Yum-yum!" She spoons the pureed carrots, a lurid orange, into their open mouths. They've stopped crying now and both of them have fixed their big round blue eyes on her face. They're like plump little birds in a nest, mouths open, waiting.

"Your Daddy loved us very much," she tells them, in her high-pitched voice. "He loved you both so much. People said terrible things about him, but they were all lies. He was a good man. He didn't do anything bad. It was all made up by an evil witch."

She spoons the food into the babies' mouths as they smile and gurgle back at her. She remembers how she'd tried to run down Erica with her car that night. After Erica left the gift for the twins and Patrick had been so unnerved by it—she knew she had to stop Erica from going to the police in Creemore. That night she'd told Patrick she couldn't stand the crying anymore and was going to the movies for a break, and left him on his own for a while to cope with the twins. She drove to the theater and bought a ticket, but left again. She told Patrick later that she'd slept through the whole movie. But she drove to Newburgh. She knew where Erica lived—Patrick had told her earlier. She had no plan; she was too

stressed and sleep-deprived to come up with one. She was sitting in her car, dithering about whether to press her buzzer and what to say to her, when she saw Erica come out of her building. When Erica started to walk toward the road, Stephanie followed in her car at a distance.

She acted on impulse. Erica was walking alone, on the side of a dark road. There was no one around. Stephanie found herself gripping the steering wheel, flooring the gas pedal, all her rage trained on the lone figure in front of her. She never meant to hit Erica, only to scare her away, but it was a close call—in her fury, Stephanie had almost not veered away in time.

She'd driven home, shaking all the way, shocked at herself, at her almost fatal loss of control. But what she'd done had the opposite effect from what she intended. Erica went straight to the coroner.

But at least Stephanie now knows the truth about Patrick. And she **is** grateful, really. Just like Erica said she would be. Better to know.

The twins smile and gurgle back at her. But Erica has become a problem again.

Stephanie will figure something out. She has to.

# 60

Erica drives back to Newburgh, rather pleased with herself and with how things have turned out. She couldn't have predicted this turn of events, but she knows how to roll with the punches. She goes where the opportunities are.

Patrick had never meant anything to her. They slept together, that's it. She'd never cared for him in the least, and he'd never cared about her. It was purely physical, the selfish satisfaction of needs, for both of them. But when Lindsey died . . . that had surprised her, and made her think. She thought about how convenient Lindsey's death was for Patrick. She thought it might have been the perfect murder.

There had been no look of triumph, no silent glance between the two of them at the scene of the accident that day. But she'd watched him and wondered. She thought he was acting a part. He'd

never told her he was unhappy with his wife, but she'd deduced it on her own. If he was so happy with his wife, why was he sleeping with her? And why did he seem so unenthusiastic about the baby? It didn't take a rocket scientist to figure it out.

She didn't know for sure, but as soon as she suspected that he might have killed his wife deliberately, she decided to snub him and keep it in her back pocket for the future when he would have money. Patrick was smart and ambitious, and she knew that one day he would be successful. That he happened to marry a rich woman was simply a bonus. She shouldn't have been surprised—he wasn't that different from her. He was every bit as much of an opportunist as she is. He just had better luck. Well, until his luck ran out.

She'd bided her time until Stephanie had come into her money. And then she executed her plan. It didn't go as expected, because Stephanie had been stubborn and unwilling to pay.

But it can all still work out nicely, Erica tells herself, now that Stephanie has killed Patrick. She has no doubts about **that** at all.

In the meantime, she has other things on the go. Niall has been avoiding her calls. He's proved more slippery than she expected. But she'll talk to him eventually, and when she does, he's not going to like what she has to say.

And she's got the Mannings wrapped around her

little finger. They'll do anything to protect that boy from the truth.

NANCY STARES OUT her living-room window, hiding behind the drapes. She and Niall are freaking out.

Erica has tried to call Niall again; she even showed up at the office, but Kerri was instructed to say that he was out. It worked, but only because he's stopped driving his Tesla to work, so Erica can't tell when he's there. Niall's using Uber a lot these days. But it's a short-term solution.

Erica has them living in fear, and they hate it; in this they are united.

Nancy is aware that keeping Erica from Niall at work makes them more of a target at home. Erica knows where they live. She's already been here. It's just a matter of time before she shows up again. Nancy spends much of her day watching out the window like this.

The only upside—Nancy doesn't think her husband will be straying again anytime soon.

They both perceive Erica's hovering presence as a serious threat. They can't live in fear forever. Something must be done.

GARY MANNING SITS quietly in his car—a leased Lexus—in the underground parking lot beneath

the office tower in downtown Denver where he works. It's already dark out. He's putting off going home. It will be another late night of tears and histrionics in the basement and he doesn't know how much more he can take.

He loves Cheryl and he loves Devin. He's their boy. He's a fine boy, and they're not going to let his birth mother fuck him up by telling him things he doesn't need to hear.

Gary thinks about watching Devin on the soccer field the other day—how proud he made him feel. He couldn't be more proud of him even if Devin was his own flesh and blood.

And now this godawful mess. Erica demanding more money to keep her mouth shut. He'd like to go to the police, but he can't. Imagine the effect of the publicity on his business. They paid her a hundred grand to get Devin. They'd made a deal with the devil all those years ago. Erica knows they're not going to go to the police.

Gary hates to see Cheryl so upset all the time, but he understands it. She's terrified that they will lose Devin, that contact with his birth mother—and learning the truth about his birth parents—will traumatize him. It might even turn him against them. She's probably not wrong. Gary can't bear to lose the little family that took them so much time and effort to build. And Devin knows something's up; yesterday he'd asked him why everyone's acting so weird lately. He's a smart kid.

Gary's had trouble getting the money together. He can do it, it will just be difficult. But his family comes first.

If only Erica Voss were dead, all his problems would be solved.

# EPILOGUE

**The Aylesford Record,**
November 9, 2018

Authorities have determined the identity of a woman whose body was pulled from the Hudson River early this morning. The deceased woman is 31-year-old Erica Voss, of Newburgh, New York.

Orange County police recovered the body earlier today near the Newburgh-Beacon Bridge, after receiving a call just before 7:00 a.m. from a jogger who noticed the body floating in the river.

Ms. Voss was in the news recently when she gave evidence at the inquest into the death of Lindsey Kilgour, in Colorado in 2009.

The cause of death has not yet been determined.

SHARI LAPENA is the internationally bestselling author of the thrillers **The Couple Next Door**, **A Stranger in the House**, **An Unwanted Guest**, and **Someone We Know**, which have all been **New York Times** and **Sunday Times** (London) best-sellers. Her books have been sold in thirty-seven territories around the world. She lives in Toronto, and **The End of Her** is her fifth thriller.

# LIKE WHAT YOU'VE READ?

Try these titles by Shari Lapena,
also available in large print:

**An Unwanted Guest**
ISBN 978-1-9848-2751-7

**Someone We Know**
ISBN 978-0-593-15223-2

**A Stranger in the House**
ISBN 978-0-525-50131-2

For more information on large print titles, visit
**www.penguinrandomhouse.com/large-print-format-books**